Anne of Survivor

Anne of Survivor

Nkrumah Mensah

NEW YORK

LONDON • NASHVILLE • MELBOURNE • VANCOUVER

Anne of Survivor

© 2025 Nkrumah Mensah

Published in New York, New York, by Morgan James Publishing. Morgan James is a trademark of Morgan James, LLC. www.MorganJamesPublishing.com

Proudly distributed by Publishers Group West®

ISBN 9781636984520 paperback
ISBN 9781636984537 ebook
Library of Congress Control Number:
2024941309

Cover Design by:
Carolina Leon Valderrama

Interior Design by:
Christopher Kirk
www.GFSstudio.com

Morgan James is a proud partner of Habitat for Humanity Peninsula
and Greater Williamsburg. Partners in building since 2006.

Get involved today! Visit: www.morgan-james-publishing.com/giving-back

To anyone who's been told they can't.
If you want it bad enough, you can, and you will.
I believe in you.

Prologue

Sisters

She stood on the deck shivering, trying to forget as a cool breeze off the water whipped across her face. The memories, however, persisted . . . demanding to be recognized despite her pain and tiredness. Anne looked at her hands. No longer the smooth porcelain hands of a prim and proper lady, within a day, they already bore the evidence of her new life: dry, cracked, and bleeding. Tears pricked the inner corners of her eyes, but she did not dare let them drop farther. Instead, steeling her resolve, she slowly and ever so gently moved her right hand beyond her left shoulder and onto her back. There it was. There was where she held her reason for running, and she would never forget.

Daddy's dear girl, Philana-Narie—Anne, to those who knew her best—was both the pride and misery of her family and friends. A pretty little darling, with thick chocolate curls and devilishly beautiful gray eyes, she knew at an early age the power she held over people. Oh, those luminescent gray eyes hid many secrets and were tickled by many fancies. She always did as she pleased, often embarrassing friends and family alike. Then, as usual, when her time of reckoning came, her parents dared not punish her for her small crimes. After all, she was merely a child with an overabundance of energy and life. Besides, as she grew, her wildness seemed to be leaving her as her charm increased.

Ethana, on the other hand, had always been a rather mousy-looking child with her blonde-brown hair and her pale, almost sickly looking, skin. Unlike her radiant elder sister, she kept to herself and never strayed too far from the house, so it was difficult for anyone to notice her at all. However, as Ethana approached her sixteenth birthday, she ventured out *a bit* more. Allowing the sun to eventually kiss her hair, making it more golden blonde, and her skin to drink in the rays, becoming both grand and healthy-looking. Ethana bore no childhood scars that marred her appearance or any sun damage from overexposure. She was simply lovely, like her mother, and was catching up to Anne in both beauty and allure.

As children, they were an interesting sight together. Loving sisters as they were, Anne always looked after and protected Ethana. When a crowd drew any-where near, Ethana would shy away from them, and Anne would eat them up. She, Anne, was always the entertainer and always a crowd favorite, so much so that she knew Ethana envied her and over time, even grew to resent her. Anne knew Ethana wished she could be so loved by everyone and loathed the fact that even their parents seemed under her charms. At times, Ethana must have felt neglected and even . . . forgotten.

Chapter One

Upon the Eighteenth

Three weeks earlier.

Thaniel, came bounding out of the manor and flew across their well-manicured yard to the carriage. "Reyna, Anne, you won't believe who left not five minutes ago!" he yelled as if catching his breath was unimportant.

"Thaniel, dear, calm yourself before you choke on the air." His wife shook her head as she handed him the wisteria she had just purchased from their trip to Haru's and climbed from the buggy.

"Reyna, you don't understand," he said as he assisted her descent. "The duke was here while you were at the marketplace. He said he has been keeping himself informed of the affairs of the young women in town. He knows Anne is coming upon her eighteenth summer, and he is contemplating a marriage between her and his son!"

Reyna's beautiful blue eyes lit up, and her mouth stretched into an exquisite smile. "Really? Well, when will we know if he has chosen Anne?"

"He will be here again Sunday next, accompanied by his wife and their son, Oren."

"But today is Saturday! That means we've only a week to prepare. Thaniel, how on earth are we going to get the estate ready within a week?" Reyna panicked as the two of them headed toward the manor house.

"We'll have to manage, I suppose," Reyna answered herself. "However, first things first; I must decide on a menu and a color scheme." Reyna continued leading the banter as they approached the house, leaving the girls to unload the carriage.

Anne gently stacked a few boxes and placed bags within bags to make for an easier carry with fewer return trips. She was deep in thought, wondering what the duke's son was like and if they would share the same dreams. It was only Ethana's hand on her shoulder that brought her back to the present.

"Anne, I asked if you were excited at all! I swear you are not yourself today. If I were you, I would be bouncing off the walls like a mad woman—well, either that or losing my lunch. I do believe I would be quite nervous about meeting the duke and duchess. And to be married to their son! What luck . . ." Ethana continued with her mindless chattering.

Anne had never heard the girl talk so much in her life. She simply rolled her eyes and gathered as many boxes and bags as was physically possible and set forth toward the manor house. One had to believe Ethana would, at some point, run out of things to say, but Anne supposed she had a great deal to convey because of her near lack of speech for her first sixteen years. Thus, she made no attempt to quell her sister's babbling as it followed her into the house and then into the kitchen.

"Can you imagine living in a palace and having people constantly wait on you? How lovely would that be! Don't you agree, Anne?"

Finally, a break.

"Ethana, I am not yet worried about such things. The duke has yet to choose me for his son, and only then will such matters relate to me," Anne spoke as she handed a bag of potatoes to the cook, who smiled at the two girls as she stowed away the food.

Over the next week, Reyna had both Anne and Ethana fitted for new dresses, gave the cook the menu for the duke's dinner, and had the house and yard staff clean the estate from top to bottom. All six bedrooms were dusted and aired out; linens were changed, and windows were cleaned. The living area, dining room, library, and parlor were also dusted, with their windows cleaned, rugs washed, and the piano (in the parlor) tuned.

Now Saturday again, the ladies of the manor were once more on their way to the market for the fourth time that week. They needed to see about combs for Anne's hair, pick up Ethana's shoes from being repaired, and decide on flowers. Anne and Reyna went to choose the flowers and told Ethana they would meet her at the shoemaker's.

"Anne, what do you think of the tulips or the stephanotis and the roses?" Her mother asked as she glanced over the selection in the little shop.

"Mother, let us not be too presumptuous as to choose the most popular wedding floras." Anne smiled a little smile. "But let us choose the candytuft, foxglove, and poppies." She knew well the meanings of flowers and chose those most likely to ward off the duke and his family. "Oh, Mother, the sweet peas are also quite pretty right now. Besides, the pink and white of the flowers will make a wonderful addition to the cool blue you have chosen for the manor's decorations. Hmm, we should probably add a few of the lavender sweet peas as well. A touch of something different."

Haru looked at Anne with bewilderment before she spoke. "Anne, you do understand what you have chosen?" she asked, for she, too, knew their meanings—the indifference of the candytuft, the insincerity of the foxglove, and the swift departure demanded by the sweet pea. The poppies meant fantasy and oblivion, which was also an odd message to send when one wished to marry. They were all truly beautiful flowers, and many would easily miss their meaning these days, but Haru intimated she couldn't believe Anne would have forgotten.

"Of course, I understand, and I would like to add some fir for greenery." Anne shot Haru a warning glance as she handed her a field bunch of fir whose meaning begged for *time*.

Reyna seemed quite happy with Anne's selection and glad her daughter knew more of the language of flowers than she did. Her knowledge was limited to what was pretty and what was not, and which flowers were best for a wedding. Anne knew her mother had never been interested in botany or flower meanings. "Yes, these are all very lovely, dearest. An excellent eye she has, does she not, Haru?"

"Yes, Reyna. She does have quite a gift when it comes to flora," Haru replied with a hint of sarcasm that eluded Reyna but not Anne. She just hoped, for Anne's sake, that the rumors of the duchess's floral ignorance were true. If not, Anne would embarrass her entire family.

"Well, Mother," Anne began as if she suddenly remembered Ethana was waiting for them, "we really should be on our way. We still have to meet Ethana about her shoes and stop by the jeweler's." Then, glaring at the florist as she gently nudged her mother out of the tiny flower shop, Anne spoke to Haru: "I trust you can have our order ready for us to pick up on our way out of town."

With a nod from Haru, they were gone.

Sunday . . . the day of rest or the day of unrest? Anne thought to herself as she unceremoniously threw on her exquisite light blue gown and slipped into her shoes. She felt like some sort of prized cattle, getting ready for the big show as she sat at her vanity and looked at herself in the mirror. Her hair was swept up at her temples and held back by two princess-like pearl and crystal combs. Around her neck, she had placed her favorite strand of freshwater pearls instead of the beautifully crafted pearl and crystal choker her mother had chosen just the other day. Her makeup was flawless, with its peach and rosy hues, making her look far lovelier than she felt.

As perfect as she was, there was one thing left to do before leaving her room. Anne looked to the small cedar trinket box on her table. She ran her fingers lightly over her initials on the top before opening it. The miniature jewelry box had been given to Anne when she was four years old, to hold her favorite treasures, like pebbles, feathers, and petals. Now, however, it held a small love poem from Devin, a rather romantic and tenderhearted boy she knew from Sunday School.

Two years her elder, he'd left town that many years ago to attend university in Sagedor. She had always thought him very sweet but found him lacking in boldness. The next treasure was a piece of fabric from her sister's dress. When Anne was thirteen, she would race all over the yard and jump over old logs, large rocks, or what have you. Well, one particular day, Anne was determined to get Ethana out of the house, telling her sister if she did not come outside, she would hurdle the wooden fence only a few meters from the side door of the manor. Ethana was beside herself. She begged Anne not to do it but refused to go out, so Anne took a running start, jumped, and *nearly* made it over. The tip of her left shoe snagged the fence, and she fell, face first, to the ground. She had been smart enough to cover her face when she realized her fate, but she scraped her right leg and knuckles badly. Ethana flew out of the house, ripping the bottom of her dress as she went. She then wrapped Anne's bloody leg with the cloth and helped her elder sister inside.

It was the first time Anne had ever seen her sister take initiative, and she believed seeing it was worth the bloody leg and a week in the house. She kept a piece of the cloth to remember that very special day.

Her last treasure, a tiny stone no more than a half an inch to an inch in diameter, was a true treasure. She picked up the small dark stone with its flecks of royal blue, aquamarine, and several shades of green. She had always thought that it was lucky and made it her good luck charm. Well, today she would see just how lucky it was, she thought as she stood and placed the stone in one of the many folds of her lace bodice. Then she fixed herself back up, looked herself over in the full-length mirror, and made her way out of her room and down the stairs to her left.

"Dearest, where have you been? You know the duke and his family will be here at any moment!" Reyna looked as lovely as ever in her silk ivory gown and her diamond necklace that had once belonged to Anne's grandmother.

"Sorry, Mother. I was hurrying the best I could." Anne looked at her mother, who seemed more than nervous about the meeting. Then, just as she was about to tell her not to worry, Ethana glided into the foyer from the kitchen.

"Everything is fine, Mother. Verna has everything under control and told me to tell you not to worry. She also says this is the most magnificent feast she has ever made." Ethana was also dressed in silk, like her mother and Anne, but the color was as delightful as the most delicate pink rose. Anne noticed how the shade enhanced the color of her cheeks and complemented her hair. She looked as fresh as the new spring and smelled deliciously of freesia. Never had Anne seen her look so radiant, and she was happy that Ethana had turned into such a beauty because she had always worried about her sister shriveling up and dying in the manor alone and miserable. With the way she was looking now, her parents would have no problem finding her suitors.

Then, with a little smile, Anne thought how wonderful it would be if she could pass the duke's son down to Ethana. If only she could.

Chapter Two

Decisions

*E*verywhere the royals went they arrived in style. Duke Saben's carriage was wrapped in a beautiful black with gold trim and had deep purple drapes. They had not one but two drivers and four magnificent black horses. Anne watched as Ethana's eyes grew to twice their normal size and she could tell her sister was trying not to drop her mouth at the grandeur of it all. As for her, Anne was quite unimpressed, or to say more appropriately . . . she felt emotionless. The carriage pulled before the manor and stopped in front of the family, with all four outside, awaiting the duke's arrival.

Once the horses had halted, and the buggy came to a complete stop, one of the drivers, dressed in a charcoal suit and hat, flew down from the driver's seat to attend to the royals. He opened the door of the buggy and, with help, out came Duke Saben. He looked grand in his dark gray suit and shiny obsidian boots. He turned to the driver and told him all was well, with which the man took to mean the duke would help the others. The second to emerge from the car was Duchess Bronwyn, wearing a sparkling lavender gown and a small diamond tiara. Finally, sliding and then stepping forth was their son, Oren.

Oren was a slight man, and upon seeing him, everything in Anne's being revolted. He was wiry, with dull, dark hair, pale skin, and depressing brown eyes. All Anne wanted to do was run, but her feet would not move, though her heart pounded the breath from her lungs. Her mind screamed, but her face remained unaffected.

Ethana, stealthily leaning to whisper in Anne's ear, also found Oren a very sorrowful creature but a beautiful one. "Oh, Anne, is he not tragically handsome, more like the reluctant hero from a story, perhaps? So much pride and dignity in those sad eyes," she told Anne dreamily. Then she sighed and whispered, "How tragically romantic."

Thaniel stepped forward to welcome the duke and his family. He merely bowed his head, raised it, and said, "Thank you for blessing us with your presence. I hope you accept what is mine is also yours and that you enjoy the evening we have arranged in honor of your presence."

"Thank you, Baron de Ranger. I am sure we shall enjoy ourselves immensely," the duke stated. After standing completely still for a moment, he moved to his wife. "I would like you to meet my wife, the Duchess Bronwyn." He then nodded to his son. "And my son, Lord Oren."

Reyna stepped forward. "Your Graces, my Lord Oren, it is a pleasure to meet you." She curtsied. "I am Reyna, and these are my daughters, Lady Philana-Narie and Ethana." Anne's mother motioned toward her and Ethana. They too curtsied. "Please do come in. I am sure dinner is ready to be served." Reyna ushered the family into the manor house as Thaniel told the drivers where they could park the carriage and then where they, too, might get something to eat.

"Reyna," the duchess began, "I was recently made aware that your last name, though spelled R-A-N-G-E-R, is pronounced Rawn-jzhā."

"That is correct," Thaniel said as he had come up from behind. "My family originated in Île-de-L'est. Therefore, *er* is pronounced 'ay.' Reyna's name is also quite unique; I'm not sure of the origin. Do you know, darling?" Reyna smiled and said it was an old family name, but as far as Anne knew, her mom's family had always been in Ryland.

"I see." The duchess nodded her understanding. Then to Reyna, she said, "You have such a lovely home. And these flowers, how beautiful."

Anne was disappointed the duchess seemed not to know what the flowers meant. She thought all upper royals had to know such things. She grimaced a little but kept quiet and followed the elder women into the dining area. The duke insisted Thaniel sit at the head of his table and Reyna at the foot, saying that it was the only proper way. The large oak table was slightly off balance because of the number of people present, having three people, the duke, duchess, and Oren, on one side and Anne and Ethana on the other. To compensate for the unevenness, the seat between Anne and Ethana was kept vacant.

Anne had overheard the dinner menu for the evening was a mixed green salad to begin, then sweet venison with a carrot sauce, steamed mixed vegetables, and scalloped potatoes. For dessert, they'd have a delicious pound cake with chunks of baked apple and lightly covered with a sweet applesauce. Only the best wines would be served, and at the end, tea would come with the dessert.

Once everyone was properly seated, Thaniel nodded for the salads to be served. As the servers were getting the first course ready, the duke began his gentle questioning of Anne.

"So, Philana-Narie, I hear you are quite the student. Your teachers praise your fine artistry when it comes to quilting and arrangement." He took a sip of water from the goblet before him.

"Thank you, Your Grace, but there are many girls who share the same eye for detail that I possess. However, your notice of mine is greatly appreciated." Anne gave the man a slight bow of her head.

Then the duchess spoke up. "Philana-Narie, your mother has told me the flora for the evening was chosen by you. I must say you have excellent taste in flowers, and they so complement the arrangements your mother had previously prepared. Did they teach you this in school as well?"

Anne wondered if the salads would ever come. "How to choose and arrange flowers, yes. However, I learned the meanings of flora on my own, with the help of a few gardeners and florists." Just then, the servers resurfaced with the salad plates. But if Anne believed food would keep royal tongues from wagging, she was mistaken. Between bites of salad, the duke and duchess continued their investigation.

"Philana-Narie—" the duchess began, to Anne's annoyance.

"Anne. Please, just call me Anne." She didn't mean to be so rude, but the way they continued to say her proper name was driving her crazy. Not that she hated her name; she simply thought it was too much of a mouthful to be said more than three times in one evening.

The duchess, startled by the interruption, cleared her throat and began again. "Anne. If you could do anything in the world right now, what would it be?"

"Are you sure you wish to know the truth?" Anne asked, knowing no one at the table was sure to like her answer. She, on the other hand, really couldn't have cared less. Oh, if only her parents weren't so bent on her marrying Oren.

"Yes, child," the duke spoke up. "The truth is always the correct way to go, and never do we want to hear anything less from you."

Anne could feel the weight of her parents' eyes on her, likely praying she would not embarrass them. But if the truth was what the royals were looking for, how or why would she deny them? "I wish I could attend the boys' school." There were gasps around the table, but she continued. "I merely wish to learn more than just how to decorate a home, how to build a menu, to sew, to quilt—a mere sliver of the basics the boys are taught. I want to learn advanced literature and mathematics, as well as science." She thought the duchess was going to faint.

The duke merely puffed out his chest, exhaled loudly, and said, "Miss de Ranger, you should be glad you don't have to worry about knowing such things. Many men wish they didn't have to spend hours working problems given to them by their teachers. Besides, a woman's mind is not biologically capable of handling such complex studies, nor are they strong enough to handle the stresses that work demands. It is, of course, the reason the Lord made it a man's burden to toil so long and hard."

Everyone at the table agreed with the duke—her mother, her father, the duchess, and Oren. When Anne looked at her sister, she saw the disbelief she saw written all over Ethana's face. She had told Ethana on numerous occasions she would like to go to the boys' school, so her shock couldn't have come from that bit of old news but because she had actually spoken her dream to the duke. Well, Anne didn't care about the duke's rank, his snobbery, his opinions, or his sad-looking boy. She didn't like being called stupid, and from then on, she was going to play herself instead of the role of the perfect little daughter.

The salad bowls were taken, and the main course was brought to the table. To Anne's great happiness, her last response had lulled the questioning royals, and no one spoke for nearly five minutes. After that, it was up to the men to talk politics and the women to speak of everything pretty and nice. Reyna told the duchess how amazing Anne was when it came to quilting, and if they had time that evening, how she would like for her to see the masterpieces Anne had finished the month before.

Meanwhile, Ethana told her mother and the duchess of the new sort of spice brought from the East and how they were learning how it accompanied dishes. Anne, on the other hand, felt she had nothing to contribute and therefore listened in on the masculine conversation happening on the other side of the table.

"Your Grace, do you mean to tell me the prince is missing?"

"Not exactly, Baron. There have been rumors concerning Sagedor breaking the terms of our peace agreement; therefore, I believe he may have gone to Sagedor to gain some sort of intelligence," Duke Saben replied as he ate the cauliflower on his fork.

"A spy? Really? You believe the prince has gone to Sagedor to find out if they are planning to attack us?" Anne's father seemed to be having as difficult a time believing the prince would do this sort of work directly. Surely, the king would not send his only son and heir into such a potentially dangerous situation.

"Perhaps. I mean, it would explain his disappearance. You see, Prince Nolan has not been seen at court for several months, and I cannot readily believe he would simply give up his duties unless there were a greater need for him elsewh—"

"Right. I'd run." Anne cut off the duke before she realized what she was doing.

"Excuse me?" The duke seemed angry. "But I do believe you know nothing of the situation and should get back to talking about flowers. Leave men's topics to men."

There was that condescending tone again, and before her mother could stop her, Anne was fit to be tied. "You think I don't know what's going on? It's as plain as the noses on your faces! There is a rumor of an upcoming war with the North, but was not the prince educated in the North? Why should he wish to fight the very people he respects—the people who taught him all the higher knowledge he possesses? Staying would mean he would have to fight; therefore, fleeing is the only other option."

If the duke was not angry before, he was now, and his face showed every bit of that anger. "You have no right to say our prince would run out on his country, and if I were not on friendly terms with your family, I would make sure you were punished for what you have said here today!"

Anne felt a bit scared, but her anger was running at a higher level than that of the fear. "Well, Your Grace, since you believe women are simpletons, then you should have no reason to worry about what I have said. And as for my keeping to women's talk, someone had to join in on your two-way conversation since it was more than obvious that your son would not. In fact, perhaps he would be more interested in women's talk!"

With that, Anne was up from her chair and on her way to her room, leaving her parents to make the apologies she would have never made herself.

The royals stayed only after being promised Anne would be whipped for her behavior and after Reyna made the greatest apology speech known to humankind. Therefore, the rest of the evening went as planned minus one Lady de Ranger. The royals ate, talked, and left without seeing Anne's quilt work. Then, once everything was cleaned up, Thaniel had one last thing to do before going to bed. He had to deal with Anne.

Anne was lying in bed, staring at the ceiling from under a cast of graying moonlight. She knew her parents were infuriated, but she wasn't sure just how angry until her father walked in unannounced.

"Anne—" he began before she cut him off.

"Daddy, I'm really sorry. I just—" He didn't let her finish.

"Don't you ever, I mean ever, interrupt me again!" Thaniel had never yelled at Anne before, nor had he ever looked so dangerous. "Do you not understand that this world is not your playground? You cannot simply decide to make it as you wish it to be. There are rules, Anne, and with those rules, one must make compromises! Now, what you did tonight was inexcusable, and you must pay the price for your actions."

That's when Anne took notice of the whip at her father's side.

"They told you to do this to me, didn't they?" She couldn't believe her father was going to go through with it. She wanted to cry, but instead, she stood, turned her back to him, and began to remove her dress.

Her father seemed to be swallowing awfully hard, and when he managed to tell her that undressing would not be necessary, Anne thought she could hear a quivering in his voice. He just wanted her to lean against the footboard of the bed. Anne did as she was told. In the cool gray light of the moon and the room's stunned silence, Anne placed her face into her hands and received eighteen lashings as was suggested by the duke. She had to admit; it wasn't as painful as it would have been had she removed her clothes, but some lashes did make it through her dress to sting her skin.

When he finished the job, he left the room and allowed one of the servants to see to her wounds.

Anne, not once in the presence of her father or their servants, winced or cried. However, later, alone in the watchful quiet, she wept. Her heart ached, and for the first time, she felt lost and confused. Though the young woman who had dressed her wounds had done well, her back ached too, but the pain from behind did not come close to the despair she felt from within. She couldn't believe her father had actually done as the duke demanded. She felt as if her family had turned on her, and now she was all alone.

The next morning, a letter came from the duke. He wrote to thank the de Rangers for a lovely evening and to ask if Ethana would be available for tea at his palace. He said he and his wife were quite taken with the younger girl and would like to see her again. Reyna was more than ecstatic, but Thaniel was concerned about what the duke might be proposing.

"Reyna, we cannot marry Ethana until we settle things with Anne. It is the only proper way."

"Yes. And it was always the way for young ladies to mind their tongues when in the presence of men." Reyna looked extremely crossed. "Anne had her chance, and just as with everything else, she threw it to the wind. I am tired of her defiance, Thaniel, and from this point forward, the child who behaves the way she should will win all the prizes." Reyna left Thaniel standing in the dining room with letter in hand.

Shaking his head, Thaniel remembered he had forgotten to tell Verna to have food taken to Anne. He was sure she would not be down today.

Verna, a much older and plump lady, had been the manor's cook for as long as Thaniel could remember. She was a sweet, short thing, barely clearing five feet, and having the loveliest crystal-blue eyes. Verna was like a grandmother to Thaniel and had always spoken her mind. However, this morning, he would have rather she kept her opinions to herself.

"Verna," he said as he entered the kitchen, "will you please take some breakfast up to Anne? I'm sure she will not feel much like coming down today." He then grabbed a sliced carrot and tossed it into his mouth before grabbing a larger one.

"Dur it yerself," Verna spat at him. Her eyes were not the clear blue he'd always loved; they were now deeper, looking somewhat clouded over.

"Excuse me?" He put the larger carrot down.

Verna turned away from her pot, in which she was making stew, to give Thaniel her full attention. "Ye hert dat poor gerl lass night fer no reason! Nah, ye want me te go up thur an' fix da mess ye made! Well, I say dur it yerself, ye no gud coward dat ye are!" Then she moved back to her pot.

"Verna, don't ever speak that way to me again if you wish to remain here," Thaniel fumed.

"I'll speak at ye enna way I chuse! Ye may be da man of da manor nah, but thur was a time when I wiped yer boddum, an' ye called me mum when yer's weren't 'round te be found, ye spoiled boy! Nah, if ye think yer a man nah, p'haps ye shud act like one an' go apologize te dat gerl of yer's! I'll not dur it fer ye, even if ye whip me once more dan my seventy-three yurs!" She was waving a spoon at him. Then she went back to her stew.

Verna had never raised her voice to Thaniel before; however, he did remember a time when she had exercised her opinion on the poor gardener the year the potatoes were slight. Now, not quite knowing what to do, but knowing he didn't want Verna yelling again, Thaniel picked up the plate of bacon, boiled eggs, and a roll, which lay on the large oak table, and left the room. He knew he should apologize to Anne, but he also knew that he wouldn't. She had to learn her lesson, else nothing would ever change.

Thaniel ambled up the small staircase to the second floor and turned to his right so he was facing Anne's door. Wondering if he should knock, he stood there for a moment before deciding he should. He made a slow rap at the door. "Anne, I have some breakfast for you. Is it all right that I bring it in?"

There was no answer. He knew she was quite likely furious with him and would give up eating if she felt it was the only way to gain revenge.

"Anne, this is ridiculous. I'm coming in," he stated as he opened the door to a sad, soundless, and sullen room. The thick velvety curtains on the facing wall had not yet been drawn, and the light filtering through made the space look misty and foreboding. He was sure Anne had not left her room that morning, so where the devil was she? Thaniel went to her dresser to set the plate down as he contemplated the impossible, but before the plate touched the table, a note caught his eye. He lifted the paper, which was small and quite worn. It almost felt like a piece of old cloth. The outside fold had that day's date, and on the inside, a heart wrenching goodbye. Thaniel dropped the plate as he read the note, sending it crashing to the floor.

> *Well, I suppose you have found my note. I am not sure of anything I wish to say, so you must bear with me. The events which took place last night were indeed terrible. I must say I regret the way I behaved, though I still believe all my statements to be true and honest to the best of my knowledge. I am sure the duke no longer wishes me for his son, which I am also sure is for the best. However, in light of everyone caring more for the duke and his family than they do for me, I have chosen to relieve you of the burden I apparently cause. Perhaps with me out of the way, you can peddle Ethana to Oren. They seem more suited for one another, anyway. As for my lashes, I am sure they will serve as reminders of your new bitterness toward me and will keep me from the sickness of wishing to return.*
> *~A*

Thaniel couldn't believe she had truly left and suddenly found it difficult to breathe. He fell to his knees, one of which smashed the boiled egg that had landed dejected upon the floor, with its insides accenting its outside, now fleshy white with a crumbly yellow—the same shade as crushed dandelions. Thaniel did not notice the egg. He was too busy trying to decide what to do.

Anne was tough. He didn't believe she could survive on her own for too long. A pretty girl with her upbringing and that ill temperament of hers could easily find trouble—if she hadn't already. He wondered what she was doing now and where she might be.

Anne looked around the marketplace. In her haste to leave before sunrise, she had forgotten to grab the simplest of necessities: food. She did, however, have eleven gold pieces and five silvers. If she spent wisely, it should last her at least two weeks, so a job must be had.

Dressed as a man in the clothes she had stolen from the laundry, she opened the large jacket to see the gardening boy's name just above the inner pocket. She smiled, thinking she should have known the clothes belonged to Henry. He was always forgetting to pick up his laundry once it was cleaned. Reaching into the pocket, she pulled out a silver coin and proceeded to the baker's. She was sure he would have some delicious muffins or Danishes, warm and ready to eat. Besides, he had tables in front of his place, and the walk from the manor to the market had made her incredibly tired.

Once in the bakery, the warm aroma of fresh bread, rolls, muffins, and the dozens of other pastries filled Anne's nose but further emptied her stomach. As she allowed her eyes to rover over each delicious item the bake shop had to offer, she hoped Dermot wouldn't recognize her. The old man had been selling bread at the market for years and was always one to hand her and her sister free cookies whenever their mother stopped in. If anything, he and Haru, the florist, were the two people at the market who knew her best, so she held her breath as she moved to the counter.

"Excuse me, sir, may I have one of your rolls and a muffin?" Anne asked in her best masculine voice, which wasn't bad at all.

Dermot turned from the counter where he had been adding the chocolate stripes to freshly baked éclairs. "Of course. What sort of roll and muffin would you like?" His eternally cheery disposition always made Anne smile, but this time, she chose to purse her lips and imagined what would happen to her if she were caught. Then, with a steady hand, she pointed to the roll she wanted and told him a blueberry muffin would be fine. Again, Dermot smiled. "So, you new around here?"

Anne wasn't expecting any questions and almost gave herself away when she said no but quickly recovered when she saw the inquiring look on Dermot's face. "I mean to say I have been here once before as a child and always thought it the most wonderful place on earth."

To that Dermot laughed. "I felt the same way when I first visited here. Then two months later, I gave up my career as a law enforcer, moved here, and became a baker." Anne already knew the entire story, and it was that knowledge which helped her to answer his question, which was, "So, are you a sailor then? I must say you don't look like one, but then again, you never know these days." He handed her the roll and muffin in a small brown bag.

"Yes, of course." Anne thought that was a brilliant idea. She could become a sailor! "We are only here a few hours, so I am sorry, but I should probably be on my way. How much do I owe you?" She looked to the old man expectantly.

Dermot waved his arms about in a dismissive manner. "Ah, don't worry about it. I'm sure you'll be back again, and when you are, perhaps you can treat me sometime."

Anne smiled. "Well, thank you, Mr. . . . ." she pretended not to know his name.

"Dermot. Everyone just calls me Dermot. And what may I ask is your name, my boy?"

A simple question to which Anne hadn't an answer, so she chose the first thing that popped into her head, "An—Andrew. Yes. My name is Andrew. Thank you for the roll and the muffin, Dermot, but I really must be on my way." With that being said, Anne ran from the bakery and, though extremely exhausted, felt it best to keep moving.

Safely down the street, *Andrew,* she thought to herself, was a divine name for her altogether, and she was quite pleased with how quickly it came to her. As she picked at her muffin with her thumb and index finger, she thought more about what Dermot had said about her being a sailor. It was a grand idea. If she found a ship in need of help, she would receive free passage from this dreadful place. Of course, she knew absolutely nothing of sailing, but she would learn all there was to know if she could just get on board. With that decision made, the only thing left to do was to find a ship. Smiling, Anne made her way to the docks.

When Thaniel finally caught his breath and came back to his senses, he ran from Anne's room to find Reyna. He went first to their bedroom, only to find a young girl making the bed. Then he returned to the kitchen, where he received only strange looks from Verna and her staff. He also searched the grounds, the linen room, and the sewing room. Finally, he decided to ask Ethana if she had any idea where he could find her mother. Slowly, he walked up the stairs, hoping not to say anything to upset his overly sensitive daughter while attempting to discover the whereabouts of his wife. Just down the hall and to the left of Anne's room was Ethana's, and finding himself before her door, he gave the heavy wood a soft rap.

"Yes?" Ethana's voice came from the other side in the form of a question.

"Ethana, it's your father. Would you mind if I came in?" Thaniel was leaning against the wall with his left hand on the door.

"Oh, yes." Ethana opened the door. "Father, Mother and I have been going over what I will wear to the duke's palace today. It would help a great deal if we could have your opinion. I just want to make sure I look positively wonderful."

The entire time Ethana spoke as Thaniel entered her room, he heard not a single word. He was busy looking at his wife, who was sitting on the edge of Ethana's bed, and wondering how he was going to break the news to her. "So, Father, what do you think of this?" Ethana held up a white dress with little pink flowers trimming the skirt.

Thaniel wasn't really looking at the dress but through it. He was entirely engulfed in his own worries. "Anne is gone."

Reyna stood. "Thaniel, what do you mean *she's gone*? Have you sent her to market?"

Angry that Reyna didn't seem to quite understand the scope of what he was saying, Thaniel erupted into a full rage. "No, Reyna, she hasn't merely gone to market! She has left home, quit us, run off forever! We were too hard on her last night. I should not have whipped her and knowing our daughter as we do, we should have supported her last night!"

Reyna sighed before she spoke, presumably to avoid exciting Thaniel any more than he was already. "Thaniel, I understand you're upset that she's apparently gone, but where can she possibly go, really? I'm sure she will come to her senses in due time and return home. As for her punishment, I think it was truly the best thing we could have done for her. If she does not learn what it is to be in her place, then she will never learn. Now, let's get back to the issue at hand and help Ethana dress for her tea at the duke's." Reyna turned to Ethana, who had dropped the dress at her feet and was rubbing her arm nervously.

Thaniel couldn't believe what he had just heard. He had thought Reyna would help him find their eldest daughter, but she seemed only to care about the possibility of marrying Ethana to the duke's son. She seemed completely unconcerned about Anne's disappearance.

Upset, angry, and afraid, Thaniel tossed Anne's note on Ethana's bed before his wife. "Here . . . read this. I hope it shames you as much as it shamed me. Now, I am going to look for our daughter before she gets hurt. If you help me, wonderful! However, if you do not and she ends up in some sort of irreversible trouble, I'll have you know, I will blame you!" Thaniel stormed out of the room, slamming the door behind him.

The sound of the door slamming echoed in Reyna's ears. She couldn't wholly contemplate her husband's words. She stared at the door for the pulse of several heartbeats. Reyna had never been so shaken in her entire life but felt it was her duty to tend to their youngest daughter instead of wasting time searching for the eldest. "I do believe your father is overreacting. This is probably just another one of Anne's jokes, and she will be home before nightfall. I'm sure there is absolutely no reason to worry."

Reyna picked up the dress Ethana had dropped upon hearing of her sister's disappearance. "Hmm . . . I do believe this is the best dress to wear for tea. You'll be beautiful."

Ethana touched the airy fabric of the dress and whispered she wished they were out with her father, looking for Anne. It seemed she didn't believe this was one of Anne's jokes, nor did she believe her sister would ever come home unless she was forced to do so. Ethana, unlike her mother, believed Anne would get as far away from town as possible and never look back.

Chapter Three

The Search

*A*nne reached the docks an hour later. She supposed she would have arrived sooner had she not gotten confused whether it was north of Dermot's or south of Dermot's. The dock was just the sort of place her mother would never have allowed her to go, and now she knew why. Everywhere she looked there were people of a questionable manner. Women walked around seductively, with one end of their skirts up, showing a bit of leg and bodices that looked way too small for their ample bosoms. Anne had never seen such blatant sexuality and wasn't sure she liked it. As she drew closer to the wooden sidewalk leading to all the boats, a rather scantily dressed woman approached her.

"Helo, deary, ya lookin' for sum compny?" the half-naked blonde asked. She was not very clean; her makeup was enough to paint murals, and she smelled of rotten fish.

Anne covered her nose with her sleeve and tried not to lose her breakfast. Then, realizing what she was doing wasn't at all polite, she put her sleeve down and did her best not to breathe in the odors too deeply. "No, ma'am, but thank you for the offer." Anne really wasn't sure what to say to the lady. She just wanted her to go away.

"Yer quite a nice boy, ya are." The woman touched a dirty-gloved hand to Anne's cheek. "Is there anythin' I can help ya with?"

Anne really looked at the woman now. She had to be in her twenties. Her hair was curled but matted at the same time. She had big beautiful brown eyes and suddenly, for some strange reason, Anne had the urge to help her. "What is your name, miss?"

Anne's question clearly startled the lady, who backed away. "Why?"

"Just wondering. You see, I am hoping one of these ships will offer me employment. I thought if I knew your name, I might be able to send money to you. Then you would no longer be forced to do this sort of work." Anne imagined herself walking up and down the dock, selling her body to stay alive, and again almost lost her breakfast.

"Go on. Ya won't send any money ta me." Then the woman ignored her with the wave of her hand.

To that, Anne merely reached into her pocket and pulled out one gold coin and one silver. Not many things in the market could be bought with a mere silver, but Anne believed the gold would help the lady get away from the dock long enough for her to send more. Anne opened her hand for the lady to see. The older woman's eyes grew to twice their normal size; yet again, she backed away. "I'll give this to you under several conditions," Anne began. "You must agree to all the conditions if you desire the money."

The woman looked at her suspiciously but no longer backed away.

"First, you are going to have to tell me your name and your place of residence. Second, you must promise to stay away from the docks. Third, you must do as I tell you to do with the money I provide. Do you understand?" The woman nodded. "Well, then, what is your name?"

"Laveda, sir." She curtsied, and her language and tone changed. "I live in Swinfen's Bar, up the road, with my sister, Sophie. The address is 11 Rampart."

"Does your sister work the docks as well?" Anne hated to think of saving two people when she barely had enough to save herself.

"No, sir. She doesn't much like me doin' it as it is. But I can't take care of her and me if we don't got any money. Ya see, sir, my sister is only eight, and she can't walk because of a sickness she had when she was five. We ain't seen our parents in three years, and I don't rightly know if we ever will again." The lady seemed so tired then . . . and so sad.

Anne couldn't imagine life if her parents had left her and still couldn't believe that she had left them. But to wake up one morning and find the people who are supposed to care for you gone . . . that would be awful. "Laveda," Anne spoke, trying to keep the emotion from her voice. "I want you to take this money and use it to buy food and shelter. I do not want you coming to the docks, nor do I want you to wear all that paint on your face. You are to go home now, wash your hair, body, and clothes. Take care of your sister in the same manner. If anyone asks where you got the money, tell him or her you found it. Do not spend it like you're mad because I don't know when I can send more. Along with the money I send, I will send lessons; you will read and learn all that I send. Do you know how to read?" Anne suddenly thought to ask. When the girl nodded, Anne continued. "Good. With any hope, eventually, you will obtain more respectable work. Do you understand?"

"Yes, sir, but what do ya want in return?" Laveda seemed weary.

"Nothing," Anne replied and then had an urge to question the young lady again. "Laveda, how old are you, and how much do you make walking the docks?"

Sighing before she answered, she seemed to age ten years. "I'm sixteen, and I only make three or four coppers a week."

Sixteen! Anne never guessed the girl to be younger than her—and four coppers a week! Goodness, that wasn't even half a silver! So what Anne was offering the girl was more than she would make in half a year! How could anyone live on so little? Anne reached into her pocket once more and pulled out another gold coin. She handed all three coins to Laveda. "Now, I want you to take this money to the marketplace. Go to a bakery and tell a man named Dermot you need to change the three coins I have given you into coppers. Tell him a friend of Philana-Narie's sent you. Once you have the coppers, I want you to take what you need for the week and hide the rest. Use the money sparingly and do not bring attention to yourself. Do you understand?" When Laveda nodded, Anne did too. "I must go now, but I will write to you as soon as possible."

Anne began to take off but then realized she hadn't even told the girl her name, so she stopped and went back to the downright stunned teenager. "Laveda, my name is Andrew, and I must ask you to tell no one of our agreement." She placed a soft hand on the girl's cheek as Laveda began to cry, then she turned to make her way to the ships.

Thaniel didn't know where to search for Anne, but the only place to start was the market. So there he was, looking over all the shoppers to see if his daughter was among them. Having no success scouting the area from his carriage, Thaniel parked it near the florist and went in to see Haru.

The younger lady was moving about her shop, making displays and hanging signs. Looking at her now, Thaniel couldn't understand why Haru had yet to marry. She was rather attractive with her jet-black hair and deep brown eyes, which, at the moment, were staring right at him.

"May I help you, Thaniel?"

Her question brought him back to reality. "Yes." He shook his head. "Haru have you seen Anne? She's run away from home, and I'm not sure where to look for her."

"Run away?" Haru lowered the sign in her hand and looked at him in disbelief. "No, Thaniel, I haven't seen her. Why on earth would she run away from home?"

Not wanting to seem like a monster in front of the young florist, Thaniel did his best to evade the question. "It's a long story. Perhaps someone at the school may have seen her." He left Haru's question unanswered and hurried away.

Thaniel asked every summer student at the school if they had seen his daughter, to no avail. He checked the library, her favorite reading spot, and all the dress shops, shoe stores, and cafés. The only other place to look was Dermot's, but he had a sinking feeling she would not be there either.

When he walked into the bakery, Dermot looked up and smiled, making Thaniel's heart sink even more.

"Hello, Thaniel! I'm quite surprised to see you here. Has Reyna finally given up on doing all the shopping?" the ever-happy man asked gleefully.

"No," Thaniel replied sadly. "Dermot, Anne is missing. I only came here to ask if you had seen her, but as happy as you are, I suppose you haven't." Thaniel sat on a chair near the window.

Dermot walked from around the counter to join him. "Missing? What do you mean she's missing?"

Though exasperated from hearing that question over and over again, Thaniel told the old man everything, including the contents of the letter she left behind. "I can't believe she's gone, Dermot." He was crying now. "How will she live? Where will she live?"

Before Dermot could say anything in return, an unattractive woman walked into the bakery. She smelled of fish and was rather dirty. "Hel'o, I'm lookin' for a man named Dermot."

A little confused, Dermot stood and coughed a bit, because of her stench, before replying. "I'm Dermot. May I help you?"

"Ya," the lady nodded. "I was sent here by a friend of Philana-Narie to get coppers for these coins." She held her hand out, and in her palm were two gold coins and one silver.

At hearing his daughter's name, Thaniel jumped up and nearly grabbed the young woman. "Have you seen my daughter? Where is she? Is she all right?" He bombarded the girl with questions she could not answer and scared her half to death.

Stammering, the girl tried her best to answer the tall man before her. "I don't rightly know who she is. Alls I know is a gent gave me three coins and told me to trade 'em in for coppers. I ain't even sure how he knows her." The girl was moving away from the hysterical man and closer to Dermot, apparently feeling a bit safer by the owner's side.

Dermot put a hand on the girl's shoulder and patted her. "Do you know the name of her friend, then?"

"When a gent comes up to a girl like me and offers her money for nothin', she don't ask questions. I took the money an' thanked him. Told me I'd keep my money better if I switched it to coppers. That way, nobody would question where I got a couple of golds."

Dermot nodded.

Thaniel didn't think the girl was lying; in fact, she seemed rather frightened of him.

Dermot again patted the girl on the shoulder. "Okay, dear, why don't we get you those coppers?" Dermot then took her coins and returned to the other side of the counter. "Miss, I am going to need to get more coppers from the back. Please stay here. I'm sure you'll be fine."

The lady nodded.

A teary-eyed Thaniel once again addressed the filthy woman, who was now in the center of the room. "So you haven't the slightest idea who my daughter is?"

Laveda answered him carefully . . . perhaps tenderly. "I am surry, sir. But I hadn't even heard her name until the man mentioned her today at the docks. And lookin' as nicely dressed as ya do, I don't rightly believe you or yer family visit there much."

"You are quite correct," Thaniel responded sadly. "In fact, I can't imagine my daughter would even associate with anyone who would go to the docks at all."

Then, slightly changing the subject, he asked, "Will you do me a favor?" When she didn't nod, Thaniel continued and hoped she'd at least listen. "My daughter has run away from home. I am sick with worry and have been searching the town for hours. Please, if you see this man again, ask him about my daughter. If he doesn't wish to let you know where she is, at least find out if she is safe."

"Sir, I don't have much, and if I do see him again, I don't wanna make 'im mad. He might help me sum more."

Thaniel could see her situation. "Listen carefully. I am Baron de Ranger. I live southwest of the marketplace on an estate called Indira. If you hear anything about my daughter, please bring the information to my manor. I will pay you well for your help."

"I don't need no money, Baron. I can take care of meself," Laveda stated, then narrowed her eyes. "If I do my best to find out about yer daughter, I'd want you to help me with my sister." She moved closer to Thaniel. "A sickness made it so she can't walk anymore, and I want something better for her than I have to offer."

Just then, Dermot came from the back with a small brown bag of rolls and several copper coins. "Here you are, young lady. The bread is a day old, but it's still quite good." He handed her the rolls as well as the coins.

"Thank ya, Dermot." She accepted the food and coins, then turned back to the baron. "Well, Baron, do we have an agreement?"

Thaniel nodded, and the girl nodded back.

After, she ran out of the bakery and toward the docks.

"Ethana, it is so good to see you again, my dear," Duchess Bronwyn greeted her young guest. "I am sorry, but Oren is a little behind schedule. It does, however, give us time to talk amongst ourselves." She smiled.

"And where is My Lord today? I hope he is well." Ethana struggled to keep her mind on why she was there instead of where she'd rather be—in town, searching for her sister.

Waving Ethana to a seat with a gracious hand, the duchess spoke, "Oh, he is cleaning up from his riding lesson. He really should be joining us momentarily. As for the duke, he had pressing matters to attend to."

Ethana nodded, though she could not have cared less about whether she saw the duke again or not. She felt had Duke Saben not ordered her father to punish Anne, she would not have run away. Then, noticing she might have been too quiet for too long, she thought she should comment on the beauty of the palace grounds. "Your Grace's gardener must be exquisitely skilled, for your grounds are quite lovely."

"Yes, Armond and his crew are rather extraordinary. I was so impressed with these gardens that I added this tent here for afternoon teas."

"I can see why you chose this area for the tent—as near as it is to the lavender, you can continuously enjoy a pleasant fragrance, even once teatime has concluded." Ethana smiled faintly. She had never found small, formal chats so difficult before. She felt as though she was feigning everything and prayed the duchess could not read her true thoughts.

The duchess smiled and then spoke carefully in a hushed tone, "Ethana, you do realize the duke and I have decided that you would be best for our son?"

Ethana knew this was the true reason she had been asked to the palace but couldn't bring herself to acknowledge that fact now. "But, Your Grace, what about my sister?"

"My dear, as lovely as your sister appears, I'm afraid she has the soul of a gypsy. Now, I know you must love her, and I don't mean to offend, but her manners are quite appalling."

Before Ethana offered a response to the duchess's comment, Oren approached from the back doors of their grand estate. She noticed he was dressed in the same manner of suit he'd worn the night before. It was in style for men this season, but it seemed to overwhelm Oren's slight figure and quiet demeanor. Ethana watched as he came closer to where she and his mother sat; however, she wasn't looking at him as if he were the most handsome man alive but trying to find the reason for her attraction to him the night before.

Perhaps it was romanticism triggered by meeting with royals or because of the soft light of the evening that had made him so enticing. Now, in the truth revealed by the morning light, he seemed too thin and too pale and left her wanting.

Once he reached the tent, he kissed his mother on the cheek, then turned to bow to her before returning his attention to his mother.

"Mother, there seems to be a slight problem in the kitchens, and Mrs. Sproule would like your help making everything right." Oren stood straight with his hands clasped behind his back. It was the first time Ethana had heard him speak. His voice was not as deep as most men and quite monotone.

The duchess, looking annoyed, stood and commented on how nothing ran smoothly if she took a break. Apologizing to Ethana, she strolled toward the palace. Oren, on the other hand, slowly moved toward his mother's vacated seat and sat down.

"So, I hear your sister's run off," he stated as he spread lemon curd on a crumpet.

Ethana was shocked by the point the conversation had just begun. "How did you know that? My family just became aware of her disappearance a few hours ago."

"Well, servants talk." He took a bite of the sweet roll. "A few of them went to the market this morning and overheard your father searching for her. You know," he continued, "her leaving may be the best thing to ever happen to your family. I mean, she would have eventually pulled you all down to her level."

Not believing what she was hearing, Ethana didn't know what to say. She never imagined someone of such a noble upbringing could say something so callous, so mean. It took her a moment to respond, but when she did, she was less than kind.

"I must beg to differ, My Lord. My sister is the core of my family. She is the only one who can keep us together, and I fear if she does not return soon, we shall all suffer."

"Nonsense," he said before saying something beneath his breath.

"I apologize, Lord Oren. I missed your complete response."

"I said, 'Women are too blinded by their emotions to see the truth.' Your sister was a plague upon your family. Now, I know you must have loved her because she was your sister, but her habits were those of a peasant. I, for one, am glad she is gone so you are no longer exposed to her influences."

Ethana could feel heat rising to her cheeks as her breath became labored. "And what influences might those be, My Lord?" Her voice was strained as she tried to keep it level.

"All that nonsense she spoke at dinner about wanting to go to the boys' school and study what men do. It is not proper, and any woman I marry will have to know her place."

Deciding she was in the wrong place after all, Ethana rose gracefully, coolly, from her chair. "My Lord, I do apologize, for I must be on my way home. You see, I, apparently unlike my sister, *do* know my place, and it is not here. I should be with my father, helping him search for Anne."

As she turned to walk away, Oren stood and yelled, "Ethana, don't be foolish! What you can have, what you can achieve, you can do it here. If you throw it all away, you are just as ignorant as your sister."

Ethana smiled to herself before turning back to answer. "I would rather hold company with my sister than be in the company with you and your sort. You may think her ignorant, but she is intelligent enough to know more things political than yourself. This means she can manage both women's talks as well as men's; whereas you, thus far, have only been able to share gossip. Perhaps my sister was correct in saying that you should stick to women's talks."

Ethana once again turned her back on the intensely rude young man and walked to where her carriage awaited.

Chapter Three

Masks

*A*nne was having an awful time finding someone who would hire her with no experience. Though she swore to learn all there was to know about sailing, many of the ships' captains didn't want to waste their time. There were only two ships left to query, and she was almost certain she knew what their answers would be. To make matters worse, she was regretting giving so much money to Laveda.

"Okay, Anne, only two ships left," she spoke to herself. "One has to take you in, or it's over. You'll have to return home." As Anne approached the first of the two ships, she was confronted by a rather large and strange-looking man. He wasn't really large around the middle, but in height, he was enormous. And though Anne had never seen a Black man up close, she was sure he wasn't of African origin because surely, if so, he would have a darker complexion.

"Is there something I can help you with?" the man asked in a rich bass voice. Anne was afraid to respond but gulped down her fear before asking to speak with the captain. "The captain is busy. You may deal with me in his stead."

Heart sinking, Anne mustered up the courage to present herself to the best of her ability. "My name is Andrew," Anne said in her masculine voice as she thrust her hand forward. When the man didn't accept it, she retracted it before continuing. "I would like to inquire after employment upon your vessel."

The giant crossed his arms. "We are always looking for capable men. Do you have any experience with large ships such as this?"

Anne had been afraid that might come up. "No, but I am a hard worker and learn quickly." Anne was about to add that she would do almost anything, but the man had already begun to walk away.

She couldn't stand it anymore! This was one of the largest ships in the harbor. She knew they must have a need for someone to clean or cook. She would gladly do either rather than go home. Desperate for a job, she followed the man onto the ship. Once onboard, she yelled at him, "Hey, listen! What you just did, I found to be rude and dismissive! Now, I need work, and I will do almost anything! If *you* are unwilling to help me, at least allow me the opportunity to make my plea to your captain!"

Just then, a shorter man, still nearly six feet tall, came to stand next to the giant. His face was smiling and warm, in stark contrast to the stern expression of the other man. "Kenward," the man began, "what seems to be the problem here?"

"Captain, this boy wishes to join our crew; however, he has no experience," the larger man respectfully addressed his shorter companion.

"Really?" The captain smiled. "Boy, how old are you?"

Anne had no idea how old she looked and didn't really know how to answer. However, she didn't want to seem nervous or less than confident. "Old enough to be on my own," she replied with a bit of defiance.

"Well, I thought it was only women who hid their ages," the captain said, and all the men on deck laughed.

Anne was finding this whole experience humiliating; all she wanted to do was leave. "Listen, I can see that none of you are willing to offer me work, so instead of wasting both your time and my own, I'll be on my way."

"Wait one minute," the captain caught her attention as she turned away. "Kenward, how is a young man to learn about the sea if no one offers him employment on the sea?" The captain was now facing the monstrously huge man.

"I am not sure, Captain. However, perhaps he could go home and read a book or ask his father to help familiarize him with small boats before he attempts to undertake a ship of this size."

Rubbing his bearded chin, the captain agreed. "True, he could do that. But I do believe he would learn faster if he were to join our crew." He again looked at the man named Kenward. "We can start him out with the simple jobs, which none of you wish to do, and in his free time, he could learn the ins and outs of sailing and trade. What do you think?"

Kenward, blunt and with purpose, replied, "I think it is a waste of our time, Captain."

"Hmm. Well, I don't. And since I'm the one in charge, this young boy, starting this instant, is a member of this crew," the captain announced to everyone on deck. "It will be our responsibility to ensure he becomes the best sailor possible, and if you disagree, you may take it up with me, privately, in my cabin." Then, turning to Anne, he asked, "Well, boy, what is your name?"

"My name is Andrew, and I thank you for this opportunity. I will not let you down."

"You had better not. Like every new crewmember, you will make five coppers a day, which equates to three silvers and five coppers a week. As you learn and become more helpful to me and the crew, you may earn up to several gold pieces per week. Do you have a problem with this?"

Anne couldn't believe how little she would be making, but what other choice did she have? "No, that sounds reasonable."

"Good." He nodded before calling forth some of the crew. "Jerah, Marid. Andrew, these two men will teach you most of what you will need to know—as well as Kenward, whom you have already met. For the first few weeks, however, you will swab the deck and help Bêrk in the galley. Any questions?"

Anne had no idea what the captain was talking about. How did one swab, and what was a galley? Knowing the crew would probably think her an imbecile for asking such questions, she chose to keep them to herself. "No questions."

"Good. Jerah, show him where the supplies are kept and how to clean properly. Welcome aboard the *Survivor.*"

Laveda ran through the marketplace as fast as she could but stopped in the middle when she saw a boutique. Remembering the deal she had made with Andrew to bathe and wash her hair, she realized she didn't have anything with which to clean herself or her sister. Thinking long and hard, she remembered she had two hundred and ten coppers in her skirt pocket, more than she made in a year! She could certainly buy a bar of soap and a comb. Believing it couldn't be more than two coppers, she entered the boutique.

Everything inside was ornate and smelled wonderful. Laveda, not forgetting that her sister was home alone, didn't wish to spend her time shopping too long, so she went directly to the owner of the shop. "Helo, misses. I need some help buyin' some soap. Oh, and a comb."

Ms. Failand, a rather stout woman in her fifties, had never turned anyone from her store and was very proud of that fact. However, the stench coming from this young woman was almost more than she could bear, but rather than kick her out, Ms. Failand held her breath and assisted her customer. "Yes, dear, soap. We have many types. Is there anything in particular you would like the soap to do for you? Moisturize . . . *scent*?" she said, emphasizing the latter.

"I just want it to clean me up a bit. If you haven't noticed, I'm a bit unkept, and I promised a friend of mine that I'd clean up a mite. Ya know, wash my hair, comb it, and take a bathe." Laveda was looking around as she spoke.

"Yes, dear. Well, how about this: I will put together a bunch of things you will need, and you can go from there? Does that sound all right?" Ms. Failand moved away from the fusty young lady, more to get a breath of clean air than to collect the girl's much-needed supplies.

"Well, that's fine. Just don't expect me to buy too much. I aint got a lot of money, ya know." Laveda waved a finger at the older woman.

"Oh, no. I will take care of everything. Just tell me how much you have to spend."

Seeing how fancy the store was, Laveda thought two coppers wouldn't be enough to get soap and a comb, so she upped her previous estimate. "I can give ya no more than ten coppers. That's really all I have to spare at the moment." She was now resting the bag of rolls Dermot had given her on a table as she took the ten coppers from the small bag in her skirt. She took no notice of the look on the woman's face.

Ms. Failand's eyes were wide. She obviously couldn't believe the girl expected to buy soap and a comb for so little. They both knew one rather small bar of soap cost five coppers alone. Ms. Failand rubbed her neck as she seemed to contemplate what to do. Laveda knew the woman could help her and hoped through her assistance, she'd become a cleaner person. Then, perhaps, she might find a nice young man to take her in. Maybe Laveda should mention that; it could be Ms. Failand's first good deed of the day.

Before she opened her mouth, the woman spoke. "What if you're merely looking for handouts or some sympathetic schmuck to swindle?" Shaking her head, the woman ignored her own question and moved to help Laveda.

Ms. Failand put together a bag of items Laveda might need: one oatmeal soap, one lavender, a parsley hair tonic shampoo, a lemon verbena hair rinse, rose hand cream, and a medium-sized wooden comb.

The price for the package she handed Laveda was one gold and five silvers, but she said she'd take what the girl had to offer and call it even. "Here you are, dear. I have added a few other products to your bag, which should help you clean up nicely."

Laveda was flustered and, if honest with herself, a bit scared. "But I haven't the money for anything extra, I told ya!"

Ms. Failand smiled. "I know. However, you are a new customer and new customers deserve special attention. Think of all the extras as gifts, and perhaps later, when you have come into a bit of luck, you'll come back and see me." Ms. Failand, being a bit daring, took the girl's hand and gently pulled her to a nearby counter where she took everything out of the brown paper bag. "Now, dear, you must listen carefully. When you clean up later today, I want you to start with this beige soap. It cleans the skin and will soften any rough areas. Then wash your hair with this parsley shampoo; it will not only clean your hair but help it grow." The older woman was holding up a small brown glass bottle. "Once you have rinsed your hair with clean water, I want you to put in this lemon hair rinse. Let it set for at least ten minutes before rinsing your hair again with clean water." She pointed to a different bottle, this one light green. "This purplish soap, I have given to you for your clothes. It will keep them smelling fresh. And this small jar is a cream. Use it on both your hands and elbows after you have dried off from your bath." Ms. Failand then put everything back in the bag. "Any questions?"

"Yes. Do I get a comb? And how much do I have to pay ya?" Laveda stared at the goody bag.

"I placed a comb in the bag. All you owe me is ten coppers. And, my dear, I hope everything works out for you." Ms Failand continued to smile.

Laveda was beginning to think this was her lucky day. First, a strange man decides to take care of her, then that guy Dermot gives her a bag full of rolls. And now, this woman is going to give her more than she ever hoped to receive for ten coppers. She wasn't sure what to say but did her best. "Thank ya, ma'am. I promise I will come back when I have more money, and I will spend a lot here." Laveda handed Ms. Failand the ten coppers then grabbed her two bags from the counter and left the shop.

Thaniel returned home sadder than he had ever felt in his life. He couldn't believe Anne was gone, and he prayed she was safe. He hadn't been home a minute before Ethana was bounding upon him. He couldn't feel anything but disbelief and an emptiness within his chest; he wasn't sure, but he believed Ethana was hugging him—it sure felt like a hug. He wasn't sure of anything anymore . . . what was his life without Anne, his darling girl? He was too numb to respond and merely stood there motionless. The next thing he knew, he was sitting in the living area in his chair, but how he got there, he did not know, nor did he care.

"Father, please say something," Ethana begged as she sat at his feet. He didn't know Ethana's fear: *What if Anne was dead, and he was too upset to speak?* His fear was paramount: what if, when he found her, she told him how much she hated him and that she would never return home? Ethana couldn't seem to take it anymore. "Papa, please!" She sat up, grabbing her father by the chin, forcing him to look at her. "Did you find Anne? Is she okay? Why isn't she home?" she yelled her questions until he cried. Then Ethana began to cry. "She isn't dead, is she?"

Thaniel looked at his younger daughter, then hugged her tightly with his right arm as he smoothed her hair with his left hand. "Did everything go well at the palace? Do they want you to marry Oren?"

Ethana pulled away from him. "What does it matter what happened at the palace?" she sobbed. "Anne is gone! My sister is gone! And I don't even know if she is dead or alive because you won't tell me!"

Thaniel watched as Ethana's sobs turned into otherworldly wails of sorrow. He placed a hand on her left shoulder and held back his own tears. "Ethana, I can't answer questions to which I have no answers. I couldn't find Anne anywhere." Then he got up from his chair, petted her head, and went to his bedroom.

Anne was so tired. She had never worked so hard in her life. Jerah, the man who was teaching her how to clean, had a tender heart. He was an older man, maybe sixty years of age, and had always lived at sea. He said the sea wasn't an easy place to make your fortune, nor was it an easy place to live, but since salt water was in his blood, he just couldn't give it up. He told her she would need to prove her worth to the crew; otherwise, they would walk all over her. At the time, when he'd told her that, she was ready for anything. Now, after scrubbing every inch of the 240-ton vessel on her hands and knees while members of the crew walked (with their dirty boots) over the area she'd just finished, she wanted to cry. It took her all day to scrub and mop the deck, and she still had to help Bêrk in the galley.

Bêrk, Anne figured, was one of the youngest men on board. The captain also looked young, but Bêrk looked as though he had just been freed from schooling. A thin, almost wiry man, Anne wondered if he'd lost weight swabbing the deck when he first came aboard. His hair was brown with a few red highlights here and there, and his eyes were blue. He was not at all terrible to look at, but in the state Anne was in, she wasn't too interested in the looking. "I am supposed to help you with the evening meal."

Bêrk turned and smiled. "Yep. Although, I bet you would much rather go to bed. I heard how much misery the guys were giving you earlier."

"Really? Are they always so hateful, or is it just me?" Anne sat on a stool near the counter where Bêrk was chopping vegetables.

"Nah. They are really great guys; they just like picking on the new kids. You know, kinda break 'em in." Then he stopped chopping to wave the knife in Anne's face. "I can still remember the rubbish they did to me; fish guts on the deck while I was scrubbing, hiding the knives in the galley, moving supplies to the crew deck. They were merciless." He laughed.

"Well, then," Anne began, "are you going to put me through it as well? Are you going to leave me here to cook by myself or have me carry twenty plates at a time?"

"Nah. You see, I've only been on the ship about two months, so what they did to me is still fresh in my mind." He was chopping again. "I thought I would just show you how things are done in the galley. Then you can turn in early. If you wake up a bit before dawn, you can have most of the deck done before anyone else is up. And you won't be too tired to help me out tomorrow." He finished chopping the last of the carrots before continuing. "So what do you say to getting straight to business?"

Anne nodded, and the lesson began. Bêrk informed her that, while at sea, the crew ate salted beef and crackers and had lemon water. The salt preserved the beef for long periods; the crackers were easier to keep than bread, and the lemon juice was to prevent an awful condition called scurvy. However, when they were at port, he was allowed to buy a few vegetables to add variation to their diet; this was also to keep everyone healthy. He said when she returned to help him the next day, he would show her how to salt the beef to make a jerky, and where they kept the brandy, which the sailors received for dinner. Finally, he handed her a small bowl of vegetable stew. She was to eat and get some shuteye. That night, she fell asleep in a cubby at the southeast corner of the galley.

The next morning, she did as Bêrk suggested; she awakened just before dawn to work. Every muscle in her body ached, but she refused to stop. By dawn, she had finished scrubbing every inch of the 110-foot deck and was beginning to mop as the first members of the crew surfaced from below. By lunch, she had finished all her duties, including collecting the trash, emptying the bedpans, and mopping the crew's quarters. After lunch, she went to Jerah and asked him to teach her as much as he could about sailing, and from one to four, she learned nautical terms, such as *port, stern, hatch, batten down*, etc. She learned the *Survivor* was unlike any ship in the harbor—being somewhat of a cross between a fluyt and a clipper. It had the pear shape of the fluyt, which made it perfect for getting into tight spots and for quick loading and unloading; however, with its three masts, it was as fast as any clipper ship. He wasn't sure who designed the old dear but appreciated every curve and line.

Just before it was time to help Bêrk in the galley, she took a few minutes to write a letter to Laveda. She told the girl she was on the ship *Survivor* and that she would hopefully send her four silvers a month. Anne also wrote, to keep people from wondering how Laveda was paying her way and not working, the girl should disappear for a few hours a day to keep up pretenses. However, she was to continue to stay away from the docks. Having said all she felt needed to be said for the time being, she signed her new name to the letter, Andrew Pallas, and ran to hand it to the ship's messenger before speeding off to the galley.

Bêrk worked her to the bone. She would have to salt eight pounds of beef and juice more lemons than she had ever seen in her life, which made her wince as the juices penetrated the cracks and cuts in her hands. And it wasn't even what they were having for dinner. He told her it was best to have most everything done before they went out to sea. That way, when the men were tired and hungry, they didn't have to wait for a meal. Tonight would be the last night they enjoyed fresh vegetables, and he hoped the apples and berries he'd purchased would keep for another few days before they would have to be thrown away. Once Bêrk had finished chopping the carrots, potatoes, basil, and broccoli, he tossed everything into a large pot and cooked the soup for more than sixty men. While the soup was simmering, he helped Anne juice as many lemons as they could, then they put the juice in a huge glass container that was bolted to the wall. Anne noticed the container was already half full, and Bêrk told her he had been working on the lemons for three days.

When the soup was ready, Bêrk called in five other men, who helped with serving the crew every night. As Bêrk spooned out the soup and placed a soft piece of bread in each, the five servers would grab as many bowls as they could, sometimes four to five at a time. Then they carried them into the meal hall, which was also the crew's quarters. Anne, not wanting to seem like a sissy, did her best to grab four bowls. If she could just concentrate on not dropping them, she would do fine. However, right as she got to the door, Bêrk gave her a warning. "Be careful, Andrew, they like to trip the new guy." Great, now she had something else to worry about.

The first few times Anne went out, she didn't drop a thing. She was beginning to think no one was cruel enough to trip the new guy when he was holding a hot bowl of soup and was feeling pretty darn good until . . . it happened. Dyson, one of the meaner men of the crew, tripped Anne as she was walking toward Kenward, and she dropped his bowl at his feet. Luckily, she didn't drop it in his lap; otherwise, he may have ended up with a pretty nasty burn. Although, that was the only good thing about the whole situation because Kenward was angry. He slammed his fist on the table then yelled that she needed to be more careful because they didn't have food to waste. She tried to tell him she'd been tripped, but he wouldn't listen. He told her she was done for the day, and she could sleep above deck without dinner.

Upset, Anne walked away from the tables in the center of the room, went over to her mat, picked up the blanket they had given her, and went above deck. All Anne wanted to do was cry. She was tired and hungry, and she knew she would have to get up before dawn on an empty stomach and do it all again. With her dry, cracked fingers, she touched the upper left side of her back and felt the scabby gash in her skin, remembering why she was there. She would not cry. She would look on the bright side. The good thing was, she thought to herself, as exhausted as she was, she would soon be asleep. Smiling at that thought, she wandered over to the port side of the ship and lay down, covering herself with her blanket.

The chill woke Anne up earlier than she had hoped. It was freezing outside, even though summer was just a few weeks away. Trying to get warm, she sat up and drew her legs to her breasts and wrapped the dirty gray wool blanket tighter around her slight frame. The entire time she sat there, she believed she was alone, but when she heard a slight shuffle toward the aft side of the vessel, she quickly shot a glance to her right. Or, she thought the sound was aft, but just to her left, or port side, only a few meters away was Captain Doran. He was looking out over the sea, toward the other ships. She wasn't sure if he knew she was there, so she did her best to remain quiet.

The captain, she had to admit, was a rather good-looking man. He was tall, without being scary like Kenward, and had dark brown hair and eyes. His beard was nicely trimmed, and he was always impressively dressed, albeit somewhat casually.

Anne watched him as he stood there and wondered what sort of adventures he had been on, or if he had ever fought pirates. O' how marvelous that would be! She would absolutely love to fight off pirates by his side and save the day! Caught up in her own fantasies, she didn't realize when the captain said something to her.

"You know, it is impolite to stare," he mentioned but never looked in her direction. Wondering who he was speaking to, Anne looked to see if anyone else was around. "Why are you sleeping above deck, anyway?" he asked, still facing the sea.

Knowing now he had to be speaking to her, Anne stood and moved toward him. "Last night, Dyson tripped me, and I dropped a bowl of soup at Kenward's feet. Kenward then told me I had to sleep up here."

Doran shook his head. "Did you get to eat dinner?"

"No." Then switching the subject, she said, "I'm sorry, Captain, but which ship is it that draws your interest?"

Again, Doran shook his head, but this time he turned to look at her. "I come here every morning before dawn to think. I just find it easier to contemplate life's many peculiarities when everyone is asleep and things are quiet." Then he looked back out to the sea where several ships were making their way to and fro.

Anne stood silent for another moment, wondering if she should leave him alone but decided against it. "I didn't see you here yesterday."

He smiled. "I try to get here before the new kid gets his early start."

"Oh. Well, speaking of early starts, I suppose I should begin swabbing the deck," she attempted a half-hearted joke. Then, "Um, before I leave, may I ask you one last thing?" Doran once more looked to her, thinking he was staring at a young man—this time with a wry look and one raised brow. Taking that to mean yes, Anne asked her question. "Have you ever seen a pirate?" She knew she sounded more like a pre-pubescent schoolboy than a man, but she didn't really care. When he gave her an odd look, Anne thought perhaps she should explain why she had asked such a peculiar question. "Please, do not believe I wish to come in contact with any; although I am not afraid of a fight. I was just wondering if you had seen them and what they were like if you had."

Smiling then, Doran explained, "Andrew, pirates are precisely the sort of people a captain hopes never to come across, and luckily, I have had the great fortune of having not seen one. However, if we do happen to come across a pirate ship, I want you to know my men's safety comes before anything we may be hauling." He had turned completely toward her and was moving his hands as he spoke. "You see, unlike some of the other ships at port, my ship has many family men aboard, and dead, they can no longer support their wives, children . . . even mistresses." He winked. "Of course, there are some men onboard, like Dyson, who hope to die in a blaze of glory; however, my first concern is, and always will be, my men. If the pirates merely wish to steal our merchandise, then they can have it."

Anne was not at all expecting this sort of response from a ship's captain. Weren't they supposed to be all bravado? She wasn't quite sure how she should respond. "Well, I'm sure the men appreciate that."

"Do you?"

Treading carefully, Anne spoke her mind. "Actually, I am quite surprised by your response, and I must admit, were I you, I would try to protect our cargo. Not because I don't worry about our loved ones at home, but because I feel if we roll over and hand them what they want, they'll expect us to do so every time. If that happens, the crew won't have to worry about working aboard the *Survivor* because the *Survivor* will not survive. The pirates would prey on us every chance they could, and soon after, the merchants wouldn't send their goods via this ship because they'd realize we were all cowards."

"You make a very interesting point." Doran smiled.

Anne hadn't noticed the captain's facial expression, and therefore continued to re-emphasize her point. "Of course, I do. And perhaps you should further consider what I have said and contemplate tactics to help the ship and crew in case of any such situation."

"Thank you for the advice." The captain still had a smile in his voice as he spoke.

Still missing the smile, she nodded. "You're very welcome. Now, if you'll excuse me, I should begin my daily chores." Anne, wrapping her blanket tighter, started toward the supply closet.

Halfway there, the captain called to her, "Andrew! Once you have finished your morning duties, I would like you to join me in my cabin for breakfast. Perhaps then we can further discuss *tactics*." Then, as if trying to hide a chuckle, he turned back to the sea.

When Thaniel entered his bedroom the night after Anne's disappearance, he found Reyna on the floor, trying to muffle her sobs. Seeing his usually resilient wife in tears nearly ripped Thaniel apart. Reyna was usually the one to make all the tough decisions in the family, but now, he could see she was just as lost as he was. That realization was almost more than he could bear, for it meant Anne was not coming home. It meant the last hope was shattered. He'd almost felt—prior to seeing her there—that if someone believed Anne would be home, it would be Reyna. Now knowing how Ethana felt and seeing Reyna this way, he was left feeling hopeless. Instead of joining Reyna's side, Thaniel fell to the ground in the doorway and wept whole-heartedly for the loss of his daughter and over the events that had led to her disappearance.

Ethana heard the sobs of her father and, becoming more frightened, ran to him. She held him in her arms and rocked him back and forth as her mother looked on. Slowly, she caressed his head and asked herself what Anne would do if it were she who was missing. Surprisingly, putting herself in Anne's shoes was not as difficult as she believed. She knew she had to be daring, fearless, and bold. It was in that moment that she decided to ask the king and qqueen for help.

Chapter Four

Resettled

*F*rom the time Laveda returned home on that wonderful Monday afternoon until Wednesday morning, she had been cleaning. Her sister Sophie and the bar's owner, among others, could not imagine what had gotten into her. She did not waste time giving explanations. She wanted to have everything in her room cleaned before she bathed herself. She felt there was no sense in cleaning up if she were just going to lie back down upon a filthy bed. Therefore, Monday after splitting her money into two separate purses, and hiding one beneath the floorboards and the other under a piece of furniture, she ripped all the sheets and blankets from her bed. She then took her meager bug-infested mattress onto her balcony and beat it over the ledge. Doing so in such a manner released many roaches, spiders, and other creepy-crawlies, which had been living inside. Leaving the mattress on the balcony, she collected and got rid of the trash in the room.

Sophie, her poor sister, was lying in the corner of the room on the filthy blankets where Laveda had placed her. Laveda knew her sister didn't know who or what had lit the fire beneath her petticoats and wouldn't be surprised if her sister was afraid of what it might mean. Laveda hadn't taken to cleaning in at least two years, and Sophie probably wondered if her elder sister was doing so now to invite clients to their room.

The first day, Sophie didn't say a word. She merely lay on the blankets and watched as her sister swept, dusted, and threw things away. The next day appeared to be laundry day, and Laveda woke Sophie so she could retrieve her blankets.

Laveda watched Sophie look about the room in amazement. She had cleaned every cobweb, removed all the trash, and washed the few dishes they owned: two small cups, a chipped bowl, and an old plate. Laveda had placed their mattress back on the wooden slats where it belonged. Then she lifted the now awake Sophie to the bed to get to the blankets.

"Laveda, what're ya doin'?" Her younger sister looked frightened.

"Sorry, Sophie," Laveda kissed the top of her sister's head. "Things are turnin' around for us, and we need to be ready to accept our blessin's. These need a good washin'." Smiling, she took the blankets to another room for cleaning.

Laveda had been gone for at least an hour. When she returned, she was carrying three dripping wet, tattered blankets. They smelled of something sweet but not too unpleasant. Laveda walked past the bed to the balcony and heaved the blankets over the banister. Afterward, she went into a brown bag, took out a roll, and handed it to Sophie, apologizing for not having fed her sooner. She then grabbed what little clothes they owned, a different brown bag, and headed back out.

After all was done on late Tuesday afternoon, Laveda finally took a rest. She and her sister were still dingy, but at least all the blankets and clothes were clean and nearly dry. Just as Laveda was about to crash on the bed next to her sister, there was a knock at the door. Laveda jumped up to see who it was while Sophie sat, obviously listening.

Laveda had received a letter, and Swinfen, the barkeep/owner, didn't seem too happy about it. "Shouldn't be sittin' around waiting for love letters. Ya need to be workin'!" Swinfen was always like this, gruff and ill-tempered.

"Yes, sir." Laveda kept her eyes down as she accepted the letter. "I promise to get back to workin' soon. Ya don't need to worry 'bout nothin'; rent will be on time."

Swinfen looked about the room through the open door and smiled. "Make sure it is. And if you're plannin' to do business out of this room, ya better know you'll need to pay extra for that."

"Yes, sir. I understand," Laveda responded meekly. When the barkeep finally turned to leave, she shut the door. Then she frantically opened the letter. It was from Andrew. He'd been able to find work at the docks on a ship called *Survivor*, and it would be at port just another few days as repairs were made and cargo was picked up.

"Laveda, what is it?"

Hearing the fear and concern in her sister's voice, Laveda looked toward Sophie and contemplated how much to tell her.

"Laveda, please," Sophie begged. "Whatever it is affects me too. I understand I often look like a piece of furniture, but I am not. Please, tell me what has happened. Why are you suddenly behaving this way?"

Remembering her promise to Andrew, Laveda dodged her sister's question. "Aren't you tired of the filth? I know I am." But when Sophie crossed her arms and raised her brow, Laveda knew she had to let her little sister in on her secret. She and Sophie only had one another, and if she couldn't trust her sister, she really had no one.

Sighing heavily, she picked Sophie up and moved her to the center of the room. The walls of Swinfen's were thin, and she couldn't risk being overheard. In the voice of a field mouse, she told her sweet sister all about the handsome young man she'd met at the docks and how he promised to take care of her as long as she did a few simple tasks.

"You like him, don't you?" Laveda blushed, and Sophie sighed. "All right. I pray, for both of our sakes, that he is genuine. But please, dear sister, be careful."

Wednesday morning came upon them, and Laveda had made a deal with Tyra, another prostitute, the only one with a wide enough barrel for bathing. The deal was Laveda would do all of Tyra's laundry; and, in turn, she could use Tyra's tub for an entire day. The first one to bathe was Sophie. Laveda handed the girl the bar of beige soap and told her to wash herself as she used a large bowl she had borrowed to clean her sister's hair. After Sophie was all cleaned up, Laveda told her to relax in the water as she combed the tangles from her hair. Then she dried her sister off with one of the lighter blankets and carried her back to their room.

Once there, she dressed Sophie and rubbed some of the lemon rinse through her dark hair. While Sophie napped, Laveda hung the wet blanket over the banister of the balcony and went out to take her bath.

It took her forever to change the water in the tub, but once she was relaxing her weary body, she felt it was all worth it. Laveda took her time cleaning up, ensuring she covered every inch of her body. She wanted to be as close to perfect as she could be before heading to the docks to speak with Andrew. She knew, of course, she had promised to stay away, but surely, Andrew only meant for her to stay away from what she used to do while there.

The thought of seeing him again brought a flutter to her stomach, and soon, she found she couldn't wait. Feeling she was as clean as she was going to get, she worked on her hair. As she lathered it up, she ran the comb through it, only to discover how matted her hair had become. Dismayed and upset, she realized, because of the knots, she was going to have to cut her hair at least three inches. Suds dripping from her matted locks, she jumped out of the tub, dried off, and found a pair of scissors on a stand by Tyra's bed. Quickly, she cut out her naps and made her hair even. She then rinsed her hair in the fresh cool water she had placed in the large bowl before beginning to bathe.

Afterward, she dumped the used tub water out over the balcony, put the lemon rinse in her hair, refilled the tub to clean Tyra's clothes, washed them, again tossed the water, and hung Tyra's things over her balcony. With a big smile, she wrapped her naked body in her blanket and ran to her room to rinse her sister's hair and get dressed.

Meanwhile, on *Survivor*, Anne finished her duties in record time. She wanted to clean herself up a bit before joining the captain in his cabin. *Best foot forward*, she thought to herself. She was already quite nervous about this *little* meeting and didn't want the added worry of whether she was presentable or not. Therefore, she washed her face and re-braided her hair into an acceptably masculine rope, and upon her arrival, Anne gave the door to Captain Doran's private cabin a firm rapping. When her knock was met with a low "Come in," she entered.

Captain Doran was sitting at the head, if there was a head, of a square wooden table. He was drinking something and reading a newspaper. Without looking up, he put his mug down and motioned her to sit at his left. "Andrew, what think you of the royals?" he asked through the paper.

"The royals, sir?" Anne asked, feeling completely thrown off by the question.

"Yes, the royals." Doran now folded his paper and looked unwaveringly upon his companion.

Anne, not knowing what had brought this about, waded into the conversation. "Well, Captain, I believe the royals are merely people like the rest of us." She paused, thinking of what else to say. "They have duties, instincts, and desires like everyone else. I think the only difference between the average person and a royal, besides the obvious monetary status, is that the average person is likely to make more of his own decisions."

Intrigued, the captain continued the conversation. "Really? So you believe a royal is a slave to his or her counsel?"

"That depends on the royal, sir." Anne fidgeted. "Do you mind if I make an example?" When the captain nodded, she continued. "The way I see it, sir, is most of the older royals *were* slaves to their counsels. They did not much care for the intricacies of running a country and left such business to others. However, I feel those times are behind us. The new royals, Prince Nolan and Princess Orianna-Loni are strong-willed. They speak their minds and do what society says they shouldn't." She paused again.

The captain sat in silence. Anne carefully broke the silence. "Captain, what is the reason for this conversation?"

Doran tossed the newspaper on the table and leaned back in his chair, folding his hands before him, and giving her his full attention before speaking. "My dear boy, I often enjoy speaking of the news early in the morning. If you look at the first page of this paper . . ." He tossed it to Anne. "You will see the royals have been asked to help the de Ranger family find their daughter. It appears the child has run off, and her sister is pleading for her safe return. When you entered, I was just asking myself if I believed the royals would help this family."

"I understand the news, whatever it may be, can be of interest. But how does this particular story affect a ship's captain?" Anne was feeling a bit nervous and hoped the captain would not discover she was, in fact, Philana-Narie. Then again, how would he? She was sure she would have remembered him had they met before.

Placing his hands on the table, the captain rose. "You're correct. It does not concern a ship's captain. However, I have met the de Ranger family on several occasions and have always known them to be happy. It is a pity to hear they must endure such sorrow now, and I pray the royal family lends some assistance."

Surprised, Anne had to know how the captain knew her family and if they had met. She couldn't imagine they had, but *what if?* "They are titled, are they not? How came you to meet them, and when you made the family's acquaintance, did you happen to meet Miss de Ranger?"

"They are minorly titled, and I am a gentleman. I know many people. As for their daughter . . ." He trailed off for a moment, making Anne feel oddly warm and nervous. "Philana-Narie—Anne, as many call her—" He smiled, and she warmed further at the mention of her name. She cast her eyes down until the heat passed. "Not really. As I recall, she was a mischievous and energetic wisp of a girl, always running about the manor. I did happen to spy her and her younger sister once as I was departing one fine afternoon. Apparently, Anne had fallen and hurt her leg; Ethana, her sister, was helping her into the house. I remember . . ." He chuckled. "Despite her injury, Anne was laughing." Deep in memory, the captain took on a far-off look. "Two very pretty girls, as I recollect. Thaniel and Reyna, their parents, are blessed to have such beautiful children."

Strolling to a nearby cart, the captain gently lifted a teapot and poured some tea for Anne-turned-Andrew. "Now," he handed her the teacup, "let us discuss the reason you are here."

The captain sat back down and then verbally answered a rapping at the door. "Yes. Enter!" Neville, the captain's helper, arrived to serve breakfast.

Finding it difficult to switch gears so suddenly while the captain ate, Anne stammered a bit before rediscovering her verbal footing. She told the captain she felt everyone aboard should know how to wield a sword. She figured, as damp as the ship could be, gunpowder would be hard to keep, so swordplay might be their best defense if under attack. "Sir, Marid knows how to fight. Perhaps he could teach the few men onboard who already know a bit of swordplay to become better. Then, the ones he teaches can break off and teach others."

She also spoke of guarding their cargo, how during an attack, having several men stand as defense would be helpful. The only problem she could see with the idea of a defensive team was if someone on offense needed help; those who were supposed to be on guard might rush in to lend assistance. "We must train those men to protect the keep and pray the offensive will protect the ship as well as their own persons."

"You speak of no gunpowder, but what of the cannons and the muskets?" the captain seemed interested in her ideas, even though swordplay was nearly outdated.

"Sir, the cannons are for long range. I am speaking in terms of being boarded. But to touch on the cannons, I'm sure you have that covered. Continue to save dry gunpowder for them. I do not discount the usefulness of gunpowder. I just don't believe we can keep enough dry for every man's musket."

"Perhaps you're right." Doran looked at her thoughtfully. Anne felt a bit uncomfortable under his gaze and looked down at her plate before turning to the window. "Andrew, I must admit I have never been one interested in battle. What of you? You seem to have quite the grasp on strategy, yet you know nothing about ships. Is your father a soldier, or is this merely where your interests lie?"

Anne was still looking toward the circular window of the cabin. She was feeling a bit strange in the captain's presence, almost as if she was suffocating. *What to say,* she thought to herself, *what to do?* Her gray eyes followed the sun's light fingers as they caressed the shelves of the room. Then, as if feeling the captain's gaze meet hers on the atlas resting upon his desk, she spoke. "Captain, my interests lie not in one place or another. I thirst for knowledge, no matter what it might be. As for my father, I have always known him to be a gentle man of books and commerce; although, the last time I saw him, he shared with me his more explosive side." She turned to look Captain Doran in the eye. "I believe there are some men who relish the thought of war and others who desire it less than a little. But when it comes to protecting one's life or way of life, all become warriors, whether they like it or not."

The captain looked her in the eyes. The silence in the room seemed suddenly deafening, and Anne's stomach felt queasy. The heat she had been feeling since she'd entered his room seemed to engulf her. Her heart was beating twice its normal rate and suffocation was, she believed, near. She was just about to break eye contact with Doran when there was another knock at the door.

Doran looked away first. "Come in."

Jerah entered the room. "Capt'n, I's wonderin' if our youngin was ready for his lessons. An' to inform 'im he has a visitor awaiting 'im on the dock."

Anne gave herself a little mental shake to allow everything to sink in. "Visitor? For me? But I know no one." She looked between the captain and the interloper.

"Well, ya may not know her, but she 'pparently knows you." Jerah wore a grin so large, it split his face in two.

The captain rose from his seat and ran his fingers through his dark hair, making Anne's temperature compete with that of the sun. She looked away.

"Well, Jerah, he is all yours," said the captain. Then, with a smile, he added, "and hers." Stretching a bit, he looked to Anne. "Andrew, thanks for your input. It was very . . . insightful. Now, be on your way. I believe your lady awaits."

Anne jumped up quickly, nodded to the captain, and escaped. She had no idea what was wrong with her. Perhaps she was getting ill; although she hoped not.

As she and Jerah walked up the three steps to the main deck, Anne was thankful for the cool air on her face. It helped to chill the heat she felt bubbling from within.

"Ya all right, Andrew? Don't seem yerself. Not as I know ya too well, but from what I can tell, somethin's amiss with ya."

Anne smiled at Jerah's concern. He was a very sweet man indeed. "I'm fine, mate. I just believe I ate more than I should have." She slapped him on the back. "So who do you believe has come to see me?"

Jerah pointed to the dock at a pretty blonde dressed in a simple lavender dress and holding a piece of paper. Anne, a bit confused, looked at Jerah. "I'm sorry, but I don't think I've ever met her before."

"Well, if you don't want her," Dyson chimed in, "*I'll* take her." His face revealed his mind was deep in lustful thought.

An attractive, masculine man, Anne could imagine Dyson being a cad, charming the ladies out of their virtue and leaving them behind. "Never you mind, Dyson. I'll speak with her." No matter who the woman might be, no one deserved to be used; Anne would not allow it. Walking past the drooling man, she made her way down the plank and toward the dock. As she drew closer and closer, the girl did seem familiar, but Anne was still having difficulty placing her. "Hello, Miss. May I help you?"

The girl smiled, looked down, and spoke at her feet. "You don't recognize me, do ya? Well, who can blame ya, looking the way I did?"

Anne took a step forward to nudge the girl's chin upward, and when her brown eyes met Anne's gray ones, Anne remembered. "Laveda, I thought I told you to stay away from the docks." Anne was not harsh with the girl, but her voice conveyed her concern.

Laveda fussed with the paper in her hand. The paper, Anne could see now, was the letter she had written to the girl. "I'm sorry, Andrew. I just wanted ya to know what I've been doin' the past few days, and to show ya how I looked." Her face was innocent and full of the desire for approval.

Anne stepped back and looked the girl up and down. She then walked around her and lifted Laveda's braid to her nose. Anne could see she was nervous, so she put her braid down and placed her right hand on the girl's left shoulder as she continued her inspection, eventually moving it down Laveda's arm to grasp her hand. Lifting it, Anne smelt it and smiled. "Lemon, lavender, and rose. Laveda, you've exceeded my expectations. You look and smell wonderful." Anne slowly put the woman's hand down and saw Laveda blush. She had to admit a blush wasn't what she had expected from the girl—gratitude for the compliment yes, but a blush?

"Thank ya, Andrew." Laveda lifted her left hand to her lips in a rather shy gesture.

"You're welcome. I only wish I could get you better clothes to wear." Anne looked at the girl's worn dress.

Laveda, too, looked at her dress, and with such a sadness that it nearly broke Anne's heart. Again, she lifted a finger to Laveda's chin to nudge it up. "Laveda, you look lovely today, without all that makeup and grime to hide your true age. As for your clothes, it is better you wear what you have for now. You still live at Swinfen's, and we wouldn't want to draw any attention to you until you are no longer there. Do you understand?" Laveda nodded. "Good. Now, there aren't too many *ladies* out here, so you stick out like a sore thumb looking the way you do. Therefore, you should return home," Anne released her chin. Again, Laveda nodded.

As Laveda turned away, she whirled back around as though she'd remembered something. "Wait, Andrew, I nearly forgot to tell ya about a Baron de Ranger."

Anne's heart froze.

"Yes, Laveda." Anne's voice was cool.

"I met him Mundy at Dermot's. He heard me say yer friend's name and went mad, somethin' about her being missin'. I didn't tell him yer name."

Anne looked down and closed her eyes for a moment before looking at the girl again. "Laveda," she spoke in a hushed voice, "the de Rangers live approximately five miles southwest of the marketplace at a place called *Indira*. Now, I want you to either go there soon or write them a letter tonight. Tell them Philana-Narie is fine. Tell them she is being well taken care of and that the man you met will tell her to write to them soon."

Laveda looked far away for a moment.

"Laveda," Anne said as she grabbed the girl's shoulders, "did you hear me?"

"Do ya love her, Andrew?" The girl looked up sadly.

"What? Laveda, you don't know what you're talking about. She and I have an agreement. I help her, and she helps me. So whatever you do, do not tell her parents she has attached herself to some strange man. I can tell you with utmost certainty that a relationship is the furthest thing from her mind. Do you understand?"

Laveda seemed to perk up. She kissed her beloved Andrew on the cheek and then ran back toward town.

"Goodness, Anne, how dense can you be?" Anne whispered to herself. "You stupid fool. Now the girl's in love with you." As Anne turned around to walk back up the plank, she noticed nearly everyone on the ship had been watching her interaction with Laveda. She shook her head and surveyed the faces as she walked onto the ship. She could just hear the jokes now, but as she stepped onboard, she wasn't prepared for the first one to come from the captain himself.

"Wow, if that's how you are with girls you don't know, I'd love to see how you are with the ones you do." Doran was smiling, and the crew gave a thunderously hearty choir of laughter.

Chapter Five

A Fresh Start

Ethana waited impatiently at Indira for a response from the royal family. She wanted desperately to know what Duke Saben had told the princess about what had occurred the night before Anne's disappearance. Ethana could still feel the heat of anger she felt when she arrived at the palace on Tuesday afternoon and found Saben there. To her great dismay, the duke and Oren were having tea with Princess Orianna-Loni. As the princess was pressed for time, and her parents were unavailable, Ethana was forced to make her plea before the two piranhas. The princess had been kind enough to hush their horrid comments while she spoke, but throughout her speech, Ethana still felt less than confident. Then, on top of it all, the princess said she would have her answer the next morning.

Well, it was now two in the afternoon and still no word. The post was late, and Ethana couldn't stop pacing at the front door. Deep in thought, she started when there was finally a knock at the door. Unceremoniously grasping the handle, she threw the door back to find a lady in a beautiful jade cloak standing before her. The woman's face was hidden by her hood, so all Ethana could see were her hands and the scroll she held in them. "May I help you?"

The lady glided past Ethana to enter the manor. "Shut the door," she murmured. Once Ethana had done as she was told, the lady threw off her hood to reveal herself.

"Princess!" Ethana immediately dropped into a low curtsy. "Your Highness," she remained in her stooped position, "to what do I owe this honor?"

"You owe it to my brother, the prince. Now stand." The princess was dressed in a magnificent ivory gown with a decorative rope of the same color but entwined with gold, wrapped about her waist, knotted in the front with the strands left hanging. The cloak she wore was lined with a golden fabric and held together about her throat with a single golden gardenia clasp. She looked like a fairy goddess, with the hair at her temples braided back with ribbon and her large dark curls caressing her shoulders.

"Your brother, Your Highness?" Ethana asked a bit confused. "I heard the prince was away, perhaps in the North Country."

The princess looked at Ethana like she was an imbecile. "Where did you get such a foolish idea?"

Feeling a bit dim-witted, Ethana chose her words carefully. "During Sunday's dinner, Duke Saben was telling us how the prince was involved in secret intelligence work in the North. When my sister openly disagreed, she was punished for it. The incident is the reason she left." Ethana was close to tears but knew if Anne were in her situation, her sister wouldn't dare cry, so neither would she.

"Well, it would appear your sister and my brother have something in common, then." The princess looked annoyed, perhaps because she had not yet been asked to sit someplace.

Noticing her royal visitor's dismay, Ethana invited her into the drawing room where they could sit and speak in peace. Once they reached the heavily portraited room, Ethana asked the maid who had been cleaning the room to leave and notify Verna they had a guest; she wished to have some tea sent. Her duties fulfilled for the moment, she sat on the velvet chair next to the sofa where the princess sat and gave the older woman her full attention.

"Ethana, it saddens me to tell you I am not sure how much help the royal family can provide, as we are unsure which direction your sister may have gone or if she is still in the country."

Ethana's heart sank into her empty stomach. She hadn't eaten since the day before and was feeling she may never eat again. All she wanted to do was go to her room and weep the way her parents had done two days earlier.

Princess Orianna-Loni looked at Ethana with sorrow in her eyes. "Ethana, please do not despair. I admit, when you first came to me, I had no intention of helping you. I feel this whole situation is sad, yes, but I don't believe we can find her. However, it appears your family is acquainted with someone of great importance to my family and the court. This gentleman has persuaded me to take an interest. It is on his behalf that I have sent eight men out, two in each direction, in search of your sister."

Ethana blinked rapidly in an attempt to hold back her tears. Then she swallowed down the lump in her throat before speaking, "Thank you, Your Highness. This means a great deal to me. Is there any way I can thank this gentleman, personally, for being so kind to my family?"

The princess's lovely face immediately changed from straight-forward business to something darker, perhaps displaying a bit of annoyance. "I'm afraid not. The gentleman has not been at court for some time, as he is avoiding his duties. And, much to my dismay, he will be absent for quite a bit longer." Princess Orianna-Loni stood.

Since it appeared the princess was prepared to depart, Ethana slowly rose to show her guest out. As she and Princess Orianna-Loni drew closer to the front of the manor, Ethana could hear her father speaking with someone. Curious about whom, and anxiously hoping it might be Anne, Ethana moved more swiftly. When they arrived in the foyer, much to Ethana's dismay, Anne was not there. Her father was standing in front of the door speaking to a rather young blonde and another girl who was sitting on the chair in the foyer typically used for mere decorative purposes.

Ethana watched as her father became aware that he and his guests were no longer alone. Upon turning around and seeing her and the princess, he immediately bowed. "Your Highness," he stammered, "I was unaware of your visit. To what, may I ask, do we owe the pleasure of your appearance in our humble home?"

"I have come to speak with your daughter, Baron. Yesterday, she brought to my attention the disappearance of your eldest, and I merely came by to inform her of the palace's stance on the issue." The princess nodded before flickering a glance toward the other ladies in the room.

Ethana noticed the glance did not go unnoticed by her father, who didn't seem ready to explain who his guests were. He spoke as he motioned to the other girls, "Ethana, Your Highness, I would like you to meet Laveda and her younger sister, Sophie. I met them through Dermot and promised to help them in any way I could manage."

"That is quite noble of you, Baron. I must say not enough of the fortunate help those who are less so," Orianna-Loni spoke as she pulled up her hood.

Thaniel murmured, "I only hope someone is out there helping Anne."

Anne's day was going smoothly. She supposed being seen with Laveda was the reason since almost every single man and, she hated to think about it, a few of the married ones, had asked her for tips on how to woo lovely ladies. Their newly found respect for her supposed prowess meant they no longer impeded her work and, warming up to her, gave her the nickname "Guppy"—small, pretty, and loved by the ladies. Anne was surprised by her instant popularity and amazed at how quickly she could work when she was happy. It seemed time just flew by, and, in only a few hours, she found the basics of sailing rather easy—actually, pretty fun. She completed her work so quickly that she had a half-hour of free time before she had to be in the galley to help Bêrk with dinner.

With all her morning and afternoon duties completed, as well as a bit of nautical vocabulary words studied, Anne decided to look out over the dock and drink in her last few moments of peace. She watched as the people ran between the town to the ships. She sadly darted her eyes over the easy ladies of the port and then wondered what she would have done had the captain not given her a chance. Would she have returned home? She closed her eyes and took a deep breath.

"Are you going to miss this place?" Captain Doran's voice was close, nearly at her ear.

Anne froze. Her hands began to sweat as she held the side of the ship, and she wasn't sure she wanted to open her eyes. She did not say a word.

"I hope you're not sleeping standing up," the captain teased.

Anne finally found the courage to look at Doran. "No, Captain. I was just savoring the last few quiet moments of the day."

Doran smiled and looked along the port just as Anne had been doing a few moments prior to his arrival. She watched him and wondered what he was truly like, where he was from. What were his family and friends like? How did he get into this sort of business? And finally, just how well did he know her family?

"You're staring again." Doran smiled but kept his eyes on the boardwalk.

Flushing, Anne looked away. "I apologize, Captain. I tend to blanket myself in my thoughts and do not realize I am staring at all." Anne tried to concentrate on the dock but found herself more often than not glancing sideways at her captain. There were many men onboard with dark features, but many of them also carried a sort of inner darkness to go with those features. The captain, however, seemed warm and lighthearted. He often joked with members of the crew, and on more than one occasion, he had even teased her. She was finding it a bit difficult to understand how he'd become a ship's captain. Most were straight-speaking and no nonsense.

She looked down at her hands. Her knuckles were raw, and her fingernails were all broken and jagged, nothing like the delicate hands she once knew. She then took a careful glance at the captain's hands. They were much larger than her own. His fingers were long and slender, their nails clean and well cared for. Noticing the captain's sudden movement, Anne quickly looked back to her own hands.

"Well, Andrew, it should be just about time for you to head down to the galley. I'm sure the men would like their supper on time."

Anne looked up and noticed him grinning at her. He had a beautiful smile, and her eyes lingered there for a while before she gave herself a mental shake and abruptly headed off to the galley. As she lumbered down the deck, she silently scolded herself for her odd behavior. Why on earth was she so nervous around the captain? There was truly no reason for it. None at all.

Doran watched as Andrew walked clumsily toward the galley. He had to chuckle a bit at the youth's nerves. If he didn't know any better, he would think the young man was afraid of him, yet the lad always spoke with such honesty. In his experience, men who were afraid found it difficult to speak as plainly as Andrew did. He glanced back at the dock, only turning again when he heard someone approaching him on the right.

"Sir, I have received a message from the palace requesting your appearance there tomorrow afternoon." Kenward stood a mere few feet away, hand outstretched to pass the message to the captain.

Doran sighed. Surely, it was another letter from the princess. She had been requesting his presence for the past few months at several banquets and ceremonies, and thus far, he had found a way to politely decline every invitation. However, with each new invite, the excuses were becoming increasingly difficult to conjure. "Thank you, Kenward," the captain accepted the letter and turned back to the docks.

Doran didn't notice Kenward grimace as he watched his captain. Finally, Kenward asked, "Captain, are you going to accept the invitation? I mean, you haven't been to court in nearly four months."

"My dear friend, I have no intention of returning until I have completed the task at hand. If the princess wishes to see me, she can come to the docks while we are at port. Not that I believe she would ever be seen within ten miles of here. Besides, we are leaving here tomorrow morn." Again he sighed. "I will write to her tonight to inform her of my plans. She can then notify the rest of the palace."

With that, Kenward walked back toward the crew quarters to eat. Doran stayed above deck a few moments longer before turning toward his cabin. He shouldn't waste time in responding if he wanted to send it off before they left port.

Reyna had been lying in bed since the night Thaniel had returned from his first attempt to find Anne. Alone, in the unbearable quiet, her mind continually reeling over the events of the past few days, she despaired. The moment she realized Anne was not returning home, she'd even forgotten to ask Ethana about her second meeting with the duke and duchess. She knew she should probably show more interest in her younger daughter's future affairs, but at the moment, her mind was filled with Anne. Tears gathered at the corners of her eyes as she envisioned her eldest wandering in a forest all alone and dressed in Henry's work clothes. Turning on her side, she cried for her past behavior and how she had spoken to Thaniel upon hearing of Anne's disappearance.

Thaniel, her darling husband, loved Anne so dearly. Of course, he loved Ethana as well, but Anne had always been *his* little one. He loved her boldness, cleverness, and wit. When Anne was but six years of age, he'd told Reyna he didn't believe he would have been happier had they had a son instead. He often spoke to Anne about trade work and took her fishing and hiking. They would race around the manor and share interesting facts they had read in one of the many books in the library.

Reyna knew, very well, this was the reason she had also blamed him for Anne's behavior the night the duke and his family came to dinner. If only he had treated Anne more like a girl, perhaps none of this would have happened. Choking back a loud sob, she shook her head. Knowing her daughter as she did, deep down, she knew no matter how Thaniel treated Anne, she would have turned out just the same. Adventure and curiosity were deeply rooted within her soul. Had he not tried to take Ethana fishing? Had he not tried to include her in all the activities he and Anne had shared and enjoyed? In truth, Anne was to her father as Ethana was to her. Anne relished exploration and excitement, loved to read, and desired to learn just about everything. Reyna knew she should not have been surprised by Anne's desires, nor the way she had behaved that horrible night.

Reaching for the handkerchief on her nightstand, she gently picked it up and folded the blush colored material into fours and dabbed her eyes and blew her nose, only to have fresh tears surface as she remembered the look on Thaniel's face after he had punished Anne. Never in her life had she seen such torment, and never before had she witnessed her husband cry. Of course, since that night, he had wept every day and sometimes twice or more. He no longer slept in their room, preferring to sleep in the front of the manor . . . just in case Anne returned. She remembered how she had scoffed at his pain over what he had done. Remembered how he'd tried to talk to her about it; her cold response was to say Anne finally received what she had always deserved.

Reyna lay back down and placed her face into her pillow as she wept anew for the loss of her family's happiness.

Just then, there was a soft rapping at the door. A few seconds later, Verna appeared in the room. "My Lady, I 'ave brought ye sum suppa," the woman spoke as she closed the door behind her. "Reyna, it's not rie healthy te go so long with nah food nar drink. Please, eat somethin', deary." Verna placed the tray of food on the nightstand.

There was barely any light in the room, for the sun was being chased from the sky by the rising moon. Finding a few candles within the nightstand, Verna placed them on their holders and set them alight, illuminating the stand and the edge of the bed.

Looking at Reyna then, Verna shook her head. Reyna guessed the woman had never seen such sadness in all her days. Of course, when Thaniel's mother had lost her firstborn, she was probably tremendously heartbroken, weeping for many a night and day. However, in that situation, the child was gone, and there was nothing to do but move on. In this instance, things seemed much worse. It was the suspense, the not knowing, the blame, and the regrets that were tearing the de Rangers apart.

And Reyna didn't even know Verna has heard Ethana talking to herself, asking, "What would Anne do?"

"One step at a time," Verna said to her as she took a cloth from her apron and gently wiped away Reyna's tears. She stayed until Reyna ate most of her food, then she tried to convince the lady of the manor to leave her room when the sun rose again.

Thaniel, Ethana, Laveda, and Sophie sat around the dining table silently eating their meal. Thaniel glanced around the table in quiet contemplation. Laveda had told him and Ethana that her benefactor had promised to tell Anne to write soon. Though Ethana wanted desperately to believe the young woman and said as much, Thaniel was unsure whether they truly could or should trust her. Then again, what choice did they really have in the matter?

Thaniel looked back down at his plate and thought over the events of the afternoon. Once the princess had gone, the rest of them had retired to the drawing room, where Verna had set up the tea tray. Over tea and biscuits, Laveda told them everything her mysterious friend would allow her to say.

Thaniel noted Ethana's excitement, as she could barely remain in her seat. Thaniel had tried to get more information about the stranger to whom they were instilling all their trust; however, much to his dismay, Laveda remained true to her promise to this Andrew character. Thaniel had even offered to take her and her sister in if she gave him the information he requested. Still, she refused.

Just before supper, Ethana asked her father to be patient, believing the young lady and her friend were the answer to their prayers. If she was correct, if this was true, why did he still feel uneasy? Since Laveda had brought them word that Anne was fine and would write, Thaniel promised to care for Sophie.

Over supper, Ethana sat wondering how she was going to care for their new ward, Sophie, and look for Anne at the same time. Though she trusted Laveda's word that her friend would have Anne write them, she still had the urge to look for her sister. She just wanted Anne home, but in thinking of Anne, she also felt a strong desire to help the two girls at the table too. She was torn. Ethana knew Anne would not hesitate to help and smiled at what she believed Anne's methods of teaching might be. Also, perhaps her father was right in hoping that if they helped these two girls, the Fates would take care to watch over Anne. Deciding her last thought was the most positive she'd had all day, she was resolute about doing all she could for Sophie.

On the other end of the table, Sophie believed this to be the best meal she'd ever had in her life and had to force herself to finish it because she really wanted to hide some in her skirts for later. But somehow, she knew that would be frowned upon. Glancing at her sister, Sophie's heart sank. As long as she could remember, it had always been just the two of them, but tonight, Laveda would be gone, and she'd be left with strangers.

She'd wished Laveda had told her of the deal she'd try to make with the baron before they'd arrived but also understood why she hadn't. If she had been told

62

sooner, she would have made it difficult for Laveda to bring her all this way. At the same time, she didn't want her sister to leave. What if something happened to Laveda? How would she ever know? Then again, if something did happen, what could she do about it? It wasn't as though she could run for help. Heck, if anything did happen to Laveda, and she was at Swinfen's, there was nothing she could do at all. There wouldn't be anyone to take her in, and she would eventually be thrown into the streets. If she was honest, this probably was the best thing for her. *But to be left with strangers and not know whether I'll see Laveda again . . .* Sophie closed her eyes to hold back her tears.

Of all the people at the table, Laveda had to be the happiest. She'd found a nice family to care for her sister; she was in love with a handsome and generous young man, and she had money enough to take better care of herself. Not having to worry about Sophie was a huge load off her petite shoulders, and though she was going to miss her sister, she knew she was doing the right thing.

Finishing her meal, she thought about what to say to Sophie before she left. Then she wondered if the baron would mind her returning to visit Sophie from time to time. Looking to him for a moment, she smiled. Of course he wouldn't mind! He seemed such a kind man. Besides, coming around would help Sophie feel better about staying. She sighed and thought of the time. She had better be on her way since it was already late. She wiped her mouth with her napkin and cleared her throat. "Baron, My Lady, I think I should be goin' now."

Ethana was startled by Laveda's voice after everyone had been so quiet, and though she heard what the girl had to say, she couldn't believe it. "You can't mean you are going to walk back to town in the dark!" she exclaimed.

"Well, I haven't got no choice. I gotta get back to Swinfen's, else he'll be thinkin' somethin's goin' on." Laveda pushed her seat back.

Thaniel was immediately on his feet and pulling the girl's chair back for her. "I insist you stay the night, Laveda. It is not safe for a lady to wander alone at night."

"Ahh, I'm nah much of a lady." She winked. "'Sides, ye've done enough for me already, an' I have to return the wheelbarra I used back to Nyssa before mornin', else her husband find it missin'."

Standing, Ethana, ran her hands down her dress and looked to her father. "Father, could you take her as far as the market? I mean we can't really let her walk all that way."

Thaniel nodded. "Laveda, I will retrieve my cloak and meet you in the foyer."

"But, sir," Laveda called after him. Ethana assumed she didn't wish to be any more of a burden to them. They had already done more than she had probably ever dreamed anyone would do for her, and now, after taking in her sister and feeding them both, she probably thought it too much that he was going to give her a ride.

Apparently, Laveda, Ethana witnessed, wasn't going to allow it.

"Baron?"

Her father continued out of the dining room, so Laveda turned to her. "Please tell 'im I'm all right on my own."

"I will do no such thing." Ethana placed her hands on her hips. "We are already missing one person, and I am determined not to lose another. Now, you stay here with your sister while I leave a few instructions for the kitchen staff."

When Ethana disappeared, Sophie cast her sad brown eyes upon her sister. This was the first time they had been alone since early that morning, and she was going to make the best of it. "Laveda, please don't leave me."

"Sophie, ya know this is what's right. Ya'll be fine here. These are good people, and they'll take good care of ya . . . better than I can do." Seeing the tears welling in Sophie's eyes was almost more than she could bear. "Please don't, Sophie. I'll visit ya as much as I can." She went to hug the younger girl.

"Ya promise?" Sophie asked as she held onto her elder sister.

"I promise," Laveda stated, as if it had been an oath to the Lord himself.

Just then, Ethana reentered with an attractive red-haired boy in tow and holding a bag of food, which she handed to Laveda. "Laveda, Sophie, this is Henry. He does a few odd jobs around the manor but can usually be found with the gardener. He is going to carry Sophie up to her new room."

Giving Sophie one last hug, Laveda again promised to visit as soon as possible. Then the young girl was whisked from the room.

Laveda hadn't expected to feel as miserable as she did while watching Sophie disappear with the boy, but she brushed the feeling aside as if it were something quite minor.

"Well, Laveda, we should head to the foyer," Ethana took the other girl's hand in hers as she ushered her out of the room.

Thaniel had already brought the carriage about, to the front of the manor, and was placing the wheelbarrow in the back when the front door opened. Thinking it was Laveda, he didn't bother turning around.

"Thaniel," Verna began tentatively. "I need te 'ave a wurd wid ye."

Thaniel turned to see the cook standing in the doorway, still wearing her apron and wringing her hands. He hadn't spoken to Verna since the morning they realized Anne was missing, and even then, it had been she who had done most of the talking . . . *or tongue-lashing*, he thought. "Yes, Verna?" he asked as he turned back to the carriage.

"I hate te disturb ya right nah, but Reyna needs ya."

Thaniel scoffed, making Verna put forth her best argument. "Nah, listen te me. She's just as upset 'bout all dis as y'are. Nah dat ya'd notice much, but she has takin' te starvin' herself. I've tried everythin' in my pow'r te git her te eat, drink, ar even get out of bed. She won't listen te me."

"Verna, I understand your concern, but Reyna is the last person on my mind right now." He jumped into the driver's seat of the carriage just behind the horses. "Now, if you would, tell Ethana I am ready to take Laveda back to town."

Thaniel could see rage warming Verna's cheeks but tried to ignore it. He tried until she approached the carriage. "Ye'd rather lose two dan jist one wud ya," she yelled.

"Verna, I'm not in the mood—"

She interrupted, "Ye listen te me, boy. Yer family's fallin' apart. Yah, Anne's missin', bah everyone's doin' da best dey can 'bout dat. Nah, yer wife's wastin' away because grief's feastin' on her like maggots on a purly cover'd roast. Du ye

65

tink dat Ethana can carry on if she lost her mum too? Du ye? Nah, if ya don't get in dare an' talk te dat woman of yer's, I'll drag ye up dare meself!"

"Verna, I'll see her when I get back from the market," he said with a sigh.

Apparently, his reply wasn't good enough for her. "No! Ye'll go nah. I'll 'ave Henry take dat gerl te town." With that, Verna went back into the manor.

After delivering Sophie to her room and before Henry had returned to his duties, Verna, storming into the manor, was barking orders, and she was barking mad.

"Henry, grab yer coat. Yer takin' da young lady home."

Confused, Ethana looked at the older woman, then at Laveda, and finally at Henry. It took her a few moments to realize what had just happened, and by then, Henry was off. "Verna, what are you doing?"

"I told dat father of yer's ta spend sum time wid yer mum." Then, wagging her finger in Ethana's face, she said, "Nah, I'm off ta da kitchen. If he dunna do as I told 'im, ye let me know."

"Father or Henry?" Ethana asked.

"Either!" Verna yelled over her shoulder as she stormed off to the kitchen.

Ethana had never seen Verna so angry, and now that she had, all she could do was look on as she disappeared around the corner. Then, before her shock had completely disappeared, Henry was back and ushering Laveda out the door. In a kind of daze, Ethana followed, but only to the doorway, where she watched her father give Henry instructions and say goodbye to Laveda as he helped her into the seat next to Henry.

When Laveda looked back toward the manor, Ethana waved goodbye before turning to her father as he approached. "What happened?"

"Verna says your mother is starving herself." He ran a weary hand through his dark hair. "Personally, I think she just wants a bit of attention."

Ethana had been to see her mother earlier that morning and didn't believe her father was right. Mother had looked terrible. Her eyes were red from all the crying she had done. Her hair was a mess, and she looked as though she hadn't gotten up.

When Ethana had asked her mother why she had not been up and about in the past few days, she had dodged the question and asked about Anne. When

Ethana informed her there was no new information concerning Anne's where-abouts, her mother turned toward the window and wept again.

"Father, I do not believe she is begging for attention. I went to see her this morning, and she looks . . . empty. There is no happiness in her. Perhaps Verna is right. Perhaps, if you go to her, she will at least eat."

As he continued further into the manor, Thaniel gave Ethana a sidelong glance. She could tell he was biting back what he wanted to say. He didn't seem to want to see Reyna, nor did it seem to her that he cared she was upset. Ethana wondered if he felt her mother deserved it.

Thaniel ambled up the staircase to the second floor, where the family rooms could be found. Once there, he started down the hall. Ethana, who had followed, stopped at the room across from her own, and her father, continued to the end, seeking the suite.

Taking a deep breath before walking inside, Thaniel wondered about what he might find. Then, with almost a bit of pleasure, he reached for the knob to see just how much pain Reyna was in.

The room was quiet and dark except for the nightstand on Reyna's side of the bed. Candles, dimly illuminating the edge of the king-sized, four-poster bed, allowed Thaniel to see Reyna facing the other direction. As quietly as he could, he closed the door behind him before venturing deeper into the room.

"Reyna?" he questioned softly. When there was no reply, he settled himself at the foot of the bed, only an inch or two from her feet. Now being this close, he didn't believe her to be asleep. So he eased himself further up the bed and gently turned her toward him. And what he saw seized his heart.

Ethana had not exaggerated the emptiness in Reyna's eyes. Looking at her now, Thaniel realized there was not much life in her at all. The candlelight cast eerie shadows across her features, making her look grim—and definitely thinner. Her eyes were blood-red and seemed smaller than usual, nearly swollen shut. All the hateful words Thaniel had desired to send her way vanished as he took in her appearance, and he struggled to hold back tears.

"I'm so sorry." Her small voice startled Thaniel. The way she looked, he had believed her incapable of speech. She resembled an empty shell, as if her soul had left her to find a happier home.

Thaniel found he couldn't respond. His throat, now like old bark, had turned dry, and when he tried to speak, it felt scratchy. All he could do was pull her into his arms as she wept.

Chapter Six

Letters & Lindsey

Anne helped Bêrk clean the plates and cups and put them away. Thoughtfully, she decided she did not like her introduction to the ship's primary cuisine. Being there was no longer room for fresh food, and the few fruits and vegetables they had left would only last another day or two, Bêrk got the crew back to their usual meal with the addition of a few slices of apple.

Finding the beef too salty, Jerah had suggested she rinse it off a bit in her cup of water. Thankful for the suggestion, she did as she was told. The water not only washed away some of the saltiness but also softened the meat, making it easier to chew. The only problem . . . she was then left with salty water to drink. Shaking her head now, in remembrance, she couldn't believe she'd actually drunk it. Then she smiled at the way Marid had laughed at the look on her face. He'd poured into her cup, a small share of brandy.

Anne had never had brandy before, but everyone seemed to enjoy it, slowly savoring each drop of the four ounces they each received. Anne hadn't wanted to seem like she was still "wet behind the ears," as Jerah always liked to say, so she downed the heady liquid in one gulp. The heat that had quickly surged through her was both shocking and undesirable. She'd clenched her jaw to keep both a cough and, she supposed, actual fire from escaping her throat. Tears welled up in her eyes, and she gulped air several times as she blinked rapidly.

Realizing no one was paying her any mind, she hurriedly gathered her things and rushed off to the galley. Once there, she took several deep breaths to calm her nerves before cleanup. Bêrk, who had joined her a few minutes later, was astonished by how much she'd already accomplished. Since then, they'd just about finished cleaning and putting everything away.

"Well, Andrew, I have to admit you are, by far, the best kitchen help I've ever had," Bêrk beamed. "I mean, if you haven't noticed, not many of the crew would give up the hard labor of sailing to cook."

Anne didn't reply, but she had noticed the other men who were supposed to help in the galley did so grudgingly.

"I think that's it," Bêrk said as he gave the butcher-block one last swipe. "Thanks, Andrew. I think we can leave the rest of the plates for tomorrow. Let's go an' get some sleep. We have an early start tomorrow." Then, as if remembering Andrew already got up before dawn, Bêrk added, "Or, at least the rest of us do."

Anne could see he was trying to suppress a smile and shot him a wry look that made him laugh before she went up top.

She had discovered she rather liked sleeping above deck. Sure, it was cold, but at least the air was clean; she imagined men probably smelled bad: sweaty, dirty, and gassy. Her tired body carried her over to the supply closet where she had placed her blanket upon deciding that afternoon she would sleep up top. She had also found two lanterns there as well, and looking at them now, she figured it was as good a time as any to write to her family and Laveda.

Taking the blanket and lantern to a cozy corner of the deck, she remembered most of the men would be asleep by now—especially Jerah, the elderly seaman she had borrowed a few sheets of paper from the other day. Sitting in quiet contemplation, Anne noticed a faint light coming from the captain's cabin. After long minutes of wondering if he would mind loaning her some paper, she decided he wouldn't.

Walking back up the deck toward the cabin, a cool breeze licked back the few strands of hair that had escaped her braid throughout the day. Hugging herself tightly, she wished she had not left her blanket behind with the lantern, and she picked up her pace as she moved toward the light. Finally coming to the cabin door, she was no longer sure she should disrupt.

Doran sat playing with the response letter he had just finished, wondering how the princess might take his latest declination, when there was a knock at the door. Thinking it was probably Kenward, Doran bellowed a low, "Come in," without looking up. Therefore, he was quite surprised to hear the soft, scarcely masculine voice belonging to none other than Andrew.

"Captain, I hate to be a nuisance, but I was wondering if I might be allowed a few sheets of paper and a pen."

Doran regarded the young man, then motioned for Andrew to sit opposite him at the table. "Andrew, we have an early start tomorrow. I would have thought everyone was either sleeping or at least beginning to turn in for the night."

Nervous and fidgeting, Anne moved forward. "Aye, sir. I, too, was preparing to rest when I decided to compose a couple of letters. I would like to have them sent before we leave this port." Anne had no idea why she was suddenly so nervous. It was a simple request, and she really had nothing to hide . . . well, other than her true identity. But that wasn't the reason for her current state; she was not afraid of being discovered. So . . . what was it?

Under his steady gaze, she warmed from the inside. Frightened by her response, she looked down before speaking again. "Sir, I will gladly reimburse you for anything I use and would not argue if you felt the need to take the reimbursement from my pay."

Without speaking, Doran stood, strolled over to the desk behind him, opened a drawer, and pulled out several sheets of paper. "Do you also need envelopes?" he asked, without turning to face her.

"Yes, sir. Two, if you can spare them." Anne watched nervously as the captain reached inside a cubbyhole and extracted two envelopes. Then he picked up a quill and inkwell before turning back around.

She stood to receive the items. "Thank you, sir." But he waved her back down. Confused, she sat.

"Andrew, I was going to leave this for tomorrow, but since you're here now . . ." Doran began as he placed the writing materials on the table before regaining his seat. "I have been mulling over what you stated regarding the defense aboard *Survivor*. I find your ideas sound, and if you can set aside some time tomorrow to sit with Marid and come up with a training program, perhaps we can get this form of defense in place as soon as possible."

Speechless, or nearly speechless, Anne took a few moments to calm her excitement before responding. "Thank you, sir. I will speak with Marid tomorrow, at first opportunity." When Doran smiled at her, her heart beat even more erratically. Feeling she needed to escape, she pushed her seat back to get up; however, her legs felt numb, and she stumbled a bit before placing her hands firmly on the table.

"Andrew, are you all right?" Doran was on his feet and shooting her a look full of concern.

Doing her best to smile, Anne raised her hand lazily to wave off his worry. "I'm fine. Just a bit tired." She reached into her pocket to pull out a silver to pay the captain for the paper and pen.

It was Doran's turn to raise a hand. "Keep your purse, Andrew. A bit of ink and a few sheets of paper will not bankrupt me."

Anne retracted her hand from her pocket and thanked the captain again before gathering the paper, pen, and ink still on the table. Having everything she needed, she murmured goodnight and started out, but the captain stopped her again as she was about to exit. "Andrew, try not to stay up too late composing love letters." He chuckled.

Befuddled, Anne asked, "I'm sorry, sir. Love letters?"

"Well, I just assumed you were going to write to your, um, lady friend." Apparently seeing more confusion in her eyes, Doran smiled before clarifying, "The young blonde who came to visit you the other day? Come now, Andrew, you haven't already forgotten her, have you?" he teased, a mischievous glint in his eyes.

Anne could feel her embarrassment rising in her face. Of course, she hadn't forgotten Laveda, but her *lady friend!* Astonished by his mistake, she felt the desire to set him straight. "I assure you, Captain, the young lady I spoke with the other day is no more *my lady* than I am the king of Atlantis. Believe me when I say she only came here to thank me for assisting her on the very day I came to your ship."

Doran chuckled. "Must you always wish for the truth to be known, no matter what?" Anne gave him a confused look. "Truly, Andrew, if I had made that comment to any other man onboard, they would probably boast about their prowess and throw in a few other feminine names to boot." He shook his head. "You know, I am going to have fun searching for a more suitable place for you among the crew." Then, looking down at the letter he had been playing with, he said, "Andrew, your point is well taken. Well, I am sure you would like to get to your correspondence, so I'll let you be. However . . ." He lifted his envelope from the table. "Do you mind sending this off to the palace when you send your letters?"

"The palace?" Anne questioned softly, staring at the envelope.

Doran cleared his throat as he moved around the table. "Andrew, let me explain. In the past, I was quite a favorite at court, and," halting before her, he continued, "there are a few young courtiers who would like the blessing of my presence. However, I find, these days, I am quite too busy and too weary of the niceties required at royal functions." He waved the response before her as if she were a mule and the letter a fine ripe carrot.

Accepting it, Anne neatly folded it between the sheets he had given her. "I will, of course, do as you ask, sir." Doran was so close, her nose twitched at the scent of his cologne: the warm yet airy scent of musk and wood married with something sweet . . . *Vanilla,* she thought. She could feel her temperature rising and her lungs strained as though they weren't getting enough air. She closed her eyes for a moment to calm her heart and hold back the suffocation. She wanted to leave.

"Ah, Andrew," the captain chuckled, "have you ever met a well-bred lady? One who would lay down her life to take care of you all your days?"

Hearing his question, another sort of heat engulfed her. She recognized it, felt her mouth go dry, and embraced it. "Permission to speak plainly, Captain?"

"Of course," Doran said with the wave of his right hand as he pulled back the second closest seat from where she stood with his left and lazily deposited himself in it.

Able to breathe a little easier now that he was farther away, Anne tried to calm herself before attempting to make her point. "Captain, I have met all sorts of women—"

"Really?" he smiled *knowingly* at her.

Anger surging through her again, she couldn't stop herself from rolling her eyes. "Listen, with all due respect, *sir*, I don't see why any woman should have to, how did you put it, *lay her life down*, for any man. Women have their own dreams, ambitions, and desires just as men do."

No longer smiling, Doran leaned forward. "Andrew, it is a woman's job to care for her man and eventually their children."

Scoffing, Anne shook her head. "If that were the case, sir—if men always needed to be *taken care of*—then we would be married the moment our mouths tired of our mother's breast! Ahhh, but we are not so quickly wed, in fact. Some men go all of their days without taking a single vow."

"You make a good point, but I think your views are a bit naïve. Perhaps you need a bit of *practice* in the art of . . . *pairing*." Smirking, he leaned back in his seat. "There are quite a few lovely ladies in Île-de-L'est. Maybe I can introduce you to one or two."

Smiling though she was, Anne knew it probably wasn't a kind one. "Sir, don't think me too bold, but I *know* you are wrong. And one of these days, I hope you find the lady who will not only capture your heart but will cause you to lay down *your* life without so much as a whisper from her pretty little rose-tinted lips." She looked unwaveringly into his eyes. "Now, if you will excuse me, I would like to get to my correspondence. . . . Oh," she added, with a quick nod of her head, "I will see to it that your own makes it to the palace." She left the cabin.

Doran stared at the closed door for several minutes after Andrew left. Never before had anyone told him he was wrong, and though he liked the young man, he wasn't sure he liked being spoken to in that manner. However, he had given the boy leave to speak plainly, so if he didn't want to hear such honesty, perhaps he should not have asked for it. Shaking off his final thoughts of their conversation like water on a hound, he thought again of his letter to the princess. He would be sure to visit Andrew in the morning, to see if there were any changes in his behavior. If there were, he could be sure the boy had read the letter; if not; perhaps he would make the young man a part of his inner circle. Having made his decision, he wearily stood to amble to the desk where all his maps lay.

Anne couldn't believe the captain was just as pigheaded as the rest of the men on the ship. She lit her lantern. To think, she was surrounded by people with whom, if given a choice, she would never bother associating. "Ah, surely you knew it would be like this," she spoke to herself as she dipped the quill into the ink well to begin her first letter.

Dearest Ethana,

Firstly, I would like to say that I hope this letter finds you in good health. Next, I want you to be assured that I am well. A dear friend informed me of the baron's search on the day of my departure from Indira. He told me to write as soon as possible, but not knowing what to say, as well as keeping up with my new duties, has kept me from doing so until now. I also happened upon a newspaper and read how you had gone to the palace to ask for help. I can't believe you had it in you to be so bold and wish I could have been peering in from the wings. Although, I am very proud of you for the courage you have demonstrated, there is no need to take up any more of the Royal Family's time. Thank you for caring about me, but I have no intentions of returning.

Ethana, please don't think me selfish. I need to do this. I need to be on my own. Perhaps, if past events had not occurred, I would still be home. However, they did, and now I am going off to find the life that awaits me. I will make a point of writing to you on occasion, to let you know how I fare. I am sorry, though, that I cannot bring myself to write to your parents. The wounds on my heart are still tender, and until they have healed or I have become numb, I shall not send word to them. Wish me luck.

Anne

P.S. Ethana, never sell yourself short. You are more than just a beautiful woman and deserve more than a loveless marriage that carries a cold title. You know yourself. Find what you desire and whom you desire. ♥~A

Folding the letter in thirds before placing it in one of the envelopes, Anne tucked the flap inside and wrote "Ethana de Ranger, Indira Manor" on the reverse. Then she began her next letter.

Dear Laveda,

I am writing you to say I shall be leaving town tomorrow morning. I am not quite sure when I shall be able to write again, but I will do my best. In the meantime, I would like you to see to your learning. This week, when you have time, please go to the marketplace and find a florist by the name of Haru. Give her the letter that follows as well as ten coppers. She will help you find the person the next correspondence mentions, and together, I'm sure they will lend you a hand, especially if you give them the enclosed gold coin to cover as many classes as it can afford. Good luck and stay out of trouble.

~ Andrew

Anne was glad that when writing the last letter to Laveda she had decided to conceal her own hand. It made what she was about to do now much less complicated.

Dear Haru,

I am writing to ask you a favor. I know I was a little less than kind the last time we met, and I do regret my behavior very much. I am sorry.

The young woman who has just handed you this letter is under the care of a friend of mine. Since he has been helping me, I promised to do all I can to help him. Laveda, the girl before you, is in need of educating. My friend has given her some money to pay for all that you and perhaps Ms. Godwin can teach her. Please, I beg of you, look out for her the way you did for me. Thank you, Haru.

Sincerely,
Anne de Ranger

Taking a deep breath and letting out a whooshing sigh, Anne placed the last two letters and a gold coin into the remaining envelope. She had one sheet of paper left, so she neatly folded it and placed it inside one of the inner pockets of her jacket and then put the quill and ink in her right outer pocket. Finally, she picked up all the letters, stood, and then reached down to lift the lantern. Although it was dark out, Anne guessed it could be no more than 10:30. The usual message boy would have gone home by now, but surely she could find someone else to deliver these letters tonight. Deciding to walk the wharf until she found someone who looked trustworthy, she made her way to the dock.

Anne hadn't walked for more than ten minutes when she saw an older man with a small tin cup in hand, swaying lightly back and forth. Strangely drawn to him, Anne decided to approach. When she was a couple feet away, the old man snapped his attention in her direction. "Sir, I do apologize if I have startled you."

Looking her up and down for a moment or two, Anne could see relief come over him. "Yer not one of them young thieves that come by these parts," he stated pointedly.

"No, sir."

"Well, suppose dat's good." He looked down at his cup then abruptly raised his left eyebrow and grumbled, "Lessen ya be one of dem cut throats. And if ya are, I ain't got nothin' worth slicin' a throat over."

Anne smiled at the older man. He was dressed in ragged clothes. His hair was a dull gray, nappy and much too long, just as his beard. She couldn't see his eyes very well because he squinted quite a bit, and the lighting along the dock could scarcely be called just that. Wondering if he would like to have something worth stealing, and thinking she would like to return to the ship now rather than later, Anne decided to employ the ragged and wrinkled man. "Sir, can you walk?"

He eyed her wearily. "Course I can walk. I can just 'bout do anythin' you can, boy! Shucks, I can even waltz. But if ya came to see me polka, yer in fer some disappointment. Dat there's one dance dat rattles my bones and makes my teeth hurt."

Anne nearly laughed outright; he was quite a feisty old man. Instead, she shook her head. "Good. Now, can you tell me whether you know the way to the palace?"

"Yah, I can tell ya." He closed his eyes and swayed again.

Anne waited. However, when he made no move to speak again, Anne asked once more. "Well, do you?"

"Yah, I know where it is." He eyeballed her. "Ya gotta be real thick not to know that. 'Sides, I used to be in the Royal Navy! Betcha did'na know that, eh?"

"No. I didn't." Anne wondered what might be the best way to approach her request. She was probably daft to think this old man could complete such an important task on her behalf. He seemed tired, and it would indeed take all night to do. Then again, she could always ask. "Sir, I am in need of someone who can deliver a few letters: one to the palace, one to Indira, and another up the dock to Swinfen's. Have you any knowledge of anyone looking for employment? I am willing to pay the person handsomely."

That certainly got his attention. "How handsomely?"

"A silver to start and a gold upon return." Then, thinking that anyone can say they delivered them and not actually have done so, she added an extra task. "Upon returning the person would have to prove he delivered these letters as well." Taking the spare sheet of paper from one pocket and the quill and ink from another, she sat on the ground, smoothed the paper flat, and began to write. At the top left, she wrote Laveda at Swinfen's and drew a long line after it, then folded it over. Beneath the fold, she wrote Ethana at Indira; another line followed. Yet again, she folded it over. Finally, she wrote *The Seal of Moonreign* and put a colon afterward before making another fold in the sheet. "Now," she spoke as she unfolded the sheet, "the proof will be the signatures of the receivers." She was showing him the paper.

"Well, dat'd be easy enough." He rubbed his beard with his left hand.

"Do you know anyone who could complete this task for me by dawn tomorrow?"

To her surprise, the old man merely continued to rub his beard. In fact, he did not speak for several minutes. Anne had believed he might like to do the task himself, but now she was wondering if she needed to continue searching for someone else. Refolding the sheet, she placed it back within her inner pocket and returned the quill and ink comfortably to the outer one before standing.

"Where ya goin'?"

"Excuse me, sir, my trespass in your space. It appears to me you haven't any idea who I might be able to employ, and seeing as I must find someone in great haste, I need to be on my way."

Shaking his head and raising a calloused and wrinkled hand, he stopped Anne from leaving. "Jus' 'cause I was thinkin', don't mean I don't wanna help. Fact is," he lowered his hand and voice, "there's a young lad with a mule jus' up the dock a bit. He don't talk, but he's not dumb. I wish I could help ya meself, but as ya can see, I'm busy."

Anne gave the man a quizzical look as he went back to his swaying. Then, feeling as though she had been dismissed, she walked up the dock in the direction he had gestured.

After leaving the old man's side, Anne had been walking for so long she was wondering if she would ever find the mute young lad the older gentleman had spoken of. She was also annoyed with all the immoral soliciting she was receiving in this seedy part of town. All she wanted to do was return to the *Survivor*. Thinking she might do just that and approach the regular message boy in the morning, Anne was suddenly knocked to the ground. Winded and instantly frightened, she tried to shove off whatever was on top of her. As she hit and pushed, however, the lump pinning her to the ground grunted and moaned, stilling her hands.

Slowly, a young man covered in rags and several torn jackets pulled himself up. Oddly enough, the first thing she noticed was his eyes; they were deep, cautious pools. He looked over his shoulder as if trying to determine whether the furies had followed him. Looking more closely as she, too, stood, Anne could see he was shaking.

"Excuse me. Are you all right?"

The man jumped as if Anne had startled him. He didn't say a word but regarded her carefully. At first, Anne thought he was a large man, but looking him over now, she could tell it was merely the illusion of one with the multiple jackets he was wearing. His hair was plastered to his head, but for someone who lived on the docks, he was incredibly clean. Wondering if this was the man with the donkey, since he had yet to speak, Anne thought it best to ask. "Sir, I was wondering if you might be the person for whom I've been searching."

He didn't speak.

She cleared her throat and continued, "An older gentleman sitting just north of here told me I could find a young man who didn't speak somewhere in this vicinity. Would you happen to be this man?"

To that, the man pulled out an old tattered sheet of paper covered with writing. He showed her one side. It read, *What do you want?*

"So you are he?"

He nodded.

Anne then told him what she was needing and how much she was willing to pay. The man nodded several times as she spoke. When she finished, he smiled and pointed to his chest. "You want the job, then?"

He went back to the sheet of paper; *yes,* it said.

"Do you think you can get back to me on the ship *Survivor* by dawn?" Anne wanted to be sure she could prove to the captain that his letter had been delivered. He showed her the *yes* side of the paper once more. Though smiling, Anne couldn't help but think something was missing. She knew she had told him everything, so what could possibly be wrong? "Your donkey," she remembered with a start. "The old man said you had a donkey."

Again the *yes* side of the tattered sheet was raised. Then, as if feeling her apprehension, he took her hand and dragged her up the dock. They only stopped when they reached a ship called the *Stalwart.* "Is this your ship?"

Shaking his head, he walked around to the other side of the miniature vessel, where large ropes helped to keep it moored. In the Stalwart's shadow lay a worn little donkey with a small rope about its neck. Quite diminutive in comparison to the ship's mooring, the donkey's rope looked like a thread wrapped around the Stalwart's lead. Anne walked over to the animal to see if she felt it could handle a night of riding.

To her surprise, as the donkey stood, she could tell, though it looked ancient, there was a quiet determination in its large dark eyes.

Inwardly smiling, Anne handed the signature sheet and the letters over to her companion. Then, reaching into her inner jacket pocket, she pulled out a silver coin and handed it to the young man. "Have you a name?" she asked.

He nodded, and for the last time that night, he pulled the old sheet of paper forth. Scribbling lightly on the upper end of the sheet as if it were wearing away, he wrote the name *Lindsey.*

"Well, hello, Lindsey." Anne extended her hand. "My name is Andrew."

Lindsey gave Anne a wry look and then went into a deep bow. When he came back up, he smiled at her, a glint of knowing in his eyes.

Uncertain what to say, Anne cleared her throat and decided to stick to the job at hand. "Um, okay. Uh, please deliver the letter to the palace first. Although the others are every bit as important, I need to be assured that particular piece of correspondence makes it to its destination." Then, wanting to get back to the *Survivor* as soon as possible, she wrapped things up. "Remember, I need to have the signature page by dawn tomorrow."

With that, Lindsey untied his donkey, hopped atop it, and moved toward her. Anne's heart was beating with a great amount of nervous energy as Lindsey reached for her and lifted her hand to his lips. Shock made her mouth drop slightly and her heart stop.

When Lindsey finally made his slow way away from the water, Anne let out her emotions with a warm wavering breath before heading back to her ship.

Chapter Seven

The Pen

*A*nne woke with a start just as the sun was painting the sky beautiful. Not knowing what had caused her to awaken so abruptly, she sat up on the deck and rubbed the haze from her eyes. Slowly, everything came into focus; the crew was crowded around something and causing a ruckus. She released a strained yawn and stood to find out what was happening.

As she approached the group of men standing less than ten feet away, she saw Lindsey at the center. Apparently, they were giving the young man a hard time for his lack of speech.

"Morning, Lindsey." Her voice made a few of the men jump. She broke through a side of the masculine wall while massaging the dull ache in the back of her neck. Sleeping above deck was hard on her body.

"You know this boy?!"

Anne couldn't believe that even this early in the morning, Kenward was such a grump. Rolling her eyes and shaking her head, she refrained from answering the question all together. "Lindsey, please excuse my comrades. I fear they don't socialize outside the crew too often."

"What do you know of what we do and what we do not?" Dyson fumed. "Less than a week on board, and he thinks he knows everything about us!"

Looking to Dyson, Anne stretched her arms over her head, making her voice sound tense and thin. "I know all I wish to know about *you*, Dyson. Now," she continued as felt her mind clear of the last wisps of dreamy visions, "I employed this young lad to make a few deliveries last night. I told him to find me here when the job was completed to receive the rest of his pay. I am truly sorry if his presence has alarmed you." To her relief, many of the men who'd gathered took their leave. Kenward did not.

"What sort of delivery was so important that it could not wait until morning?" Suspicion snuck through his voice.

"My personal affairs have nothing to do with this ship. And if you don't mind, I would like to keep my work and personal life separate."

"You just make sure they remain so, for if they do mingle, I'll be there to set *you* . . . I apologize . . . *things* right." He then turned and walked away.

Anne wasn't sure how or why Kenward believed he had so much say in what went on aboard the ship. However, unlike Dyson, she knew he was not the type to make idle threats. But there was no time to think about that now. Looking at Lindsey, she could tell the young man had been frightened. "Are you all right?"

He nodded and then went into a low, graceful bow. Driven by panic, Anne quickly grabbed his arm and pulled him upright. When his eyes shot up to hers, they were full of surprise and a great deal of confusion. Noticing him in the daylight now, Anne realized his eyes were not dark as she had believed the night before. They were clear. She remembered she had thought of them as pools; though she still believed that was a good description. His eyes seemed to be made of liquid. She couldn't tell whether they were blue or green, for they were so light in color, but there was a pale green halo about the irises. His hair was extra fine and flax-colored, and he was rather slim.

Feeling anxious, as though she believed he was looking through her and not at her, she tore her eyes from his and looked over his shoulder as she spoke. "I'm sorry about that, but if you haven't noticed, people here do not treat me that way." Then, looking at him once more, she asked, "Do you have the signature sheet?"

He nodded and reached into his outer-most jacket pocket to produce the paper. "Thank you." Anne looked over the sheet to see Laveda's scrawl and her sister's fair hand, then at the bottom, the seal of the Royal Family, with the viscount's name next to it. "You've done well."

Lindsey's eyes were trained on her face, silently questioning her. When Anne noticed the question, her breath caught in her throat. She looked away and busied herself with extracting his gold coin from her coat. However, before handing it to him, she forced herself to meet his eyes.

"Listen, I haven't the slightest idea how you know what you know about me, but you must keep it to yourself. Here, amongst these people, my name is Andrew. They know me as the newest addition to their crew, and all other information about me I keep to myself. Got it?" She handed him the coin with a firm glance, silently telling him the matter was closed, and he should refrain from bringing it up again to her or anyone else.

Lindsey took the coin from her without looking at it. He nodded his understanding as well as, she assumed, his thanks. She figured the lad wasn't sure why she'd have any desire to stay amongst such ill-mannered brutes but knew better than to ask. She obviously didn't want to talk about it. What she didn't know was that he was taking a few moments to remember her face for when their paths might cross again, and then he turned to leave.

The men on the ship were loading some cargo as he made his departure, making it a bit difficult for him to avoid getting hit in the head or the side with either their arms or large boxes, but he made it down without too great an incident. When safely on the dock, Anne looked up to see Lindsey looking back at her. He waved, then ran up the wharf.

Anne was relieved to see the young man go. She couldn't have someone ruining her escape. Soon, she would be far away from this port and completely on her own—free to explore new places and experience life to the fullest. Taking in a deep breath and smiling to herself, she decided it was indeed time to start the day. *Although,* she thought, *first things first.* She must see Captain Doran.

Anne looked down at the signature sheet she had made and ripped off the piece containing the royal seal. After all, she didn't want the captain to know to whom she had written. She placed her piece in her pocket and set out to see the captain.

Anne knocked on the door and was met with a rather angry bellow to enter. Hearing Doran's response to her knock, she wondered if this was a terrible time to stop by. But, just as before, she thought, *I'm here now, may as well enter.* Upon opening the door, Anne glimpsed Doran's bare back before swiftly turning her head. Perhaps she should come back later. "Sir, I apologize. I had no idea you were preoccupied." She kept her eyes averted and began to back out of the cabin.

"Nonsense!" Doran was shaking his head as he turned to face her. "Please, Andrew, do sit down. I was just shaving. It is one thing to have a beard, but it is quite another to be as hairy as an ape!" He chuckled. "So, how can I help you?"

Oh, how Anne wished he would put on a shirt. She had never seen this much of a man's body before and assumed the heat she felt rising within was because of her great embarrassment. Keeping her eyes on his face, she decided the quickest way to handle this was to inform him of his letter's delivery and be on her way. "Sir, I wish to tell you I sent a messenger to deliver your correspondence last night. I also asked him to bring back proof of the delivery and would like to hand it to you presently." She put forth the portion of the sheet that contained the royal seal.

Doran accepted the paper from Andrew. His astonishment upon seeing the seal and the viscount's signature next to it was not noticed by Anne. "You asked the messenger to bring you the seal as proof that the letter made it to the palace?"

Confused that he would find such a request odd, Anne tread lightly. "Of course, sir. I was too weary to deliver the letter myself, and as I was going to employ another to do what you had asked of me, I wanted to be sure the task was actually done. It would not be difficult to say that one made the delivery without having truly done so."

"Thank you for your . . . efficiency, Andrew. I honestly hadn't expected you to go to so much trouble; most would not have done so. Surely you must have paid a fair amount to have the letter delivered and signed for. Pray tell me how much it set you back so I might reimburse you."

Standing from the seat she had taken when motioned by him to do so, Anne began to take her leave. "Sir, it was my choice to handle the situation in this manner. Besides, the young man not only delivered your letter but mine as well; therefore, I see no need in accepting more than my regular payment—especially since you would not allow me to pay you for the supplies I needed."

Remembering that she still had his quill and ink, she removed them from her pockets and placed them on the table. "Thank you again, sir." Then Anne made her escape.

Ethana was still reeling over the letter she had received earlier that morning. They finally had word from Anne! Though her heart was saddened by Anne's dismissal of their parents, at least they could take solace in the knowledge that Anne was still alive. Dressing quickly, Ethana wanted to let her parents know Anne was safe. With the letter safely in her pocket, she finished combing her hair. Then Ethana made her way out of her room and down the hall. She did not stop to knock on her parents' door.

"Father, Mother, I have heard from Anne!" she shouted. Her parents were still in bed, their curtains still drawn. Ethana was happy to see they were lying in one another's arms.

"Ethana," yawned Thaniel, "what on earth are you shouting about?"

"Father, I have heard from Anne! She says she is well and would like us to stop searching for her." With that explanation, both Reyna and Thaniel were up and out of bed. Ethana thought they might knock her over in their excitement, so she took a few steps back as they came toward her. "Wait!" She threw up her right hand. "I have the letter she wrote, but I don't want you to get too excited. She is still quite upset with both of you, and I'm not sure whether she wanted either of you to see the message."

Reyna looked at Thaniel as fresh tears sprang forth and slid down her face like a babbling brook.

Thaniel merely shook his head. Then, after a few silent moments had passed, he sighed, "Well, Reyna, what did you expect? Of course she is angry with us. Why else would she run off and not send us word?" Then, turning to Ethana, he ordered, "Tell me exactly what she said."

After Ethana had finished reading the letter to her parents, her mother began a new round of weeping, and her father looked as though someone had ripped his heart from his chest. "I'm sorry," Ethana whispered.

Thaniel turned his glassy eyes on his remaining daughter. "None of this is your fault, Ethana. I know this is just as hard for you as it is for us."

"Why didn't you ask the messenger where he met her?" Reyna's scream suddenly cut through the thick air of sadness, blame deeply embedded in her voice. "Why did you not ask him where we could find her!?"

Ethana stood back and watched as her father took hold of her mother. Never before had she seen Mother this way. Fighting back tears of her own, Ethana tried to explain, "The messenger could not tell me anything. He could not speak."

Thaniel looked at Ethana. "A mute messenger?" He chuckled. "Leave it to Anne to find such a person to deliver a letter." He then gave a more hearty laugh before burying his face in Reyna's shoulder where he began to cry. "I miss her, Reyna. I want my little girl back."

Ethana, close to tears, retreated from the suite to return her parents their privacy. She had to be strong, and being surrounded by such sadness would only weaken her resolve and turn her into a puddle of nerves. Besides, she needed to write the princess to request that she to call off the search. And Sophie needed to be tended to.

"Come on, girl, chin up," Ethana spoke to herself. "No time for tears. You've a girl to look after."

The rest of the morning raced past Ethana at an alarming rate. She broke her fast with Sophie in the guest bedroom and then asked a few of the maids to help her with the young girl. Sophie was to be cleaned, her hair cut, and her nails trimmed. She also had Cipriana measure the young girl for clothes.

Cipriana, though only thirteen, was one of the most accomplished seamstresses in the household. She made all the servants' clothes and helped Ethana and Anne when they'd needed a few gowns made in a hurry. When going to ask Cipriana for her assistance, Ethana was more than certain the girl would jump for the opportunity to come up with four pretty dresses for their new ward, and much to her delight, she was not mistaken. For at least two and a half hours, Sophie and Cipriana went over dress ideas as Ethana sat back to write up the week's menu.

With dress designing and menu creating complete, Ethana felt she should discuss the matter of education with Sophie. With Henry's assistance, Ethana and Sophie sat outside by the creek. The sun was hung high in the translucent blue sky, and the air was clean and fresh. "Sophie," Ethana breathed in the warm scent of honeysuckle, "can you read?"

Sophie looked from the creek to Ethana. "Yes . . . well, no. I mean, I can read little words. Laveda taught me some." She looked back at the creek, and Ethana watched the girl study the foam forming over the stones. "Do you think the water is cool or warm?" Sophie asked before closing her eyes.

After a few seconds, Sophie opened her eyes and seemed to take notice of every flower, every tree, as if she was feasting on them.

She probably feels so free out here, Ethana thought.

Before now, Ethana hadn't given much thought to the way Sophie lived her life. She wondered just how long the girl had been cooped up in the brothel she called home. Perhaps the lessons could wait another day. Feeding the soul was just as important, if not more so, than feeding the mind.

Ethana smiled and leaning back in the grass, having decided to show Sophie how to spot animals in the clouds above.

Haru could not believe what she was reading. A letter from Anne? Surely, she should run to Indira immediately, but then what of this girl? Should she carry her along to Indira as well, or take her to see Ms. Godwin? Oh, what should she do?

"Ma'am, I don't mean to be rude, but will ya take me for educatin' or no? I'm sure I can find the way on my own. But it'd be nice if ya'd at least point the way."

Haru looked at the girl but didn't really see or hear her. A few more moments passed before she spoke. "Do you know Anne de Ranger?"

"Nope. I know 'er family, though. They're takin' care of my sister. Nice people they are."

Puzzled by her answer, Haru was even more confused than before. Her head throbbed slightly and, knowing her indecision would only make it worse, she decided to take the girl to the teacher. Besides, it wasn't as if she couldn't go to the de Rangers afterward. "I shall show you the way. It isn't too far off but can be as difficult as Minotaur hunting if one takes a wrong turn."

Laveda hadn't the slightest idea what a Minotaur was or why anyone would wish to seek one, but as she and Haru made their way through town, she thought the animal must be quite elusive. There were so many twists and turns to make, and at every turn, a new row of shops. She had no idea how she would find the school again once they arrived. At first, Laveda tried to remember the names of the stores or boutiques where she would need to turn, but after the fourth or fifth turn, though she remembered their names, she no longer remembered whether she was to turn left or right. Frustrated, and a bit scared, she looked back the way they had come and urged her brain to recall the lost information.

"Um . . . miss!" Haru called to her. Laveda did not hear her. Haru then cleared her throat. "Eh-umm, miss . . . Laveda. Please follow! We are almost there." With the turn of yet another corner and a stroll down a rather short street, they came to a stone wall with a narrow wooden door no taller than six feet. Next to the door was an old, beat-up wooden sign that read, "Open this door and soon you will know . . . the larger world and the keys it holds."

"This is the school?" Laveda asked her companion, with a skeptical sideways glance. When Haru didn't reply, Laveda mumbled to herself. "Made of stone . . . no windows . . . one little door? Looks more like a prison te me."

"Shh! I am trying to listen for the riddle."

"Riddle?"

The woman raised her hand to silence Laveda again. Just as she did, a beautiful male voice wafted down to them from above, saying, "I'm everywhere you are and everywhere you go. But only those who seek me will ever truly know."

The voice was melodious, dripping down like sweet honey poured from a jar. Never before had Laveda heard such a lovely, yet still masculine, voice. She looked around to see where it had come from, but there was no one on the street with them, and she couldn't for the life of her see so much as a hole in the wall from which someone could see them.

When the man had finished his rhyme, there was a silence unlike any other. It was as if even the wind dared not provide an incorrect reply. Nervously waiting, Laveda tried her best not to breathe too loudly, afraid she would be denied entry. Suddenly, an even lovelier voice fluttered gently on the air, like a butterfly rising and falling on the breeze. In the beginning, Laveda had no clue where it was coming from, but then, turning to ask Haru, the source was revealed. Haru's beautiful soprano soared to the top of the brick wall.

You are everywhere I am
And everywhere I go.
I do plan to seek thee,
I truly wish to know.
I think you are knowledge
And if that be the key,
Please do allow entrance
For my guest and me.

Laveda, enchanted, glanced around to see if the man would reveal himself. She was disappointed. She wasn't exactly sure what she expected, but when the small wooden door flung outward and there was no sign of anyone, she felt a little put out.

"Well, here we are." Haru gestured toward the door. "We must not dawdle; I have a shop to run." Gracefully, in her floor-length sage dress, Haru crossed the threshold of the school. Laveda tentatively followed.

Upon entering, Laveda felt jolted when she spied several acres of land with a huge building in the center. The grass was a wonderful emerald color and seemed to be rolling in the breeze. There were few trees or flowers along the outer border, but as she looked at the building, Laveda could see several weeping willows and a few other trees she could not name. The magnificent building was made of the same stone used on the outer wall through which they'd just entered. There were two grand towers and a winding drive leading to the front. Laveda had seen sketches of the royal palace and though it, too, had towers, this building seemed warmer, more inviting than even the royal abode.

Haru moved onto the small dirt road before them and waited. Normally, when school was in session, the keeper of the gate would open the door to all the students. Inside, the students stand before a great line of carriages, each waiting to transport its share of pupils up to the school. Now, however, during its season of closure, a visitor had to answer a riddle in the way it had just been given and then wait for a ride. Standing patiently, Laveda could feel Haru watching her, so she smiled in awe of the place.

Laveda looked again at the wall behind her and tried to find the person who had asked the riddle. She couldn't see any holes in the wall, nor could she see anyone sitting atop the stone barrier. Trying to uncover the magic that could hide an entire person from view, Laveda nearly missed the soft sound of horse hooves on the path.

"Come, Laveda," Haru called. "Here is our ride."

Laveda turned to see a carriage no different from the ones she'd seen every day at the market—black with four wheels and one driver. There was absolutely nothing extravagant or special about it whatsoever. *Truthfully*, she thought to herself, *I've seen more impressive carriages at the dock.* Shrugging off this bit of information, Laveda climbed in after her guide.

As they wound their way up the path to the school, the carriage gently rolled past a play area, then a small stream. Like a tour guide, Haru pointed out these features as well as a few others to Laveda. "The stream runs through this area and provides irrigation for the many gardens of Constantine Manor. It also provides us with water to drink and clean with."

Not wishing to feel stupid, Laveda dared not ask what Constantine Manor was, remaining silent.

When they arrived before a large white building with eight columns, Haru welcomed Laveda to Constantine Manor. Then they walked up the expansive steps to the massive porch where a man stood waiting with the door wide open.

"Good afternoon, Bowen. We are here to see Ms. Godwin."

Nodding, the formally dressed older man informed them Ms. Godwin could be found on the balcony in the garden beneath the styrax.

"Um, Haru, what exactly is a styrax?" Laveda asked as they made their way through the school.

"Oh, um, styrax is the natural name of the snowbell. It is that lovely tree over there that has fragrant, white bell-shaped blooms." Then, moving her hands down the skirt of her dress, she moved onto the terrace.

Laveda noticed the terrace was not completely covered in stones; the farther she ventured out, the stones gave way to soil. Soon, she found her slippers surrounded by lovely little pink and purple blossoms. Laveda wasn't sure how they had created this garden that seemed to float in the air. Sure, she had seen lovely terraces before, but they merely seemed a prettier version of her dilapidated balcony. This, on the other hand, was an extraordinary floating wonderland of scents, sounds, and beauty. She imagined herself lying among the blooms, blanketed by leaves, and with a soft bundle of moss on which to lay her head. This was a marvelous place.

"I don't see her, do you?" Haru's question was like cold water upon the head of the resting.

"How'm I te know if I've seen her or not!?" Just then, it was as if the autumn rose from the farthest corner of the terrace. Frightened by the sudden movement, Laveda took a step back.

"Moira?" Haru questioned as she moved toward the fire amongst the greenery.

"Haru! I was sure it was your voice I heard." Slowly the petite figure came forward, and to Laveda's astonishment the flame she had seen was merely a woman—an amazingly gorgeous lady, but a woman none the less. As she took Haru in her arms and spoke in a musical sort of way, Laveda became more entranced simply by being in her presence.

"Moira, I know I should visit more often, so I am very sorry to tell you I have not come on a social occasion." Haru then explained to the elegant woman the reason for her visit, and Ms. Godwin listened intently, nodding politely every so often to let Haru know she was paying attention.

Laveda, on the other hand, never took her eyes off the lady who had come to stand next to them. Never before had she seen anyone quite so striking. Ms. Godwin, though smaller than average height, was dressed in red and golden—the very essence of the falling season. Her facial features were small and could be compared to the pretty features of a child. In fact, one might think she was rather young if it were not for her eyes. *Her eyes* . . . Laveda stared. They were like, *like so many things all together.* She couldn't decide whether they matched the sea after a storm or the sky during a storm. Then, again, though the color was a gradient of hues, her eyes were clear, and Laveda thought the sage of Haru's dress, though darker than the woman's eyes, complemented them wonderfully.

"Do you think you could find some time to donate to the girl?" Haru questioned under her breath, though Laveda still heard her.

Moira smiled at and moved around Haru to meet her new student. "Hello, Laveda, my name is Moira Godwin." She bowed her head slightly before returning her gaze to Laveda. Ms. Godwin's voice was soft and sweet, and instead of piercing the air as a pointed jab, it rose and fell like a leaf on a breeze. "I am primarily the etiquette teacher at this institution; however, I am sure Anne would have me teach you to read, speak, and write properly, as well as a few things that are not normally taught to young ladies." Her lips parted in a knowing grin.

"Like what sorts of things?" Laveda asked suspiciously. She wasn't too sure of the missing girl's character, though, she had to admit, everyone seemed quite fond of this Philana-Narie. But to Laveda, anyone who would leave such a wonderful family for the uncertainty of the greater world had to be raving mad.

"Miss Laveda, Philana-Narie was the most extraordinary student I have ever had the pleasure of teaching. She is brilliant, fun, witty—quite full of life. Though I am assuming she would like me to teach you the basic knowledge any young lady of her stature should possess, that is not the information for which she often pressed me." Glowing, she continued, "Philana-Narie, Anne, could have sent you to any of her teachers for you to learn the basics, but she did not. She sent you to Haru and me. And I can only suppose the reason for this was for me to teach you everything I taught her."

When the music that was Moira's voice stopped, Haru smiled, nodded, and said her goodbyes.

Laveda watched Moira hug her taller friend. "Do come again soon. It would be good for my heart.

Chapter Eight

The Sword

There was a thunderous amount of clapping and whistling as Anne helped her opponent from the ground. Over the past three months, since they had left the port at Ryland, she had practiced her swordplay. Yet, never before now had she beaten anyone aboard the ship. Embarrassed by her weaknesses—as well as her shipmates' behavior whenever they were at port—Anne had been driven to spend all her spare time practicing. Noticing that most of the crew had been watching her bout with Bêrk and had seen her triumph, she knew her hard work had paid off.

"Well, mate, you've certainly come about. Never thought I would see the day you'd beat me—not that I'm the best there is, mind you."

Placing her sword back in its sheath, Anne chuckled. "Well, I'm sure months of nothing else but work and swordplay were bound to make me a little better than I was before."

"A little better! I swear, for a moment there, I really thought you were going to run me through!" Clapping Anne roughly on the back, Bêrk laughed. "A little better. If you keep going about things the way you always do, I'm sure you could soon take on Dyson."

Bêrk had to be Anne's closest friend onboard, and despite his defeat, he still cheered her on. "I'm not too sure about that, my friend, but if you continue to believe, then perhaps, one day, I will believe it too." The two were ambling up the deck toward the galley when they noticed Captain Doran approaching. He had caught wind of Andrew's victory and wanted to give his congratulations, but when he noticed Andrew tense up, he felt the need to also clear the air between them.

"Andrew, I would like to speak with you for a moment."

Anne looked toward Bêrk. She hadn't spoken privately with the captain since he had embarrassed her in Île-de-L'est two weeks after they had left her home port. She would never forget and, perhaps, never fully forgive him for what he had done.

"Oh, um, well, Captain, I was just on my way to the galley. Bêrk and I need to get the grub started. Don't want to keep the men waiting, ay?" With that being said, she smiled at Bêrk and tried to urge him toward the galley.

"I'm sorry, Andrew." Doran placed a firm hand on her right shoulder. "I really *must* insist."

There was no way out. Anne had to do exactly as Captain Doran commanded, and she hated it. She left home so she could do whatever she wished to do, not to be under someone else's control. Nodding once to Doran, she acquiesced and followed him to his cabin.

Anne entered the masculine room belonging to her captain when he held the door open for her. She knew her demeanor was rigid, and she dared not breathe. Though she could not imagine what he would like to say to her, she knew she needed to be prepared for the worst.

The door behind her closed and then . . . she heard it being locked.

The sound pierced through Anne's reserve and the visions of the bar she had visited with Doran at port filled her mind. She closed her eyes to the revolting images as they replayed themselves in her mind. Then, as she felt the captain move from the door behind her, she gave herself a mental shake, pursed her lips, and opened her eyes.

Doran assessed Andrew's disposition. He knew the young man had not been the same since they'd departed Île-de-L'est over two months ago. He also knew it probably had something to do with their little visit to La Belle É'toile. However, the details were a complete mystery—a puzzle, one he was going to piece together right now. "Andrew, why don't you have a seat?"

Anne looked at the seat to which the captain was referring, and then returned her gaze to his before declining. "I would much rather stand, sir."

"Very well. Do you mind if I sit, then?" Anne merely raised her left brow and slightly tilted her head.

"No? Good." Doran lowered himself into the seat on the other side of the table across from where his sailor stood before sweeping his feet from the floor and placing them upon the wood's surface. His hands were interlaced and resting on his chest.

"Now, Andrew, why don't you tell me what's on your mind?"

"I'm sorry, Captain?"

"Don't look so confused. I'm not so thick that I don't notice there has been a cloud over you since Île-de-L'est."

He could tell the young man wasn't sure what to say. He figured Andrew did not wish to discuss the situation. What Doran didn't know was that Anne didn't want it to seem as though she were hiding something. "I apologize, sir, if this *cloud*, as you so call it, has in any way affected my work."

"Ah, Andrew, I never took you for a dancer." Doran swiftly, yet gracefully, stood and turned to the tray on his desk. "Tea?"

"Um, no, thank you, sir." Out of the corner of his eyes, he watched the boy clasp his hands behind his back. "Sir, what is it, exactly, you wish to discuss with me?"

"Stop it, Andrew." The casual tone in the boy's voice made Doran snap, and he slammed his palm on the table, nearly spilling the tea held in his left hand. "I didn't bring you here to see how well you can waltz around an issue. I want to know what on God's blue waters is wrong with you! We are a team on this ship, and if for any reason I cannot rely on you, then you need to go."

Anne was quiet for a few moments. She contemplated what she would do if she were dropped off at the next port. Could she find work? Perhaps. But what if she could not? She wasn't the only person relying on her salary; she had to think of Laveda as well. She had to stay onboard. "Captain, there is nothing amiss with me. However, I will keep what you have said in mind."

Doran stared at Anne. She figured he knew she was lying. Shaking his head, he chuckled and settled himself back into his chair. "That's not good enough." He sipped the warm liquid from his tin mug. "Try again."

"Try what, sir?"

Doran placed the teacup on the table, leaned back in his chair, and trained his eyes on Anne. "The truth, Andrew. I have always known you to tell the truth; that is your gift. Do *not* let this crew or the sea take it from you. Now, tell me, what happened between you and Linette? Did you not find her sweet?" One corner of Doran's mouth curled upward, and that was it. That was the final straw.

Anne couldn't believe her captain, this man she had grown to respect in so many ways, was so horrid when it came to women! She could take it no longer. "How dare you! How dare you speak of her or . . . or any woman like that! Who gives you the right to degrade another person?"

"Degrade? I was just wondering how she was taking to her new career. You see, she used to be one of the bar wenches."

Anne was fuming, struggling to control her temper. She looked down at the seat before her and closed her eyes. An enormous wave of anger, followed by sadness, washed over her. She thought of the young girl, Linette, and how she had nervously begun to undress before Anne. How she herself had stopped the pitiable girl and comforted her when she cried, "Am I not desirable?" Anne had rocked the smaller young woman in her arms and smoothed her hair away from her tear-stained face. She then told Linette a story—one about a penniless girl who was really a missing princess. When the poor darling finally fell asleep, Anne allowed herself to do the same. However, trained by what she liked to call *life on a boat*, she rose before the sun had completely awakened and left a gold coin and a note for Linette.

> Where there is hope, there is light.
> Where there is light, we can see.
> And when we see, we find direction.

With new direction, there comes a change.

You have my hope, if you have none. Now, with this light, I beg you see. Find your direction and change your life for the better.

~Andrew
The Ship "Survivor"

Thinking back on it now almost brought tears to Anne's eyes. But this moment was not the time for tears. *Tears,* she thought. The concept startled her, and she wondered if she would ever shed them freely again.

"Have you a sister, Captain?" she asked after what seemed a lifelong silence. Her voice was small, and if Doran had not been listening and watching intently, it would have been swallowed up by the quiet.

"I have." Anne glanced up, damming the emotions from her face. Doran sat up in his chair, and the air became thick. Anne figured Doran assumed this was what he had been waiting for. Perhaps, he thought she had a sister who had been used in some way, or maybe his sailor had been witness to an awful crime. He urged Anne on. "Have you a sister, Andrew?"

"I have." Anne looked Doran in the eyes. All teasing gone, she believed she finally saw compassion in his dark eyes. Her mouth was becoming dry, and she knew if she didn't explain herself soon, she may not be able to explain at all. "Captain, I know and love many women. I listen to and understand them. I know they have hopes and dreams of their own. I also know they would rather meet Death early at their doors than live only to be of *service* to men."

She swallowed the lump forming in her throat. "I will not be a part of any mere usage of ladies, for I know what it is to be ignored and used in an ill manner." She braced her hands on the chair before her and rebuilt the dam around her heart before continuing. "To conclude, Captain, I shall admit I have been feeling poorly since we were docked at Île-de-L'est, though I did believe, until now, I had hidden it well."

She watched Doran's look of astonishment. She could not have known Doran had heard the same view from his sister. In fact, it was because of this same strong belief that his sister, aged twenty-one summers, was still unmarried. "I see. So your temperament was due to having a lady purchased for you."

Anne looked at her hands as she thought through the comment. Though she found what he said to be true, she couldn't help the hurt growing within her. At last, an answer came to her. "No."

"No?" It was Doran's turn to raise a brow. "There has been something else weighing down your spirit, then? Well, boy, spit it out unless you are now avoiding the galley."

"Forgive me, sir, for what I am about to say." Anne closed her eyes, took a deep breath, then reopened them. "I have realized it was not only that Linette was given to me, but that she was given to me by you."

"By me?" the captain questioned, laughter back in his eyes. "And how, may I ask, does the giver factor into your misery?"

Anne was insulted by his light mockery. "It matters, Captain, because I thought better of you. I would have expected such behavior from Dyson, or even Marid. But I never envisioned you, an intelligent gentleman, going to such a place, let alone *using* women as . . . as *whatever*." She could not find a word foul enough. "Now, if you feel I have spoken ahead of myself or that I am no longer worthy of being a part of this crew, I am sorry." *Well*, she thought, *that's it. He's going to make me walk the plank.* She watched as his jaw clenched.

"Are you finished?" he spat at her. Anne nodded as her heart crumbled. "What is wrong with you? You claim to understand women, yet you seem ignorant of the needs and desires of your own sex!"

"What of them? Are we to fill ourselves up while we empty others, taking from them all they have to offer!? Who are we to—"

"Stop it!" Doran once again slammed his hand on the table. He was now standing and his face was grim. "Perhaps I have allowed you to speak too freely in my presence. It is not for you to judge my character, nor is it up to you to protect every lady to grace this land. What *is* commanded of you is that you go about your duties without question. Do you understand?"

"Aye, sir." Though she felt meek, Anne remained firm.

"Good. Now, congratulations on your recent victory against Bêrk; now get to the galley before I change my mind." Anne found herself, yet again, fighting back the tears that had been threatening to burst forth at any moment. Determined to leave completely dry and with her dignity intact, she made for the door with due haste. However, before she could unlock and pull the door inward, the captain caught her attention.

"Andrew."

She did not turn to face him.

"Not that I owe you any explanations, but I have never taken advantage of any woman, prostitute or no."

Then she was gone.

Doran stood staring at the door for several moments before retaking his seat. Why had he felt the need to dispel Andrew's ill perception of him? If it had been anyone else, he might have just let it go and not given it another thought. However, this boy was different.

One word, he thought to himself. *If I were to choose one word to describe Andrew, what would it be? Naïve? Perhaps. Yet, though he seems to be naïve in some respects, he seems wise in others. Trustworthy . . . well, that is without question. Enigmatic.*

"Yes. That's the word," he whispered to himself.

Andrew was not a person one could easily sum up in one word, though *enigmatic* was an excellent adjective. He was a marvelous mixture of strength and weakness, maturity and naivety, openness and mystery. Mystery. Perhaps that was the reason he was drawn to the youth.

But his last question would keep him up at night. "What is he hiding?"

Anne was finishing the after-supper cleaning when Bêrk turned in. She hadn't told him of her conversation with the captain, feeling it would be better to keep the incident to herself. Besides, she was sure none of her crewmates would share her views on how women should be treated.

Having finished wiping down the counters, she carried a bucket of dirty water above deck to toss overboard. Since she had perfected the art of carrying a full bucket on the ship, not a drop of water splashed free from its captor, and she easily made her way to the ship's edge. Effortlessly, she lifted her burden and let the contents flow freely over the side.

Exhausted and sad, Anne looked out over the black waters of the Ladonian Channel. Over the past three months, she had been to nearly every island that made up the countries of Île-de-L'est and Yakecen. Now they were on their way to the island of Hampton, where they were to deliver their cargo of dyes from Yakecen and lace from Île-de-L'est. The men seemed excited about reaching the large island. There were many stories of beautiful women, exotic foods, and a lively atmosphere. It had been difficult for Anne to feign enthusiasm because it sounded as though there would be little time for her to spend alone.

She breathed in deeply and once more thought of her discussion with the captain. He may think he didn't use women, but in purchasing Linette's services for her, he had done just that. Anne shook her head. What should it matter to her what he did, anyway? Her heart gave a little lurch, and her face became warm.

"I hope this isn't the beginning of a cold," she spoke to herself. "Get ye to bed, Anne, else the flu catches you." Taking her own order, she went to retrieve her blankets.

Chapter Nine

Dinner with a Baroness

*L*aveda loved Sundays. It was the only day of the week she could get away from her studies to see her sister, and the de Rangers were always nice enough to invite her to stay for supper. She was grateful to them for so many things, and she hoped to repay them one day for their kindness.

Laveda walked quickly through town, for she was running a little behind schedule because of her stop to see Haru. She and the older woman had become friends, and Laveda finally felt she had someone to look up to. Of course, there was also Ms. Godwin, but it wasn't the same between the two of them. She often thought of Ms. Godwin as a goddess—someone high above her, a person to be adored beyond admiration. And how could she, Laveda, ever hope to achieve such greatness of mind and spirit? It was like wishing to become an angel; it could never be.

Laveda smiled to herself and bent her head to take in the scent of the flowers she had just purchased for the baroness. Though she had never met the lady of the manor, she was informed by letter that the baroness would be joining the de

Rangers for supper. Therefore, wanting to make a good impression, as well as wishing to show off her new knowledge of flora, she had designed a lovely bouquet for the lady.

A gust of wind whipped her hair across her face, reminding her that winter was on its way. She wondered how she would make it this far from home when the snow came. Finally arriving at her destination, she decided the question was better left for another day.

Laveda knocked only once when the door swung open to reveal Henry on the other side. "Well, it's about time you arrived." The young man smiled. "I swear, I don't believe I can endure another round of questions from your sister."

Laveda laughed, and the sound rang out beautiful and pure. Sophie was always so impatient when it came to her visits. She gave Henry a big hug before entering the manor house. "So where is she?"

"Lady Ethana took her out back to keep her mind off the door." He led her through the house. "Who are the flowers for?"

"I brought them for the baroness. I heard she would be joining us for supper and thought it would be nice if I had something for our first meeting." Laveda's speech had improved with her studies, but she was still nervous about being accepted by the lady of the manor.

"I'm sure she will love them."

They stopped a few feet before the kitchen. "Well, I really must get back to work. I trust you can find your way to the gardens from here, and I hope you have a wonderful time at supper." Henry winked at his nervous companion, and she smiled warmly in return. "And don't worry about the baroness; she's sure to love you." He gave her a smile and squeezed her shoulder before continuing to the kitchen. And Laveda made her way to the back of the house.

Sophie and Ethana were lying on their backs, staring at the sky, when Laveda approached. Laveda knew when Sophie heard her footsteps because she immediately flipped herself onto her belly.

"Laveda!" she yelled and held up her arms.

Laveda smiled as she placed the flowers on the wooden bench to her left and moved toward the cloud watchers. She bent to her knees and pulled Sophie onto her lap. "You know, I don't believe I left you here to lie about like some sort of beggar," she teased.

"I would not have been lying about if you had come on time," the girl shot back just as playfully.

Ethana sat back, watching them for a few moments, marveling at how well the two of them got along. Though she and Anne had been close, she didn't believe they had ever been as close as Laveda and Sophie. There was no competition between them, just love and acceptance; which was as it should be. The way it would have been if she hadn't been so jealous of Anne.

Laveda saw Ethana shiver before speaking to her. "Laveda, for whom did you bring the flowers?"

"Your mother," she spoke over her giggling sister. "I thought since this would be our first meeting, I should bring a gift."

"Oh, how kind of you!" Ethana smiled. "Perhaps we should go inside now that you are here. I'm sure Verna will have supper ready any moment."

Ethana and Laveda paired up to help Sophie inside.

Dinner that night went as it usually did—minus one Baroness Reyna de Ranger. Thaniel had come down to say Reyna was still not feeling up for company, and though his voice was that of someone unconcerned, his eyes were sad and his face grim. The flowers Laveda had brought seemed to glow at the center of the dining table, unaware of the rejection the others felt.

Thus the evening passed as always, with the four of them discussing how well Sophie's studies were coming along, how much Laveda appreciated everything, a comment or two on Laveda's wonderful personal changes, and new information on the missing de Ranger.

Apparently, much to Laveda's surprise, Ethana had been receiving two to three letters a month from her roving sister. "How is she then?" Laveda asked with genuine concern, for she felt she was very much a part of the family and knew they not only wanted but needed Anne to come home. "Do you know where she is?"

"I'm afraid I do not; however, she sounds well." Ethana picked at her cherry cobbler. "She never tells me how she is affording to live on her own or if she ever intends to come home. And since I haven't the slightest idea where she is, I cannot ask her anything."

Ethana's fork lowered as her once bright face fell into shadow. In that moment, Laveda felt the air in the room became thick with everyone's suffocating grief.

Chapter Ten

Kenward's Home

*H*ampton was an island of many exotics. Anne could never have imagined such a place existed. Primarily, it was a forest surrounded by beach and ocean. The people there were kind though somewhat on the sensuous side. Most had dark skin, full lips, and soft curly hair. They were truly beautiful, and their island was a place of many pleasures with strange yet tantalizing tastes and smells. The entire time they were there, Anne felt as though she were on vacation.

She spent her mornings working aboard the *Survivor*, her afternoons speaking with the natives, and her nights lying on a secluded stretch of beach to sleep beneath the stars. Though the weather was becoming cooler, she had found the brisk morning air invigorating. Like all wonderful things, though, it had to end.

"Andrew, what on earth are we to do with these?" Bêrk grimaced at a bunch of asparagus.

Smiling and shaking her head, Anne took the vegetable from her bewildered friend. "It is called *asparagus*. And the rest—corn, endive, squash, spinach, pumpkin, silver beet, and this little thing is called garlic." She pointed out each item in turn. "I spoke with the captain after researching what the native gardeners grew and asked if we could bring something new aboard. You know, to liven up mealtime a bit."

"Liven it up? Well, I hope you know how to cook all this rubbish; otherwise, meal times are sure to get a mite livelier than you hope!" He gave the veggies another skeptical grimace before turning to his own supplies.

Anne watched Bêrk and smiled; although he did a wonderful job keeping everyone aboard healthy, he lacked the desire to offer something fresh—innovative—whereas she had gone forth to try all sorts of new foods. When she found something she liked, she was not averse to asking for the recipe. She was sure the crew would be happy with all the work she had done while in Hampton.

"I don't believe I pay you to stand around smiling at your crewmates."

Anne's smile fled, and she closed her eyes as the scent woody musk kissed by light vanilla enveloped her. When she felt the wearer standing by her side, she labored to open her eyes and turn to face the captain. "I'm sorry, sir. Bêrk and I were just discussing some of the food I brought aboard."

"Ah. Well, I see you have purchased an alarming amount of vegetables." The captain looked over the food supply. "I hope you're not wasting kitchen resources on items that will not keep."

"No, Captain. Much of the items here were gifts from the farmers. In my spare time, I would help them in any way I could in exchange for whatever produce they could part with. And, fortunately for us, the produce they are harvesting now is all quite hardy."

Anne could tell she had surprised him. She knew when they usually had a few extra days at any port, the men would take leave to have a bit of fun and relaxation. Doran seemed speechless—nearly. "Um, well, thank you for your thriftiness. It is greatly appreciated."

Just then, Marid came to thin the thickening air with a mischievous smile. "Pardon me, Captain, but there is a young lady on the dock asking for Andrew."

Anne rolled her eyes and made her way to the dock. Even though she had never done anything with any woman, the crew still considered her quite the ladies' man. "I don't see why *everyone* thinks *I* have a philanderer's spirit," she spoke to herself.

107

"Perhaps it's because *you* are the *only* man aboard who has women come to you instead of the reverse." Though Anne's feet tried to continue on their speedy way, the shock of hearing Captain Doran's voice nearly stopped her, and the result was her tripping over her feet and landing face-first on the deck.

The captain was immediately by her side. He moved the hair from Anne's face and checked to see if her nose was bleeding. When he discovered she was fine, he swiftly lifted her to her feet. "Come, now, you don't want to be late for your lady friend." His brow was raised, but his face held no hint of amusement.

Anne moved quickly around him, and before long, she was standing opposite a woman she had met just the other day.

The girl went into a low curtsy before Anne, then rose, smiling. "Andrew, my father has sent me to give you these gifts. He thanks you for helping him with the shop's numbers."

Anne took the basket the girl handed her and opened it. Inside were three large jugs of liquid and a small jar of honey. She wasn't sure what was in the large clay jugs but knew honey was quite a luxury, no matter where you lived. "I am astonished by this gift. Your father has given me much already."

"Yes," the girl's smile broadened, "but if you remember the drink my mother brought to you before you left our home, then you will be even more thrilled with this."

"Are you saying this is *the* famous pumpkin juice for which she would not share the recipe?" Anne's eyes lit up. She had loved the drink so much, she had nearly begged for its design.

"Yes, it is."

Overjoyed, Anne lost all composure and gave the girl a huge hug. "Thank your family tremendously for this gift. And tell your mother, especially, that this draught is worth more than a house of gold."

They continued to chat along merrily until a harsh voice killed their delight.

"What are you doing with this man?" bellowed Kenward, and for a moment, Anne wasn't sure to whom he was referring. "Answer me, Kismet!"

"And what does it matter to you who I spend my time with?" The young woman challenged the second-in-command of the ship.

Anne looked from Kenward to Kismet and was suddenly afraid she had just hugged the large man's wife. "Kenward, nothing has happened. Kismet just—"

"I was not speaking to you," he roared. Then he seized Kismet by the arm, only to have her turn and swiftly kick him in the groin. Anne, stunned, couldn't say anything.

Busy staring at the man crumpled on the dock, Kismet's voice called to her as if nothing had transpired. "Andrew, I am so pleased you like the gift, and I hope you will come back and visit us soon." She spoke seductively as she took Anne's hand in her own, and Anne couldn't believe the girl was actually flirting with her.

Not wanting to seem rude, yet also not wanting to appear as if anything had transpired with the lady before her, Anne placed the basket in the sand and lightly patted Kismet's hand with her left one while extracting her right from the young lady's grasp. "Yes, perhaps. Although, I am not quite sure my mate here would approve." She then tried to help Kenward to his feet but was shoved away.

"You're correct. I don't approve!"

The next thing Anne knew, there was an all-out verbal assault. She could barely understand what was being said, but from the few tidbits she could catch here and there, she gathered Kismet was Kenward's younger sister. She was so relieved by the news that she didn't see what hit her.

It was dark when Anne found herself lying on her back on a sea of clouds. No—they were not clouds at all . . . pillows. She closed her eyes again and took a deep breath. Her heart seized as she took in the achingly familiar scent she could only attribute to the one and only Captain Doran. Without thinking, she shot straight up in the bed and slid her feet to the floor.

It was night, and she hadn't seen dusk. So she'd been out for a while. Anne sat on the edge of the bed and tried to regain her memory. "I was on the dock, speaking with Kismet," she spoke softly to herself, "and Kenward came." All at once, the reality of what had happened engulfed her. "He *hit* me." The horror of that final statement brought her hands immediately to her face. The left side was tender to the touch, and she winced as her fingers touched the inflamed yet hard tissue around her eye.

Never before had she been punched, and for the second time since she began her adventure, she wanted to break down and cry. She would have done just that had Jerah not chosen that very moment to enter the room.

"Andrew, are ya awake?" The old man moved cautiously into the room, a lantern held high.

Anne focused on the approaching light and calmed her nerves before speaking. "I'm awake."

"Good heav'ns, my boy—ya scared us. Been out most of the day, ya have." Jerah came to sit next to her. Then, after checking her face, he filled her in on what had happened after she had been knocked out.

"Ya know, I don't think I've ever seen the captain so angry before. He and a few of the others pulled Kenward from ya, then he had Dyson bring ya to his cabin while he tore inta ol' Kenny."

Anne listened intently as Jerah recounted the scene she had not been awake to witness. When he was done, though she had slept the day away, she felt drained.

"Well, anyway, the captain would like to see ya now. He's above deck, standin' where ya usually sleep."

Not knowing what to say, Anne merely followed Jerah out of the cabin to where the captain patiently waited.

Doran did not look at her when she arrived by his side. His gaze was steady on the silvery moon-wash upon the cheerless sea. "Andrew, what business did you have with the family Wemilo?"

"I gave bookkeeping advice to Master Noshi. He recently let his accountant go and was having a hard time managing the home business, as well as the larger affairs of the island. "

"Is that all?"

Anne looked at the captain. He was rigid, with his hands clasped behind his back and his gaze still focused on the moonlight. "Need you ask, Captain?"

Doran turned toward her, his face grim. "Andrew, ever since you have been aboard this ship, I have been rather lenient with you. I'm not sure if it is because you are the youngest or because you are so different from the others. However, whatever the reason, it has to stop. Kenward has been with me for many years, and I trust him more than *anyone* else upon this ship. Therefore, it would be best if you remained on his good side." Then he turned to walk away.

Anne couldn't believe he was making it sound as though it were her fault. She couldn't let him walk off thinking she was some sort of . . . trouble-maker. "Captain!"

He stopped but did not turn. She gulped hard. "Captain, you know my mind when it comes to the subject of women. I had no intimate relations with any of the women of the Wemilo household or with any other woman on the island. I was also unaware of Kenward's ties to the family; therefore, anything I may have done wrong was because of my ignorance, not my intent." She felt as though she was shaking from the inside out. She drew in a steadying breath. "Captain, if my being here is a problem, perhaps it would be best if you left me in Sagedor."

The captain remained silent and started off toward his cabin again, leaving Anne to stare after him, sad and dejected.

Chapter Eleven

Gifts

E ver since the end of August, Laveda had continued her private lessons with Ms. Godwin at Haru's floral shop, as she could not afford to attend school formally like her peers. She had to admit; being away from Constantine Manor was calming on her spirit. She wasn't as nervous, nor as afraid to make mistakes. This meant she learned more quickly. Besides, she loved being in the little flower shop and often stayed after to help Haru.

"Laveda, you have accomplished more in nearly four months than most of my students accomplish in a year." Ms. Godwin placed her books back into her leather bag from which they had come. "I am quite proud of you."

Laveda smiled, slightly embarrassed by the compliment. In a way, she felt very unworthy of the praise, as if she were but a handful of soil blessed by a holy priestess . . . so high was Ms. Godwin in her mind.

"Well, ladies, I must get back to the manor. I have a study group tonight. Seniors preparing for their exit examinations." She shot a knowing smile to Haru.

"Ah, yes. The poor darlings. I hope they realize how much studying they are going to need and that they should take the exam seriously."

Laughing musically and shaking her head, Ms. Godwin replied, "Each year we do our best to warn them, but whether they heed our advice, we shan't discover until the test scores are in." Then she said goodbye to her friend and her pupil before making her way back to the school.

Laveda returned home early. She wanted to lie in bed and read the new book Ms. Godwin had given to her. It was about ancient gods and goddesses from the land of the forgotten—a place to where people no longer traveled since true faith had come to their own land. She knew most people found it blasphemous to even consider reading such a text, but Ms. Godwin felt it important to know the old language, and besides, Laveda was curious.

Walking swiftly toward Swinfen's, she almost missed the young courier hurrying about his daily deliveries . . . almost. Catching him in the corner of her eye seemed to give her wings to fly up the dirt path and bring her swooping down upon the front steps, with the hope he might have a letter from Andrew.

Having arrived, Laveda remained outside for a minute or two to regain her composure. It would not go over well if Swinfen knew just how much she looked forward to her letters and packages.

Once she felt well enough to enter, Laveda lumbered in as if she had just had a very trying afternoon. Not once did she make eye contact with the barkeep owner, nor did she act as though she had seen the courier. Laveda merely made her way across the crowded room, heading in the direction of the spiral staircase leading to the ladies' rooms. She even feigned surprise when Swinfen called her to the bar.

"Laveda, bring yer freeloadin' arse to the bar!"

Laveda had never been sure why he called her a freeloader. She always paid him on time, even if it meant going hungry for a week. "Yes?" she asked exasperatedly.

"Don't give me no attitude. Look here, ya got another box." He narrowed his eyes and pushed the package toward her with his grubby hands.

Quelling her excitement, Laveda acted as though receiving the small cube was an enormous burden. She sighed and threw the box into the bag she had fashioned from old clothes so she could carry her books. Then she turned and made a conscience effort to walk normally to her room.

113

Once in her room, however, she felt free to release her joy. Without delay, Laveda threw herself on the bed and tore open the package. Inside was a beautiful handkerchief the color of fresh cream and bordered with the most delicate lace she had ever seen. She unfolded the pretty little thing, and as she suspected, two gold coins fell into her lap. Taking little notice of the money, for Andrew often sent her coins hidden in gifts, she gently ran her fingers over the handkerchief. To her surprise, she felt tiny raises in the soft fabric. Looking more closely, she smiled as she read her name and the year in a thread that was one shade darker than the cloth itself. Never before had Andrew ever sent her something so beautiful. She found it difficult to lay it down long enough to read his letter.

Laveda,

I hope this gift finds you faring well. I wish I could say luck and happiness were both on my side; however, I fear there will be difficult times ahead for us both. Some rather unfortunate events have transpired on my ship, which has led me to believe I should seek other employment. Therefore, I would like you to spend your money sparingly. The Survivor is on its way to Sagedor, and it is there I will look for another ship. Once I am secure, I will write you again.

~ Andrew

P.S. I hope you like the handkerchief; Île-de-L'est is well-known for their beautiful lace. And my grandmother once said a lady should never be without the grace of lace.

Laveda was shocked by the tone of the letter. Never before had Andrew seem so forlorn. She wondered what could have possibly happened, and if she should find a way to meet him in Sagedor. But no. Andrew certainly wouldn't like that. He had just told her to use her money sparingly, and even if she were to go, which port would she find him? Sadly, she laid the letter on her lap and picked up the handkerchief once more. *Surely, God would not allow such a good man to suffer so greatly for too long,* she thought.

Ethana had been trying to get her mother to leave her bedroom since the sun rose that morning. It had been months since she had been seen outside her room, and Ethana felt a birthday was as good a time as any to begin life again. The dining room was filled with flowers from all of her mother's dear and increasingly concerned friends, as well as with presents, letters, and pastries of all sorts. Yet they all sat there untouched.

Ethana looked about the achingly cheery room, where light filtered in from the not-too-distant windows, lending warmth and promise. She remembered how it used to be when they celebrated birthdays; there would have been flowers and glowing candles everywhere. Yet today, even though it lacked added adornments, the space defiantly carried a cheerful disposition. She wondered if it would ever feel the old way again—filled with laughter and sunshine.

As her heart sank to an all new low, there was a hardy knock at the front door. Figuring it was another gift being delivered only to sit dejected, Ethana took her time getting to the front of the house.

She was unsurprised when she noticed a messenger holding a mid-sized brown package tied together with string. Not thrilled in the least, she accepted the gift and returned to the dining room. It wasn't until she placed the package on the table that she realized how important it was. The parcel itself did not look special—compared to all the others, it looked a little shabby and beat up. However, it wasn't the package itself that had caught her eye but the handwriting atop it.

"Anne," Ethana breathed the name to herself. She knew it was. It had to be.

Leaving the gift on the table, Ethana raced through the house and flew up the stairs several steps at a time. Not noticing Cipriana coming down the hall, Ethana plowed into the young girl, causing them both to fall to the floor. After bouncing up as if nothing much had happened, she threw the young lady a swift apology and continued down the hall. Once she arrived at her parents' door, she didn't bother to knock. She entered, breathless and flush.

"Ethana, what on earth has gotten into you?" Her father gave her a stern glare.

Taking a few moments to catch her breath, Ethana leaned against the wall. But when she regained her composure, she did not speak to her father but to her mother. "You must come down quickly!" Her breath was still a bit heavy.

"Ethana, you know quite well your mother does not feel up to walking about," her father said with a bit of warning in his voice.

Ethana was glad her parents were getting along again; however, her father had taken to protecting his wife in a way he had never done before. Whatever she didn't wish to do, she was allowed to skip, but not this time. Oh, no. Ethana was sick of her mother living in this everlasting depression and continuing to wallow in self-pity, leaving her and her father to deal with everything. If she wanted to get the gift from Anne, she would have to go down and get it herself. "Well, I suppose if mother is not interested in what Anne sent her for her birthday, it's her right."

To that, her father was immediately on his feet. Anne had not written to either of her parents since before she left home, so this gift was a great symbol indeed. "Are you sure the gift is from Anne?"

"Father, I would know Anne's hand anywhere. The gift cannot be from anyone else."

Reyna sputtered a bit before she spoke, "P-please. Bring it to me." The hopeful look on her mother's face almost made Ethana give in, but she pursed her lips and stuck to her guns.

"No, Mother. If you wish to open any of your gifts, you are going to have to go down to the dining room and get them yourself." Ethana figured her dad could see what she was doing and though he, too, presumably wanted Reyna to leave the bedroom, Ethana didn't think he would force her to comply. However, before he could voice any opinion on the subject, Reyna was up and putting on her robe.

Apparently, she was too excited to stay in her room. Ethana hoped Anne had forgiven their mother—otherwise, why bother sending a gift? With her dress robe tied tightly about her waist, Mother flew past her husband and her, seeming not to care enough to give answers to the astonished looks on their faces. Down the hall, descending the stairs, and around to the right she went.

Once in the dining room, Reyna's eyes fell upon a small child, sitting at the table and enjoying a bowl of porridge.

The girl glanced at her, smiled, and said, "Happy birthday, Baroness. Look," she motioned to all the presents on the table opposite her, "many people love you very much."

A tear ran down Reyna's cheek and dropped slowly and silently from her chin to her feet. "All the love in the world cannot replace the love I have lost." Ethana and Thaniel had just entered the room. With their sudden stopping, Reyna knew they must have heard what she had said from the hall.

Taking her mother by the hand, Ethana ushered her to an empty chair at the table just across from Sophie. Once she was seated, Ethana moved to get the parcel. Reyna stared at the package as it made its way toward her. Suddenly, she didn't know what she would do if it was bad news. What if Anne had not forgiven her after all?

With shaky hands, Reyna accepted the gift, but as she tugged on the string that held it together, the shaking increased. Eventually, she placed her hands, palms down, on the table and took a deep calming breath before attempting to open it once more.

One fold after another, and the parcel paper lost its form and became straight and flat. Husband and daughter held their breaths, and the young girl looked on with increasing curiosity and excitement. Reyna removed a small box from inside the creased and faded brown wrapping paper, and it was gorgeous—a charming cherry-wood box about four inches square with a small marble lotus set in the top.

Reyna knew it must have cost a small fortune and vaguely thought about how Anne could have ever afforded it.

Ethana spoke up. "How lovely." Her daughter placed her hand upon her shoulder.

Reyna allowed her fingers to roam about the box's smooth surface, letting them rest on the intricate golden latch that united the top with the side and held its secrets within. She took a deep breath and lifted the latch to reveal what she hoped would not only pale in the light of Pandora's findings, but would also be the one thing she desired most. Slowly, little by little, light crept into the rich cherry cube until it came to expose a delicate note folded well enough to fit inside without touching any wall—the gift for which Reyna had prayed.

No one breathed a word as the birthday girl took the note from the box and read it silently to herself. Then tears, not too many, streamed down her face, though she never blinked. Handing the tiny message to her husband, she stood and left the room.

My Lady de Ranger,

Mother. I have heard of your disposition and though it tears at my heart, it also fills me with anger. You have a house to run and a daughter and husband who need you. You've no time for self-pity. I myself have wanted to curl up into an invisible ball and cry my soul clean several times over the past few months but have chosen instead to master my emotions. Being strong and holding loyalty to our causes are the only ways to survive the cruelties of life. Therefore, although I hope you like the small treasure box I have sent, my true gift to you is this small bit of advice . . . though your heart aches, get up, love your family, keep your home, and mend. Happy birthday to you.

~ Anne

Chapter Twelve

Andrew the Gentleman

*D*oran sat steadily working to organize the invoices taking over his desk, but, as focused on this task as he was, his mind would find a moment—a second, periodically—to think of Andrew. It had been weeks since he had spoken to the youth, yet his thoughts always returned to their last conversation. Should he have convinced Andrew to stay? Surely not. It would have lessened the strength of his kinship with Kenward. Besides, once they landed, where would the boy go? Doran smiled as he recollected the day Andrew came aboard; he was fragile and naïve but with plenty of courage and determination.

"Haaaa," he sighed aloud. He would miss the boy if he were to leave, but he simply couldn't bring himself to ask him to stay, either.

A knock on the door startled him back to the present. "Come in!" he bellowed irritably. Kenward entered. "Is there a problem?" Doran raised a questioning brow.

"Aye, sir." Kenward closed the door behind him. "Sir," he stood at attention as if he were upon a military vessel, "the crew is wondering about your disposition."

Doran had not been expecting this, and, if truth be told, he would have been less shocked had Kenward reported the ship was taking on water. "My moods," he stated gruffly, "are of no concern to the crew."

"Morale is falling, Captain, which *is* a concern of the crew. Because of you and *Andrew*," he said the boy's name with disgust, "the air on the ship has become thicker than homemade cream."

Knowing he shouldn't take the situation lightly, but not really knowing what else to do, he turned the concern into a joke. "Well, cream is something of a luxury upon a ship, so I'm sure they are enjoying it well enough."

Kenward took a deep breath and a more comfortable stance before continuing. "Captain, perhaps you should speak to the boy. Show everyone what he did was wrong, but there are no hard feelings between you."

"And *what* has he done?" Doran went from dismissive to enraged in the blink of an eye, not knowing or caring why he suddenly wished to bash his friend's head in. "I'm waiting, Kenward! What exactly do you perceive that Andrew did wrong?"

Kenward had seen Doran angry more times than there were stars in the sky but never over something as trivial as this. He trod carefully. "Everyone saw the way he looked at Kismet. Only a man who has tasted that which is forbidden would have such a gleam in his eyes."

Doran was not surprised by Kenward's reply—or at least not so much as he was with his own response. "You're wrong, my friend," he sighed. He wasn't sure why he felt so strongly toward someone he had known for merely four and a half months, especially after having known Kenward for six years. But he was sure Andrew had been no less than a complete gentleman to Kismet. "I truly believe he has not touched *any* woman since joining our crew and, above all else, Andrew *is* a gentleman."

Kenward protested, but Doran wouldn't hear it. "Sit down, my friend, and let me tell you a tale."

Kenward took a seat across from his captain and prepared himself for what was sure to be a waste of his time. Doran, on the other hand, leaned back and trained his eyes on his hardheaded but loyal companion. He had been through quite a bit with Kenward and trusted him with his life. *Trusted him with his life . . .* that one thought made his eyes flicker as another, somewhat related thought, flitted across his mind. *What about Andrew?*

Forgetting for a moment that Kenward was in the room, he entertained the idea, giving it a thorough examination. He had to admit that he trusted the youth and was drawn to him for some unknown reason. He liked speaking with Andrew, hearing his ideas, whether reasonable or overly idealistic. He smiled. Yes. He liked Andrew. And if anything were to happen to Kenward, he would probably turn to the boy and confide in him the way he was with Kenward now.

This revelation was shocking, and he gave himself a mental shake back into the present, where he found himself face to face with his old friend.

"I'm sorry, Kenward, I just . . ." he trailed off. He really wasn't sure how to explain what he was feeling. He shook himself again. "Never mind. Let me tell you a little more about Andrew."

Doran shared with Kenward about Andrew's first visit to Île-de-L'est, how Andrew had pitied the young girl he had purchased for him and how angry and disappointed Andrew had been in him. Then Doran recounted *Survivor's* last visit to the east islands and how he had gone in search of the girl to uncover exactly what had transpired between her and Andrew. He relayed the disbelief he felt when he found Linette working in a lace factory, and the young woman praised dear Andrew as if he were no less than an angel of mercy. How he was her savior and that not only had he given her enough money to pay off her debts, but he had given her hope for a better life. Taking his advice, she left the saloon early the next morning and never looked back. With complete clarity of mind, Doran remembered the words she had said to him when he asked what she had given the boy in return.

"Nothing, sir. He never asked for anything. But for his kindness, I would do whatever he would ask of me, and I know I shall love him forever."

He explained to Kenward that Andrew had never slept with her, as was his due, or taken advantage of her in any other way, which had made the captain feel worse about their present situation. He had to make Kenward understand. "So you see, I can't imagine Andrew would ever use Kismet as you believe."

"Captain, I see what you are saying, but perhaps the reason the boy had no interest in the girl is because she was not so innocent. Or maybe she was not to his liking. I cannot say whether she be lovely, having not seen her, but Kismet is both beautiful and pure; the daughter of the master of Hampton, a prize for any *worthy* gentleman. And Andrew is *not* worthy!"

Doran was disheartened but, again, not surprised. He tried to look through the stony heart, revealed upon Kenward's face, as he reiterated his position on the subject and made a request. "I think you're wrong, my friend, and I urge you to better acquaint yourself with Andrew. As for my addressing him, that shan't happen until the two of you are resolved amongst yourselves." Then he dismissed his friend.

Doran did not watch Kenward leave but turned his thoughts back to Kismet. He knew Kenward wished him to marry his sister, and Doran had given it some consideration in the past. All Kenward said of the young girl was true to his knowledge: beautiful, pure, possessed a great wit, and a member of one of the wealthiest families in Hampton. She would make some deserving man very happy. He just wasn't the one.

"I'm not for her," he spoke to himself, allowing the truth of his words to seep through his soul. Though he was sure this wasn't a revelation, he hadn't really given it much thought over the past few months. Since Andrew's arrival, he hadn't given any woman much thought, neither for sex nor marriage . . . odd how his mind always returned to Andrew and his philosophies.

His philosophies. Oh, how his sister would rail him about listening to a boy he barely knew instead of her, though they speak with the same mind. He smiled. *My sister would like Andrew.*

Meanwhile, Anne looked across the water as the ship made its way 'round the islands of Yakecen. It had been a rough few weeks, and she knew it would get worse still. In less than a week, they would reach Sagedor, and she would come face to face with the task of finding new employment. She wasn't worried about finding another ship since Sagedor had a fairly large port, and she had learned as much as she could while serving aboard the *Survivor*. She was much better off now than when she had come here. She breathed in deeply as her heart sank. She still wasn't entirely sure what had gone wrong.

Several more days passed, and they finally reached the harbor at Sagedor, and things aboard *Survivor* still seemed rather hopeless to Anne. But since there was so much for them to do when they reached the new port—cargo to be moved off and on, supplies to be purchased, and barnacles to be removed— Anne busied herself with each task, trying to put off the inevitable. She needed to find new employment.

It was quite late in the afternoon when she ran out of excuses and began her search for a new ship. She had been correct in her assumption; there were plenty to choose from. There were so many, she felt she could be picky about which one she'd work upon, and picky she was. The first ship, *Intrepid,* though beautiful, had a captain who seemed quite delusional. He behaved as though he were the king of the world and dressed as if he were going to a ball rather than captaining a ship. The next two, *Sea Lion* and *Round-a-Bout*, were smaller ships and paid much less than she was currently making. The fourth, however, seemed to do. *Maritime*, though a mite smaller than *Survivor*, was praised by many at the port, and Captain Morven seemed reasonable. The ship was in need of a cook, and she told him she was up to the task. She would receive four silvers a week, five coppers more than on *Survivor*, and could start in three days.

Feeling rather chipper about finding new employment so soon, Anne made her way to the closest saloon for dinner, entertainment, and drink.

The saloon was well lit and packed with roaring laughter and smiling faces. Wanting to be near people but not wishing to bring attention to herself, she sat at a table in the back; it was partially shaded by the stairs and the loft above. She hadn't been there long when an older barmaid came to take her order. Over the past few months, Anne had been to several saloons and bars, thus, she was no longer bothered by the scantily attired ladies who worked them. She ordered her meal and drink without much embarrassment.

Once the woman had gone, she leaned back in her seat and watched a group of men playing cards rather than the ladies gleefully kicking up their heels on the stage. Completely consumed by the men's banter, so different from the quiet tension that usually accompanied card play, she hadn't noticed Kenward's approach until he was sitting before her. Though startled, she stared at the larger man, praying he had not come to give her another sound thumping.

"I hear you have been seeking employment today." The man placed his glass of what she supposed was whiskey on the table. "Have you forgotten you already have work aboard our ship?"

Frightened but not wishing to give in to Kenward's intimidation, she forced herself to remain in her laid-back position as she spoke. "I am under no misconceptions of your feelings toward me, Kenward. You have never liked me, and, I dare say, the feeling has been mutual. Therefore, I felt it would be in the best interest of all involved that one of us leave. To your advantage and my disadvantage, you have served aboard *Survivor* longer. It seemed only proper that I should be the one to find other work." There. That went rather well; her voice neither quivered nor varied in any way.

Kenward's eyes narrowed. "Andrew . . ." Anne still detected anger in his voice. "I have come to apologize for my behavior and to give you my blessing."

Shock made Anne sit up in her seat. Never would she have believed Kenward would apologize to *her*, and what was this about his blessing? He couldn't mean to be stepping aside to allow a relationship between her and Kismet. *No.* But she didn't need his blessing for anything else. This was a trap—plain and simple. He was trying to catch her at something, and she was not going to allow it.

"Your blessing? I'm sorry, but I don't see how I would need or desire your blessing to work aboard another ship. I don't know who you think you are, but my father you are not."

"Don't play games, boy, for I'll not give it again! If you wish to be with Kismet, it is fine with me so long as you receive the blessing of both our father and mother!"

Ah, so I was right. Delighted in her ability to read Kenward, Anne laughed—not the roaring laughter of the other men in the saloon but more of a snicker, which only angered Kenward further. Seeing the man's hands clench, she stifled her laughter before replying.

"You poor fool." She noticed his face reddened despite his dark complexion. "Though I think Kismet a fine young woman, I'll not have her. You see, Kenward, I am of Galahad's temperament. There is no woman can waylay me from my task, and I shall *never* marry any maid, your sister included. So you see, your fretting all this while was quite unnecessary."

The barmaid returned with her vittles and drink, so Anne prepared herself to eat. She placed her napkin in her lap after wiping the fork and knife. If she had been home, she would have surely asked for cleaner utensils. Settled, she slowly cut up her stewed beef, eating a perfect square before noticing that Kenward was staring at her. Looking down, she thought perhaps this was too proper a way for a sailor to eat, but it was done. And this was, in fact, how she was raised.

"And what task are you trying to complete?" Kenward ventured.

Anne had not been expecting this question, and therefore had no response. She thought for a moment before answering. "I wish to find my purpose, and once found, dedicate myself wholly to that purpose." It was the best way she could describe why she had left home. She knew she was meant for something great, but what that was, she hadn't a clue.

No longer desirous of Kenward's company, she politely asked him to go. She needed time to herself. "If there is nothing else for you to say, I would much rather eat my meal in peace." As Kenward rose to leave, she thought to add, "If you see the captain before I do, please inform him I have taken employment aboard the *Maritime*. I will give him my reasons for leaving in person when I return to gather my things."

"Well, Captain Doran, it has been quite some time since you've come to Sagedor! Where have you been hiding yourself?"

Doran had always been fond of Captain Morven, the man who had taught him all he knew when it came to transporting cargo. Smaller in stature but booming in voice, Doran had always felt, though taller, he was the smaller of the two. He laughed and cuffed the older man soundly on the back. "Rather, I have been working between the islands instead of playing at port."

With a look of mock offense, Morven replied, "Playing! Playing! Well, I never thought you would be one to make light of my labors." But then the man, not having the ability to truly feign such an injury, laughed heartily. "Oh, my boy, you know me well."

"As well as I think you should know me." Doran had been walking up the dock, clearing his mind when Morven spied him. He wondered now, however, if the man had sensed his displeasure because his face, though still light out, had given way to a more serious mask.

"I was happy to hear you were at port, my boy, but displeased at how I came by the information," the older man began. "You see, a young man calling himself Andrew came 'round looking for employment. Now, I've no need for extra hands, but I hired him so he'd stop lookin'. Seemed to me he wasn't happy to be leaving *Survivor*, and I thought I might speak with you about it."

Doran, who wanted someone to confide in other than Kenward and Andrew, filled Morven in on all the past events and told him how he felt about the situation. Morven proved a good listener, as always, and was ready with advice when it was needed.

"Wow, sounds like you *are* in a pickle. Now, I understand why you have stuck by Kenward all this while, but friend or no, do you think you should back him when he's wrong? And if you have such great admiration for the youth, should he not be told? I know it's hard working with so many personalities, and at times, minds and opinions can clash. But, if you ask me, these men seem to be fighting over you, and only you can put a stop to it. Speak with Andrew; hear what he has to say. You've already spoken with Kenward, so listening to Andrew now is only the right thing to do. Then make your decision."

Doran had been wanting to speak with the boy for some time, and now that he was aware Andrew was serious about leaving, he knew the time had come. *Time to apologize.* Thanking his old friend, he went in search of the boy.

Laveda smiled as she watched the Baroness de Ranger teach Sophie how to knit. Sophie, though excellent when it came to her letters, was all thumbs when asked to knit, dropping stitches and so forth when she was to keep them, and keeping things when she should drop. Laveda had to admit knitting was not her forte either; she would much rather quilt or cook, but as she wasn't the student today, she could sit back and enjoy the battle ensuing before her.

It had been a week or so since the baroness's birthday, and ever since then she had been up and about; helping Ethana with the manor as well as with Sophie. Everything seemed to be coming together at Indira; the servants were happier, the lord and lady of the manor were becoming closer, and it felt as though even the air itself had taken on a sweeter bouquet. Some of the tension was gone, and they were all pleased. However, none of them were naïve enough to think all was as it should be. Sure, things were better, but life was still incomplete.

Wondering if Anne would ever return to Indira brought Laveda's mind back to Andrew. She wondered how he was doing, if he had found another ship, when she would see him again. She wanted to show him how far she had come, and how much he had helped both Sophie and herself. His last letter had worried her quite a bit . . . not for her own sake, because she knew the de Rangers would never allow any ill to pass over her or her sister. She worried because she knew he was despairing and there was no way for her to help.

"Oh, Laveda, is it really necessary for a lady to know these things?" Sophie's moan stopped Laveda's thought train in its tracks.

She smiled. "If the baroness says so, who am I to contradict? Surley, a lady of her grace and upbringing would know better than you or I." The look of despair which shadowed the child's face brought bubbles of laughter from all in the room, and for a time, Laveda's worries were forgotten.

Anne was packing her things on deck when Doran found her. She knew eventually she would have to face him but wished it would have been later rather than now. And gauging by the look on his face, she assumed he had spoken with Kenward. She turned her eyes back to her bags.

She missed the look of sadness in his eyes, so after a minute, she spoke first. "I'm assuming you have heard?"

"I have."

Doran took a deep breath before beginning what he wished to say. "I'm sorry, Andrew. I know I should have spoken with you earlier, but I was wishing you and Kenward would resolve this amongst yourselves. Then, when Captain Morven told me of your search for employment, I knew I had let you down."

Silence.

"Afterward, I spoke with Kenward, and he said he is resolved and apologized for not believing in my opinion of you. However, I fear I am the one in need of making apologies, for I should have told you that I never believed what you were accused of. Again, I am sorry and would be pleased if you would continue your employment aboard my ship."

Anne didn't know what to say. It was the second time today she had been shocked into muteness. She couldn't believe her future employer had spoken to her present one, nor could she believe Doran was asking her to stay. She knew she mustn't cry. Pushing down her misery, she steeled herself enough to respond. "And if I stay, what of Captain Morven?"

"Morven only employed you for my sake. He didn't want me to lose such an *interesting* member of my crew." Then, after a pause, Doran continued. "I'm glad he did, and I am willing to pay you five silvers a week, that is a silver and five coppers more than what you are currently receiving—not to mention five coppers more than Morven offered. With the pay raise, however, I would like you to train your replacement as you will be aiding Bêrk and Jerah in their duties from here on. So . . ." with a lighter tone, he asked, "will you stay?"

Anne couldn't have said no to Doran had she tried. He had apologized, and Kenward was apparently no longer angry with her. There were no more reasons for leaving when all she wanted to do was stay. Besides, the pay raise was nice, and she already knew the crew. She put the bag down and stood. "If you truly wish me to stay, I will."

The next morning was glorious! Anne didn't think it was possible to be any happier. The air was brisk, but with the sun shining, no one minded. Besides, it was Halloween, and the captain had given a few of them leave to have fun that night . . . so long as they finished their duties.

Anne stood, looking out to sea, enjoying the wind and spray upon her face, as she awaited the arrival of the new cleaning boy. The night before, she and Doran had engaged in a long talk about what really happened in Hampton between her and Kismet. Then they had talked politics over drinks and all was made as right as rain. Nothing could possibly bring her down now—she was sure of it!

"Andrew, I brought ya the new cleanin' boy. Capt'n says ya should get to trainin' 'im right away."

Hearing Jerah's cheerful voice, Anne turned around all smiles, only to be faced with a new, unexpected twist of fate. Was she ever going to catch a break?

Chapter Thirteen

Troubles in Ryland

Anne's eyes settled on the attractive redhead before her. Though, more seasoned in his appearance, she could never forget his face. Devin would always be Devin, the charming young poet who's held a special place for her in his heart for years. Oh, how was she to keep her secret from someone who knew her as well as he did?

"Good morning, sir. My name is Devin Lennox." He held out his hand. She took it so not to be rude but wondered at the change in his surname.

Devin spoke. "I'm sorry, but have we met before? You seem quite familiar."

It begins already, thought Anne. *Well, I'll play the game, and I intend to win.* Smiling with newly mustered confidence, she denied their acquaintance.

Although the world seemed to be moving in a positive direction, affairs at the palace were ever so frustrating for the princess. It was four weeks until the Grand

Harvest, and there was so much for her to do. So much, and she was expected, as usual, to complete all tasks on her own.

"I fail to see the point in defending him!" raged Orianna as she paced up and down the queen's sitting room. "Is it not his duty to see to the lower affairs of state and to attend formal balls and gatherings? Of course, it is," she answered for her parents. "I believe it is time you *ordered* him to take up his duties rather than playing merchant to the islands!"

King Bohden had always found Orianna amusing. She had so much energy and conviction, and if the truth be told, he sometimes felt she would make a better heir than his son, Nolan. However, today was not one of those days. At present, she was little more than an annoyance, and he intended to take the wind from her ever-billowing sails. "Speak you of duty, my daughter, when you have not fulfilled your own?"

She stopped her pacing. Father and Mother lazily sipped their tea while seemingly enjoying the warmth coming through the large window behind them. Orianna knew they were trying to pay her little attention, knowing it would only fuel her flame. Orianna watched her parents with mild loathing. She knew exactly what her father meant and knew her mother agreed. Oh, how little they understood the modern world.

"A lady does not need a man to aid her in her affairs," she spoke between her teeth, which was not ladylike in any situation, whatsoever. "I feel I have proven that already. As your son gallivants from island to island '*sowing his oats*,' as Mother likes to call it, I am here running this country! Is there any man here to assist me now? No. Also, were I to wed, whom would see to your precious son's obligations?" she yelled while stamping her foot in what promised to be the beginning of a tantrum.

Her parents seemed unperturbed by her outburst, and when they spoke, it was as though they were having a normal conversation about any number of frivolous topics. "She's running the country, my dear?" Her father added a lump of sugar to his tea. "Perhaps I have missed something. Last time I checked, I was still king, or perhaps I have died and have simply failed to notice. Tell me truthfully, my love, am I yet living?"

Without looking up at her husband, Queen Zorina answered in the same lazy tone in which the king had spoken. "Of course you are living, or at least you are as much a part of the living realm as I. Therefore, if you be dead, I must be as well. Though I do very much doubt it, else our child would not be vexing us during tea." She nibbled a lemon cookie.

Their banter only angered Orianna further, but before she could fly into another fit of rage, her father seemed to awaken from his lethargy. "Orianna, I would like you to remember to whom you speak." His tone was more alive than it had been before. "I am still the king and the law of this land. As you are my daughter, I have always given you a fair amount of leniency, and now I offer your brother a bit as well. You seem to think I am unaware of the happenings around me, but I assure you, that is not the case. Nolan shall be returning home in time for the winter holidays, and we will then further discuss his role and duties. As for the present, I thank you for looking to his affairs as well as your own, and I would have you treat your mother and myself with more respect than you have shown us today." With that being said, he went back into the laxness from which he came.

Orianna, knowing she had been dismissed, left without another word. She hated discussing Nolan with her parents because it always ended the same way. It was as if he could do no wrong; he was completely above reproach to everyone save her alone. *And it wasn't at all fair,* she thought to herself. She couldn't even take a short holiday with all the work, meetings, and charitable events she was expected to attend in his absence. Oh, how she wished he would do something to open everyone's eyes to the sort of lazy, noncommittal person he was.

Still fuming, she made her way to her apartment to complete her obligatory correspondence. However, thinking of this task only fueled her rage further. Why hadn't he informed *her* of his return? She, after all, was the one who had to make the arrangements for the upcoming holiday festivities! "Oooh, it's just like him to keep me in the dark," she spat into the air, scaring a poor servant as she stormed past.

When she arrived in her sitting room, where she did most of her writing, she ignored the writing table and paced the length of the room. She would get him back. She had to. All he ever wrote her was to enquire after the missing de Ranger child and to entreat her to aid them in their search. Not once did he mention returning to court. No! She would have remembered it! "Oh, he'll get his," she spoke to herself. But what to do? Suddenly, a brilliant thought rose swiftly to her mind and delighted her heart. Yes, she would get him, and she knew just how to do it. Her eyes squinted into devilish slits, and one side of her usually delicate mouth curled in a rather sinister way.

It had been nearly two weeks since Laveda had heard from Andrew, and she was sick with worry. Her studies were hardly a distraction either. Laveda hated mathematics and didn't understand why Ms. Godwin felt the need to teach her things of which a lady ought not be concerned: counting money, paying bills, keeping books—t'were a man's jobs! Feeling she could not absorb any more information that afternoon, she headed home. It was getting a bit nippy out, and mathematics would not save her if she were to fall ill.

Placing her books into the new leather bag the baroness had given to her during her last visit to Indira, Laveda hadn't noticed the messenger boy go by. If she had, she would have rushed home as quickly as her legs would allow to learn if there was news from Andrew. However, having missed sight of him, she lumbered back to Swinfen's.

Arriving at the bar moments later, she carried herself inside, preoccupied and miserable. Swinfen took one look at her and bellowed her name so loudly, her soul almost returned to Heaven. "Laveda, come here, ya lazy gerl!"

Laveda was not in the mood to deal with the nasty old barkeep, and though she went to him without a word, she silently prayed he'd be brief.

"Ya've got another love letter here." He waved the carrot in her face. Laveda tried to act as though the note meant nothing to her, but she knew it wasn't working, and Swinfen's smirk confirmed it.

"I know ya want it. So don't cha give me that look like ya don't."

Everyone in the bar had their eyes on them.

"Lately, ya've been treatin' yerself like a lady . . . smellin' good, combin' yer hur. I'm beginnin' to wonder wha ya've been up ta." He had come from behind the bar and was so close to her face, she could smell the liquor on his breath. "Maybe ya've got yerself some real nice gent lookin' after ya. Maybe I shud taste a lil of wha' he finds so sweet." Then, without another word, the man was on her.

Laveda kicked and screamed, but no one cared. The men in the bar merely cheered as Swinfen pushed her onto a nearby table and ripped her top. Embarrassed to tears, Laveda hit Swinfen as hard as she could with her bag, and he fell to her left just enough for her to stand. She did so and kicked him in the groin. The cheers of the bar turned to laughter when the barkeep crumbled to the floor. Then, as swiftly as she could, Laveda snatched the letter and ran to her room.

Once inside, she didn't waste time. She quickly gathered her clothes, her soaps, her rinse and cream, and took the money she had hidden in the floorboards and beneath the furniture, stashing everything in her cloth bag. She threw both her cloth and leather bags over her shoulders and ran out the door and down the stairs.

She assumed Swinfen was back on his feet and madder than ever, so on the way out of her room, she had armed herself with the chipped bowl from which she used to eat. However, it proved not enough. As she took the last step on the staircase, two men grabbed her, knocking the bowl from her hand, and they took her to the barkeep.

Swinfen was sitting on a bar stool, his face red with anger. "An' where do ya think yer goin'?" His words were slow and deliberate.

Laveda couldn't believe this was happening. She was so close to having a promising life and now this. She closed her eyes and prepared herself for the inevitable, while she prayed someone or something would intervene.

Then . . . it happened. She heard a man speak from behind. "Excuse me. I was wondering if any of you—ahem, gentleman—might know a Miss Laveda?" Laveda recognized the voice but couldn't place it for the life of her. She tried to turn her head to see, but the man to her right tightened his grip on her arm.

Laveda could hear the man's footsteps move closer as he continued to speak. "You see, I have need of her *services*, and would appreciate it if . . ." His voice paused for a moment, and he seemed surprised. "Laveda, there you are! I looked for you by the docks, but when I couldn't find you there, I didn't think you would mind my seeking you out here."

Laveda tried to speak but was cut off by Swinfen.

"If ya need to speak to this freeloader, ya've got to go through me."

The man came into Laveda's view, and she recognized him right away. Bowen was shorter and older than Swinfen, and the barkeep looked ready for a fight. Laveda swallowed hard, trying to think of something to do to prevent Bowen from getting hurt. But just then, Bowen pulled out his purse and asked Swinfen if he could purchase Laveda for *some time.* "Sir, a gentleman, such as myself, does not speak of *intimacies* aloud or with strangers." He extracted a gold coin. "Perhaps this will allow me some time with her." He handed it to the unruly man.

Swinfen, a greedy yet not an altogether unwise man, took the coin but would not allow Laveda to leave the bar. He had his men relinquish Laveda to the gentleman and told him her room was on the second floor. Then he smirked at Laveda and whispered in her ear that once her friend left, he *would* have a turn.

Grateful to have another chance of escape, Laveda gladly took Bowen to her room; however, once secured inside, she asked why he had come.

"Ms. Godwin asked me to send you word. She will be out of town for the next few days; therefore, she cannot resume your lessons until her return." He handed Laveda the letter and watched as she slipped it into her leather bag. Preoccupied, she was spared the pitying glance in Bowen's eyes.

Laveda was sad she had to put her letters away, but she simply hadn't the time to read when they were in dire need of an escape plan. She remembered hearing a story of a lady once escaping a saloon by climbing down sheets she had tied to her bed rail. Well, Laveda really didn't have sheets, so the blankets would have to do. They were a bit threadbare, but they should work. She quickly tied them together, then asked Bowen to test her makeshift rope for sturdiness. Feeling more confident about her handy work, she tied it to her balcony.

Minutes later, she and Bowen were safely in his carriage and heading toward Haru's shop.

Chapter Fourteen

Hide and Seek

Anne couldn't believe she was having so much fun. Devin, though still the sentimental boy she had always known him to be, was much more entertaining than she remembered. His wit and good humor were so positively infectious that soon everyone aboard was in on the fun.

"Come on, Andrew, surely you can do better!"

"Don't count on it, Devin. I swear he fences like a maid," screamed Bêrk in return.

Anne smiled inwardly as she got back into stance. If only Bêrk knew.

"En guard!" It was on again but over swiftly as Devin, after a particularly surprising lunge from Anne, lost his footing and landed on his back.

"A maid did you say, Bêrk? I fence like a maid?" Anne questioned over her shoulder but never took her eyes off Devin as she lent him a hand.

"Well, who would have thought a man of letters would be worse off than a maid? I mean, he's still a man, right?" Bêrk laughed.

"Apparently not, my friend." Devin smiled at Bêrk and clapped Andrew on the back. "Or perhaps Andrew is better at this sort of play than you remember; either way, well done, Drew!"

Anne paused a moment when she was referred to as *Drew*. Shaking her head, she marveled once her memories returned. Devin, though usually formal in speech, always gave his friends pet names to show his affection. *Drew*, she thought as she gathered their playthings. *I wonder what he would say if he knew he used to call me Annie?* However, as soon as Anne's thought had presented itself, it vanished without further examination because the captain had come on deck.

"Devin, how come your lessons?" Doran was all smiles lately.

"Very well, sir. Andrew is an excellent teacher; I cannot imagine being trained by anyone else." Anne wished Devin hadn't brought her up at all. Though she, Doran, and Kenward had cleared the air, somehow, she felt things were still a bit strange between them—or more to the point, between her and the captain. "Never did I think I would meet such a friend so early in my adventures," Devin continued his praise.

"A teacher is only as good as the achievements of the pupil, resulting from the teaching. Therefore, I must say the certainty of whether I be good or not remains to be seen." Anne did her best to avoid looking directly at the captain as she spoke.

Captain Doran laughed. "Devin, never mind Andrew. He is so honest, modest, and good that I would swear he was cut from the Shroud of Turin."

Anne blushed slightly, as much for the praise as for the shame she felt when he used the word *honest*.

Doran invited Devin to share a meal to get to know the new crew member better. Anne, feeling a little peevish, stormed off to put away the fencing equipment before turning toward the galley.

Once they had safely reached the flower shop, Bowen and Laveda informed Haru of the girl's latest predicament. Horrified, Haru listened intently as they painted the picture of events, so vivid, a rush of emotions nearly overtook her. She hadn't imagined that such a sweet child as Laveda had been living in such a place.

"Has anything of this nature happened to you before?" Haru gently touched Laveda's shoulder.

Haru noticed a look of sadness and shame overtake Laveda, and her heart sank. Over the past few months, she'd seen Laveda struggle to become a lady, and now, she worried Laveda felt all she was, and all she would ever be, was a used sack of bones not fit for better.

"It has," Laveda answered meekly, "but it was the first with Swinfen."

Haru's right hand involuntarily flew to her gaping mouth, and she closed her eyes. It took her a few moments to compose herself, but when she did, she asked Laveda to find a comfortable place in the back to take a nap. Laveda nodded and retreated while Haru thanked Bowen for his help.

Not wishing to intrude on their privacy, Laveda sat on the stool before the large chunky wooden table in the center of the room and read her letters.

She read Ms. Godwin's first, which merely stated her mother was ill and she had gone to Quirin to care for her. She also left Laveda with a few lessons for her to begin in her absence. Nothing too extraordinary—though she had wished Ms. Godwin had left out the mathematical lessons. Sighing at the lesson plan, Laveda went for the letter she had been waiting weeks to receive: the letter from Andrew.

Dear Laveda,

I am sorry it has taken me so long to write again, especially since I may have caused you to worry with the last letter. Well, that said, I am glad to report things are much improved. I am still aboard the *Survivor*, for things have worked themselves out, and on top of that jolly bit of news, I have received a raise. Therefore, I may be able to send you a few more coppers a month. This month, however, I have sent a mite to Ms. Godwin as payment for your education, so I hope you have enough to scrape by until December. If not, send me word immediately. Mid-month, about the same time you receive this note, I shall be on my way back to île-de-L'est; send word there, and I am sure to receive it upon my arrival. I pray all is well with you, but I shan't write again until the beginning of December—that is, unless you find need of something sooner. Until then.

-Andrew

Laveda was pleased to hear Andrew was faring much better but was saddened she would need to inform him of her lack of residence. She also realized the sooner she wrote to him, the better, because he was certain to continue sending word to Swinfen's. So without another thought, she lifted her leather bag from the floor and took from it her ink, pen, and some paper. Before she began to write, she conceded she didn't know where to tell him to respond. Would she be staying with Haru? And if so, where exactly did Haru live?

Just then, Haru entered the small room. Though light in spirit, the woman seemed slightly subdued since Laveda's arrival. "Laveda, I am so sorry for what you have gone through and hate to add to your worries now." She paused, then said, "Laveda, I wish I had room for you to stay with me, but I haven't, and though I am sure Moira has an extra room or two, I'm afraid she left town hours ago."

Laveda thought about staying with Ms. Godwin and knew it just wouldn't do. To live with someone as amazing as her would be as bold as asking permission to holiday on Mt. Olympus; she just couldn't do it. So there was only one other place for her to go.

"I shall go to Indira." There. The decision was made, and she had a good feeling the de Rangers would not turn her away.

"Are you sure they will have you?"

Laveda looked at the surprise on Haru's face, and when it did not trouble her, she knew she was resolute. She would stay at Indira unless they refused, but she doubted that would happen. "I cannot speak for them, though I trust they will not turn me away."

That was answer enough for Haru. She told Laveda she would spend some time preparing a few orders before they ventured out, and Laveda, having no objections, said she would spend the time completing her correspondence and studying her numbers. Although she was tired from her ordeal and should probably take a rest, she knew once at Indira, the de Rangers would have her do nothing but.

My Dearest Andrew,

I am sad to write that it appears as if our fortunes have merely changed owners. As of today, I am no longer resid-

ing at Swinfen's. The events that forced me to find new residence are too terrible and embarrassing for me to recount. However, please do not worry, for I am well in body and mind. As for my heart, it will mend; it always does.

Since I am no longer a resident of the old address, it would be best if you sent me word at Indira. The de Rangers are such an agreeable family; I shouldn't think they would mind. Also, though you have received an increase in wages, I would not have you send it to me. With the de Rangers, I shall be well cared for. Therefore, please save all you can; you may need it over the winter months. I am, of course, assuming the Survivor will take time off, as most ships do during the frost.

Well, I suppose I have written all I would have you know and cannot avoid my studies any longer. I look forward to hearing from you in December and hope this letter, though sad in its making, finds you well. May the angels protect and bring you home soon.

Laveda

At port, Anne pulled the letter from the envelope.

"No!" Anne exclaimed aloud. She should have known when she received a message from Laveda earlier than she expected that something was amiss. How could this happen? How in the world could her two lives be allowed to come together? First, Devin came aboard the *Survivor,* and now, Laveda was residing at Indira? No!

"Oh, this will not do," she spoke quietly to herself as she paced up and down the deck. But what could be done? She didn't know anyone with whom Laveda could stay. Besides, anyone she knew would mean including the girl in the life she was so desperately trying to leave behind. "Oh, but surely any place would be better than Indira," she exclaimed aloud once again. What if Laveda described her to the family or they read one of the letters she sent to the girl?

So caught up in the muddle in which she found herself, Anne hadn't noticed Devin sneaking up behind her until it was too late. He snatched the letter from her hand. "What do we have here?"

Shocked, angered, and a little embarrassed, Anne lost her temper. "Return my letter at once!"

"Or what?" Devin teased. Anne had never known the boy to be so playful. Perhaps this was the way he was with other men or something he learned at school; either way, she didn't like it.

"Or I'll run you through!" She lunged at him.

He merely hopped out of the way. "*My Dearest Andrew,*" he began to read the letter. "Really, Drew, the way everyone onboard speaks of you, I would have believed you a monk!" Just then, she planted her fist onto his left jaw, and they fought over the letter.

At this point—actually, over the past few days—Anne had become sick of the effort she had to expend with Devin being aboard *Survivor*. Every time she felt safe, as though he wouldn't recognize her, he would ask again if they had met before. Saying *no* time and again had become so tiresome that Anne had begun to avoid him altogether. Therefore, this interlude was unwanted on many levels. She punched him in the gut.

"Ahhh," Devin groaned as he hit the deck. Anne took back the letter, folded it, and placed it in the inner pocket of her jacket. "Come on, Andrew," Devin whined as he got up rubbing his belly where she'd rammed her fist. "I thought we were mates."

Anne rolled her eyes.

"Come on, for reasons unbeknownst to me and the crew, you've been avoiding me for the past few days. And though they say you keep much to yourself, they are in agreement that you're stranger than usual."

Anne looked at Devin—noticing his face was red, and it appeared she had badly hurt him. Feeling a small twinge of guilt, she acquiesced. "Sorry. I have been a little . . . preoccupied."

Smiling then, Devin stood a little taller. "No problem. I suppose ladies tend to do that to the men they love." Anne didn't say a word but merely raised a brow.

"Oh, you know what I mean! Come," he clapped Anne on the back, "show me about the island, and if that does not rid us of feminine thoughts, we shall have a cider or two and drink the rest away."

Anne was having a grand time showing Devin about the island. They stopped by her favorite shops, parks, and restaurants. She showed him the view from Les Marches au Paradis, the highest peak in Île-de-L'est. Then, when she couldn't avoid her duties any longer, they returned to town to purchase supplies.

The market at Déesse, Île-de-L'est's capital city, though very pleasant and full of beauty, lacked the vitality of Rowena's markets in Hampton. Déesse was prim and pretty, with its clean cobbled roads and shops decorated with flower boxes. People strolled from shop to shop without making a fuss, and if they came across someone they knew, a curt nod was sufficient recognition. Rowena, on the other hand, had its shops but also had food carts and people selling goods in the streets. The adults strolled between stores, while children ran or skipped about. Seeing someone you knew brought shouts of recognition followed by laughs, hugs, and inquiries into the health and happiness of one's family. Rowena simply pulsed with constant energy. Anne told Devin the difference between Déesse and Rowena, and though she spoke marvelously about Rowena, she felt more comfortable in Déesse.

"I suppose it's because Déesse is more predictable. You can guarantee the people are going to be pleasant and that nothing will disrupt your plans."

"But would you turn away a distraction if it proved a good one?" Devin questioned as he lifted a rather odd-looking vegetable from a cart before returning it to its resting place.

Anne thought about the question for a moment and realized, for once, their roles had reversed. She had always been the adventurous one, the one who wished for something unexpected, but now she would desire to be some place a little slower, more *predictable*. "Perhaps I have had my fill of adventures," she sighed, as much to herself as to her companion.

Devin smiled. "You know, Drew, I have never been the sort of person to seek adventure. In all honesty, I always thought with—quote, unquote—*adventure*, comes trouble."

"Then why do you seek it now?" Anne handed an older lady three silvers for a sack of mixed squash.

"Ah, now that's the question." He rubbed his jaw. "I once knew a young lady with so much spirit, I feared she'd developed wings, then fly to the ends of the earth in search of excitement."

Anne wasn't listening too closely as she gave a different woman a few coins and asked her to send a box of goods to the ship. "Ah, and what does *she* have to do with *your* adventures?"

"I loved her," he said whole-heartedly. Anne stopped to lend her full attention. "I am afraid, however, my love was and always has been unrequited. You see, my friend, she was always so bold and I so plain. I was drawn to her as Icarus to the sun, and just as Icarus, I was pulled back to earth. I suppose men are simply not meant to fly."

Anne was amazed at how much feeling he was speaking with.

"And now, I fear I have lost her. So I dare myself to fly, though I panic at the thought of crashing into the sea. If perchance we meet again, maybe she will find me changed—more to her liking. If not, I pray I find some other maid to hold my heart, a maid capable of ridding me of all thoughts of her."

He was talking about her. She was sure of it. And though she felt awful for him, nothing but pity stirred in her heart. She had to do something, say something to . . . to lessen his love for her or make him seriously consider other options.

"Devin, what if you did happen upon her, and though she found you changed, there was still no love in her heart?"

He took a deep breath and exhaled slowly. "I hadn't really thought of that. I hoped she would see the change and the love would follow." He sighed. "I just know I miss her and have for some time."

Anne felt worse and worse with each passing second. She didn't want him to change for her; that was silly. Surely, he knew so. But if not, she had to make him see. "Devin,"—there was strength in her voice—"you shouldn't have to change yourself for anyone. If this lady cannot love you for who you are, perhaps she is not so worth as you believe. You should find someone more deserving."

"Easier said than done, my friend. I mean, what if you were to discover tomorrow that your lady was in love with another? Would it not tear your heart in two?"

Anne shook her head. "I have no lady, so perhaps it is beyond my understanding. You see, my friend, I am not, nor do I ever believe, I will be in love."

Before Devin had the chance to reply, a young woman came running between the food stands, screaming Andrew's name. "Andrew! Andrew! Oh, I knew you would return!" The lady threw herself into Anne's arms, wrapping hers about Anne's neck.

"Linette," Anne unwound herself from the maid's embrace and brought her hands, more respectably, between them. "How've you been?"

"Oh, wonderful," gushed the girl. "My debts are paid. I am now working at La Belle Dentelle, just up the street, and it's all because of you!" She planted a moist kiss on Anne's mouth.

"I'm glad I could help." Anne again put some distance between herself and the young woman. Then, with great embarrassment, she remembered Devin was standing by her side. "Oh, ah, Linette! Um, I would like you to meet a friend of mine, Devin Levenax of Ryland."

Linette, being the polite maid she was, greeted Devin and welcomed him to Île-de-L'est. Though it only took a few moments, it was enough time for Anne to regain her composure, which led to a far more comfortable conversation in the end.

After a brief chat with Linette, the two had finished their shopping and returned to the ship. Devin had been fairly quiet the rest of the afternoon, but Anne merely figured it had been a long day.

The rest of the evening passed as it usually did. Anne and Bêrk took to their tasks in the galley while the rest of the ship was busy loading their new cargo. Grub was served at the designated time; the mess was cleaned, and the meat was prepared for the next day. Then and only then did Anne go above deck to reply to Laveda.

But there, in her usual spot, to the center port side of the ship, Devin sat, waiting for her. She didn't wish to be rude but wasn't in the mood for conversation. "Is there something you need?" she asked on approach.

"I believe you and I know one another, after all." Devin's tone was even but did not seem angry.

"I don't know what you mean." Anne was sure she hadn't given anything away, yet her body tensed unexpectedly.

Devin looked at her. "I knew from the moment we met that we had met before, though you denied it. But today, in the marketplace, you finally tipped your hand."

Anne's mind raced over the day's events and conversations, trying to find the moment in which she had given herself away. Devin watched her with interest, and thinking she hadn't the slightest clue, continued. "Levenax of Ryland? I told you my name was Lennox, and for all you could have known, I was from Sagedor." His tone was no longer even but now slightly strained—irritated. Anne was caught.

"I don't know what sort of game you are playing, but I demand to know exactly who you are!" Devin was standing now, approaching her. She took a few steps back and glanced about, hoping no one was around to witness the situation. Luckily for her, most everyone had already turned in, and those who were still up were out and about on the island.

The way Devin grabbed her arm, she could tell he was furious; it was rough— his fingers biting into her skin. "Who the devil are you?" His voice was low and menacing, another side to him she had not known. She felt frightened.

"Devin, please," she said, fear creeping into her voice. Then, with more courage, she tried to find a way out. "So I know who you are. What does it matter?"

It was not the answer he was apparently looking for, and he shook her. "It matters, and if you do not reveal yourself soon, I will take my concern to the captain!"

Oh, what to do? Anne thought. She couldn't tell him, but then again, she couldn't have the captain involved either. It was terrible luck to have a woman aboard, so Doran would have no choice but to leave her here. And that wouldn't do at all!

Anne must have been thinking for too long, for Devin suddenly shoved her to the deck and headed toward Doran's cabin. Panic-stricken, she did the only thing she could think of.

"There are many a rose but only one so sweet. There are plenty of clouds but only one for sleep." Devin stopped, but she continued, "The heart can hold many, but only one shall it cherish. True to love it will be or broken shall it perish."

Anne watched Devin as his poem was recited to him—the poem he had written for her. And knowing Anne as he did, he knew, more from embarrassment than love, she would have never shared it with anyone.

"Annie?" he whispered.

Anne rose from the deck and rubbed her arm. It was over. She had lost. He knew.

Chapter Fifteen

Reis

*I*t was a week and three days until Grand Harvest Day, the day families came together to thank the Lord for the fertile land and healthy cattle by having an enormous feast once all crops had been harvested. And though Laveda was thankful that this had been a particularly good year for agriculture, or so Henry had told her, she couldn't help but be even more thankful for the new life she had been given. The de Rangers were more wonderful than she thought they would be, giving her the last of the rooms available (excluding Anne's) and, in return, only asking her to do her very best regarding her schooling.

Now and then, however, she would help Henry in the garden or give Verna a hand in the kitchen. Though they told her this was not necessary, she felt she should do more than merely receive excellent marks to show her appreciation. And receive not good but *excellent* marks, she did.

With additional aid from Haru, Laveda had grasped her mathematical studies with great confidence. Before, she hadn't realized basic algebraic theorems could be of any use to a lady, but once Haru had explained to her she used them every day to calculate the profits and losses of her shop, Laveda was intrigued. She finally understood why learning such a subject could be useful to her, for unless Andrew were to ask for her hand, she was more than likely to be left to her own devises.

Not thinking on that now, she decided it was time to get cleaned up and begin the day. Being the third Sunday of the month, the entire family, including Sophie and herself, was expected to join the other influential families at St. Ursula's Cathedral in town. Laveda had not yet been to St. Ursula's, but from what her sister had implied, she didn't believe it would be to her liking: ladies dressed in their ballroom best, gentlemen suavely and coolly watching as the ladies fluttered by, eyes and ears open to all but the sermon. Or at least, that's what she had envisioned—a half-day social engagement, nothing at all like the tiny parish on the hill the family attended on all other Sundays.

Laveda sighed as she glanced over the dress Cipriana had helped her make the week before for this very occasion. It was pinkish-lavender, with lace and plenty of fabric waves and folds. Though she believed only two days ago, there was no other dress so pretty in all of Heaven, she now wondered if it was fancy enough. After all, it would be the first time she was introduced to anyone in proper society. Sighing again to push away her fears, she turned to the basin in the corner of the room and filled it with the pitcher of hot water the maid snuck in every morning. A quick wash would make her feel better.

A couple hours later, the wash was apparently not enough, Laveda thought, as she did her best to avoid fidgeting where she sat. Everyone in attendance was so gorgeous; she was finding it difficult to listen to the sermon. Sophie must have known this, for her little hand slid over to rest on hers. Laveda drew comfort from her younger sister, glad she was not there alone.

Ethana witnessed this gentle moment between the sisters, and her heart ached. She remembered when she and Anne had been that close, how Anne was always trying to look out for her. Tears welled up in her eyes, and she tried to blink them away, glancing about the cathedral as a way to dispel memories.

Looking around the large room, she noticed the royal family had snuck in as usual. They had a private entrance and were seated on the lavish balcony. The king and queen seemed to have their eyes trained on the priest, whereas the princess seemed to be listening to whatever nonsense her horrid cousin Oren happened to be sharing. Not wishing to think of anything awful to do to Oren while she was in church, Ethana turned her eyes back to the priest and his sermon.

Orianna had no idea who the stunning young woman with the de Rangers could be. She knew every courtier within fifty miles of the palace and any too far off would be attending their Sunday service elsewhere, especially since the prince was not around to be ogled. Although, she had to admit; she was rather surprised she had not noticed the woman before her cousin brought the young beauty to her attention—she tended to have an excellent eye for newcomers. Then again, she had enough on her mind with the upcoming Acceptance Ceremony, Grand Harvest Day, and the Christmas Ball, all of which she was organizing. Yes, she certainly had a great deal to keep herself occupied.

However, she thought in a rather sly manner, *the more ladies at the ball, the merrier.* She would simply have to learn the young stranger's identity after church, and God would just have to forgive her for working on the Sabbath.

Ethana and Laveda were chatting quietly as they followed the baron, who was carrying Sophie, out of the cathedral. Reyna stayed close behind, but there was much to be said to others about her long absence, and the girls, consumed with their conversation, did not take notice—not until Oren stopped them just as the daylight warmed the tops of their heads.

"Ladies," he said as he revealed a smirk and bowed.

Ethana went rigid, sending shockwaves through her companion. "My Lord, to what do we owe this . . . honor?"

"I'm afraid, Ethana, the honor is not yours but your friend's." He nodded toward Laveda. "My sweet, what is your name?"

"Laveda Reis, My Lord." She dropped into a low, graceful curtsy.

Ethana's mind sparked to life when Laveda revealed her surname and marveled at the fact she and her father had never asked before. There were few people left who knew of or remembered the true tale of Sir Llewellyn Reis, and she wondered if Laveda was one of them. However, though she wondered at Laveda's historical knowledge, there was no wondering about Oren's, for he seemed completely oblivious to the reference.

"Well, Miss Reis, I am honored to inform you my cousin, Princess Orianna-Loni, has taken an interest in you." He smiled as he spoke. "She would like for you to join her for a talk in her carriage."

Ethana watched Laveda's body language and knew she was instantly terrified.

Laveda turned and whispered to her, "I'm not ready to meet with royalty. What if I say or do something incorrectly?" Ethana knew the young woman was still trying to get used to life with her family, and they were far more relaxed than the other patrons of St. Ursula's appeared to be. Perhaps she would feel better if she had a bit of company. "My Lord, I'm sure Laveda is honored by the princess's interest in her—"

Laveda seemed to read her mind. "And I would be more than thrilled to join her. However, pray tell me, would it offend your cousin if I were to arrive with a dear friend close at hand?" She motioned to Ethana.

Ethana winked at her.

Oren found it difficult to hide his distaste for the idea, and his face showed his disdain far before his words were out. "I hardly believe that is necessary."

By this time, Reyna had joined them. "She is merely a girl, My Lord. Surely, you do not suggest she should walk with a gentleman alone?" Reyna's face was sweet and unassuming, but both Ethana and Laveda knew better than to believe she was unaware of what or whom Oren was truly interested in. "Ethana, dear, please join your father and tell him Laveda and I will be along shortly." Ethana gawked but only for a moment. Then, without further ado, she watched Laveda and the baroness escorted to the princess's carriage.

Orianna no longer rode to church with her parents, for in their later years, they preferred to take the scenic route home, and she had always desired a more direct route. Actually, if the truth were told, Orianna was not one to go 'round anything. She was, much to the royal court's pride and shame, upfront with what she felt on all subjects—always. She did not see the point in wasting time, even if it were only a minute to smell the roses as one passed them along the way.

Just as Orianna began to wonder about wasted time, she spied Oren returning with two ladies in tow: the Baroness de Ranger and St. Ursula's new addition.

"Your Highness," Oren bowed to his cousin, "might I introduce the Baroness
de Ranger and her charge Miss Laveda Reis." Once introductions were made,
Oren stepped to the side of the ladies, who were in the process of executing perfectly manicured curtsies.

Unlike Oren, Laveda's last name was not wasted on neither princess nor baroness. Reyna, just as her daughter, knew of the sad love story. The princess, on
the other hand, eyed Laveda with suspicion, suddenly determined to uncover the
girl's motives.

"Miss *Reis,* is it?" Orianna raised a brow. When Laveda nodded, she continued. "Well, where is your family?"

Laveda seemed shocked by the question. But when the princess asks a question, it cannot go unanswered. Orianna waited.

"I've no family, save my sister, Your Highness. My parents left us behind four
years ago next summer."

"What do you mean they left you behind?" Orianna asked. She noticed
Reyna listening intently.

"Well . . ." Laveda felt rather uncomfortable. "My sister and I were out picking
wild flowers in a field near our home, and since Sophie is crippled, Your Highness, my
father was to return for us within the hour. When he failed to return, I helped my sister
back to our home only to find it had been ransacked, and our parents were gone. I only
assumed they left, for much of my mother's clothing and jewels were missing, as well
as some of my father's things." The heartbreak was evident in her voice.

To the princess, Baroness de Ranger's heart seemed to fill with sadness, likely
as she thought of the two girls returning to find their home an empty shell, devoid
of the warmth and love to which they believed they would be returning. They
must have concluded they were unloved, unwanted. Reyna shook her head. The
princess couldn't read the woman's thoughts. If she could, she'd hear, "If only
Laveda and Sophie knew what had happened to their parents. Perhaps then they
would not feel so rejected!"

Although both Reyna seemed completely convinced of Laveda's sincerity, the
princess was still skeptical. She had heard Sir Reis had two children, but until

now, had dismissed it as another court rumor. But what if he did have two children, and as this girl proclaimed, she and her sister were they? She would have to research Laveda's claim, and if her memory served her correctly, there was another rumor of an old woman who knew all as well.

"Well, mademoiselle, welcome to St. Ursula's. I trust the de Rangers are treating you well, and I hope to see you again soon." Orianna gave nothing of her suspicions away but thanked Oren for escorting the women to her carriage and graciously took her leave.

The entire ride home from the church service was shrouded in an air of suspicion. It hung over the de Ranger carriage like a blanket of sheer silk; touching each rider softly and making them glance 'round to see what was there. Sophie and Thaniel, though they knew nothing of what had transpired in the princess's carriage earlier, were not immune to the eerie feeling, but they knew not to ask until they were in the safe confines of Indira. Then, once they had arrived, each person filed out as quickly as was possible. Some truths were best revealed within the confines of a private space.

Thaniel was the first to break the silence. "Will someone please tell me what's happened?" he asked as he set Sophie on a sofa in the library, where they had all congregated.

Ethana, nearly on the verge of bursting, painted the picture of events for her father, and for the part where she was not a participant, her mother took up the brush.

Thaniel could see that Laveda and Sophie seemed confused by the anxiousness of their new family, especially when all three de Rangers turned and stared at them. Laveda, who had come to sit beside her sister, fidgeted. And Sophie, poor Sophie, had looked more comfortable in the cathedral.

"Laveda," Thaniel finally chimed in once more, "your father was Llewellyn Reis?"
Laveda nodded.

"As in Sir Llewellyn Reis of the Royal Guard of Ryland?"

To that Laveda had no answer. She thought about it for a moment, but nothing came to her. She didn't believe her father was a member of the Royal

Guard, for she never saw him do more than modest farm work. "I shouldn't think so."

"What was your mother's name?" Ethana stepped forward from the background. "Solène."

To that Reyna and Ethana gasped and brought their hands to their mouths, and Thaniel closed his eyes. The three of them looked as though they might weep. Thaniel took both Reyna and Ethana in his arms and told them Laveda and Sophie should be told the truth of their parents' disappearance. To this, the two women nodded before leaving Thaniel's side to sit with the two new additions to their family.

Laveda looked intrigued, though anxious. "What do you mean by *truth*? Did you know our parents?" Thaniel knew she wanted answers to many questions, and Sophie, he saw, sat whispering her own questions to her sister, making the already long list even longer. When the baroness sat to Laveda's left and Ethana to Sophie's right, it was storytime; and all eyes trained on the baron.

Tentatively, Thaniel recounted the grand accomplishments of Sir Llewellyn Reis. He was the youngest captain of the Royal Guard, had fought successfully in three wars, had an excellent mind for strategy, and was loved by all in Ryland. However, much like many other stories from earlier times, his tale held a tragic end.

Though brilliant in his field, he was horrible at diplomacy and was not respected by neighboring royals. This flaw was his greatest foe. On a diplomatic mission to Île-de-L'est, Sir Llewellyn shamed the house of D'Écart for their lack of support during the Theron invasion. Although Theron was a small island off the coast of Ryland, its people were experienced hunters and took the lives of many of Llewellyn's men before their encampment was discovered.

Since Ryland was at odds with Sagedor and Hampton tended to stay neutral in such events, they were hoping to receive aid from Île-de-L'est. However, no matter how much King Bohden begged, the great Armée of Île-de-L'est was never dispatched. Llewellyn, a proud man, and a stalwart soldier, could not sit by and let the slight go, not when so many good men were lost. Therefore, before all the assemblage in Île-de-L'est, he let the king know, in no uncertain terms, how he felt.

Now, had this been the only thing to transpire while Sir Llewellyn was on the island, everyone believes things would have cooled down, for King Bohden made apologies for his captain. But Llewellyn was a man of great passion, and his quick temper with those who crossed him, as well as his easy smile with friends, caught the eye of King Marcel's niece.

Mademoiselle Solène was the last of her immediate family, the only survivor of the pox, which had ended the lives of her parents and brothers. Not having anyone to watch over her, she became her uncle's responsibility, and he was happy to care for her. A lucky young lady, Solène had no scars upon her face, and the king found her several suitable suitors. But if truth be told, he had already decided to give her hand to his best friend, Gervaise. Solène knew of this, and believed Gervaise, though a kind man, to be too old to make her happy. Llewellyn, on the other hand, was young, opinionated, strong, and beautiful.

Though she was positively stunning and harbored an excellent wit, she had a great deal of competition. Llewellyn was used to having ladies throw themselves at him, and though Solène wanted him to notice her, she was not willing to humiliate herself in such a manner. Besides, if the king caught wind of her amour, he would end it before it could begin.

So she took a different approach. Whenever Sir Llewellyn said something funny, she would say something equally amusing and somewhat contrary. Her plan worked. The angrier Llewellyn became with her, the more he thought about her. She had set herself apart from all the other ladies at court, and all she had left to do was reveal her true intentions.

"So," Thaniel continued the tale, "as it has been told, Solène went to Llewellyn's room the last night of his stay and professed her love for him. She explained why she had been so contrary and begged him to forgive her deception."

What Solène had not realized is through all his years as a member of the Royal Guard, Llewellyn had never truly paid attention to his adoring female fans. He thought them silly and a waste of time. In setting herself apart from the others, by not hanging on his every word, he had become interested in her. And this interest caused him to study her as she moved across the grounds, listen to her every word, and eventually fantasize about the one he could not have. But in knowing she loved him, he realized he could have her . . . and he would.

"Over the next year, they would meet in secret," said Thaniel. "And it is said, when Solène found she was with child, Llewellyn ran off with her."

The kings, Bohden and Marcel, searched everywhere for the missing couple, but they were nowhere to be found. It wasn't until thirteen years later that an informant came forward with the needed information, and both Llewellyn and Solène were captured and taken to Île-de-L'est. King Bohden put in a plea to Marcel, but in the end, Sir Llewellyn was beheaded for his crime. As for Solène, she refused her king's offer of imprisonment in an abbey and begged to follow her husband.

"On the day of her beheading, her oldest friend and confident said Solène asked her to find her daughters. They were all alone and knew nothing of what was happening." Thaniel took a deep breath. "Then she was taken to join her husband."

As Thaniel shared this history, Laveda was struck dumb, and Sophie wept softly. Never before had they heard this tale, and it was a great deal to take in all at once. She had so much anger toward her parents for leaving them behind; she wasn't sure she could change. *It wasn't their fault.* She turned the information over and over in her mind. All the pain and suffering they had gone through over the past three years was not directly their fault.

But what of her mother's friend? Why had she not come to find them? She and Sophie had stayed in their home for a month before they were finally forced to leave by the landowner. Was that not enough time to find two young girls on their own? Laveda looked up, about to pose her question, but seeing the sorrowful looks around the room, she thought it best to leave it for another time. Instead, she stood up, pat Reyna's hand, which had been holding hers, kissed her sister on the forehead, and left the library.

Chapter Sixteen

Harvest Preparation

*A*nne had done her best to avoid Devin since the night he was made privy to her big secret, and much to her delight, he seemed to be doing the same. However, no amount of avoidance could protect her from coming in contact with him no less than three times a day, and each time, she could see the pain in his eyes. Once he knew who she really was, he surely had concluded that though she cared for him, she still did not love him; and it broke his heart.

Another person she was seeing less of was the captain. Apparently, he was quite busy, completing the end-of-year paperwork and deciding when to have everyone return to work after the holidays. Usually, in their area, winter was short-lived, coming late in the fall and ending a little earlier than most others have to wait for spring. Also, it rarely snowed in most parts of Ryland, but the closer one lived to Sagedor, the more likely one was to receive a cool blanket of the delicate white flakes.

Still, Anne had to admit this year seemed different. The air was now so cold; she bore the smells and indecencies of the crew and joined them below to sleep.

And with such strange weather, she could imagine the captain's frustration in predicting the future climate.

As for herself, she was steadily sending out inquiries to find a place to stay during the months she would be idle, and she continued to carry out her usual duties. She hoped to receive a few messages when their ship reached Hampton within the week, and surely one or two of the places she wrote to would be within her budget. If not? Well, she would have to think on that later.

"Andrew!" Anne heard Jerah shouting her name as he ran up the deck to where she stood on her break. "Andrew, the capt'n would like ta have a word with ya."

This was a surprise since they had not spoken since before they'd arrived in Île-de-L'est, and though she believed he was not out of sorts with her, she couldn't imagine why they should speak now. "Me? Why would he wish to speak with me?"

"Lord knows, me boy, but ya shouldn't keep 'im waitin'."

Anne regarded her old friend for a moment, then took off toward the captain's cabin. Once there, she gave her usual three raps at the door and waited for a reply.

"Come in, Andrew," came the captain's low bellow.

Anne entered the room, and her mind spun slightly as her lungs filled with the unforgettable scent of musk, wood, and vanilla. She took a steadying breath to calm her heart, which seemed to be on the verge of seizing. "You called for me, sir?"

"Yes." Doran was standing over his desk with his back to the door. "I am sure you know the Grand Harvest is in a few days." He never looked up from his paperwork.

"Yes, sir. I am aware." She and Bêrk had been trying to come up with a menu that would both surprise the crew and remind them of holidays at home. It was often difficult to remember what was happening in the world when you were on the outside. Though the ocean was, in general, a peaceful place to work, it also served as a barrier between the crew and the lives they used to live. It was the perfect place to lose oneself, with the aid of the gentle waves, gorgeous sunsets, and being wrapped lovingly in the crisp ocean breeze.

"Well," he pulled out a navigation map, "if my calculations are correct and the weather holds up, we will be arriving in Hampton the day before." He placed the map before her to point out their position in relation to the island of Hampton.

Anne wasn't sure what this had to do with her—other than she no longer had to come up with the most marvelous dinner ever seen aboard a cargo vessel. Then again, the captain was unaware of her plans. "Wonderful, sir. I am sure the crew will be happy to learn they will spend the holiday eating more than salty beef." She tried to smile, but not knowing the nature of the discussion made her uneasy.

Doran grinned in return. "I'm sure they will. In fact, I am hoping the Wemilo family will have some of us, if not all, to dinner. However, to secure our place at their table, I was planning to give them *you*."

Anne's face must have twisted into a look of confusion because the captain laughed out loud as he spoke further, "Only to help them with the food preparation, Andrew."

Doran's low gurgling laugh grew to a healthy rumble and then released as the most beautiful sound of merriment Anne had ever heard. It brought an easy smile to her lips. "Okay, so you wish for me to help with the Harvest dinner, but what about Bêrk? Surely, he would be the better choice since he is head cook?"

"Yes, yes, but when I spoke to him, we both agreed you were more creative and knew better what flavors complemented others. Besides, you are already familiar with Kenward's family."

"Don't remind me," she said as she subconsciously framed her jaw with her hand. The memory of being punched still needled her heart. Thank goodness it hadn't left a mark.

Doran's smile faded a little. She assumed her mate was sorry about the incident, which occurred the last time they were in Hampton. She didn't know her captain had heard from Kenward, and he knew the family would be happy to see their young friend again. "If I were you, I wouldn't worry about the past. Master Wemilo is looking forward to seeing you again, and perhaps on this visit, you will have a chance to clear Kismet's mind of a secret romantic rendezvous . . . with you." The glint in his eyes told Anne he was teasing her.

Anne hated it when the captain teased her in such a manner. She knew he did so to amuse himself, and much to her disappointment, she always, without fail, gave him what he wanted. She changed the subject. "Well, I'm sure I will come up with something suitable for the dinner. So if that's all you needed to tell me, I'll return to work."

"Oh, Andrew, before you go, I would like you to use me as your guinea pig."

"Excuse me?" Anne turned away from the door to face him once more.

"Well, I would like you to cook up a few things and try them out on me before you test them on the island. Besides, I hear the galley is running low on vegetables and the like, so you can't use the crew as your taste-testers. Therefore, I would like you to bring me a new dish each night this week."

Anne couldn't believe what she was hearing, but since there was nothing she could do, she merely nodded and left the cabin.

Anne was completely consumed by the scope of her new project as she made her way to the galley—so much so, she wasn't paying attention to those around her and ran right into Devin. "Oh, I'm so sorry."

Devin just looked at her. She sensed he wanted to say something, but she was too scared to hear it. Her palms began to sweat, and she envisioned herself shoving him out of the way, running up the deck, and jumping into the channel. Then she would be safe; then, and only then, could she stay completely away from both Devin and Doran.

"Annie," Devin whispered, bringing her back to the situation at hand, "we need to talk. It's not right . . . the two of us avoiding one other this way."

He was right. He was completely right. If they were going to work and live on the same ship, it only made sense they do their best to be friendly. So she nodded her agreement and waited for him to continue.

"Good. It would be nice if we could get along until I can get you home. I mean—"

"I beg your pardon?" Anne interrupted. "I'm sorry, Devin, but this *is* my home."

She hoped Devin could see her anger growing, but she also knew it wouldn't change his mind. She still didn't love him, but his love for her would not allow him to let her continue to live such a dangerous life.

"Listen, Annie, it's not proper for a lady to live at sea with a ship full of men. If anyone were to find out, it would make you unsuitable for marriage."

Anne held back a giggle, one intricately laced with a touch of malice. "First of all, Master *Lennox*, the name is Andrew." When Devin tried to interrupt, she held up her hand. "Second, I have been living and working aboard *Survivor* for more than five months. In that time, I have learned to navigate the channel and various parts of the ocean; I have learned the art of swordplay, been punched by a crew member, worked beyond exhaustion, adored by ladies on every island, and made wonderful friends. *Here* is where I have gained the respect I feel I deserve, and here is where I will stay. Furthermore, if you *ruin* me by telling *anyone* my true identity, all I will do is thank you. For you see, third, I have *no* desire to wed *anyone*. I would sooner die than become some man's home accessory." Anne was seething with anger, and the more she spoke, the more difficult it was to control. In fact, the mere labor of her efforts was leaving her breathless.

Anne didn't know how long she and Devin had been glaring at one another, but she prayed it had been several minutes, for Doran's hand came down on her shoulder, nearly making her jump out of her skin She hoped he had not heard what she'd said.

"Now, what have we here?" The captain eyed them both carefully.

Anne was still too angry to speak, so she clenched her jaw and looked away from the equally flaming red-head, leaving Devin to do as he wished.

Devin sighed and shook his head. "A minor disagreement, Captain. *Andrew,*" the name seemed to take great effort to say, "and I were just discussing the best places to live. However, I am afraid I have offended him. I apologize." Devin bowed to Anne and took his leave.

She and Doran watched Devin go. "Andrew, do you have anything to add?"

Oh, she wished she had been the first to leave. An image of sharks ripping her happily to pieces shot across her mind. "If only."

"Sorry?"

Anne, you're losing your mind—pull it together, she mindfully berated herself before answering the captain. "Sir. Devin and I have a long history, an extremely difficult one to explain. He's like family, and just as any family, we are . . . sometimes we're friends and sometimes we're not." Hoping this was enough to satisfy the captain, Anne, too, took her leave.

Anne had never been so frustrated in all her life. It was as though the captain had asked her to make a feast out of crackers and cheese. She needed flour, sugar, fresher vegetables and fruits, and a duck! Then, oh yes, then she could give him a feast worthy to be served at the Grand Harvest. Instead, she was reduced to a mediocre vegetable stew, a sorry-looking meat pie, and a pathetic apple yam casserole. She could just see Verna shaking her head now. And the worst part was, she received no feedback from the captain.

"Andrew, Captain's wonderin' when chow is," Bêrk derailed Anne's train of thought, saving her from any more self-abuse.

"Bêrk, I'm running out of ideas. Seriously, how am I to show him how well I can cook if I am lacking the necessary ingredients?"

The head chef merely laughed and clapped Andrew on the back. Bêrk could see that she was just about finished with the captain's dinner. He didn't say another word, presumably to avoid upsetting his aggravated friend.

Anne paid no attention to Bêrk. Today, she had made the oddest shepherd's pie ever by chopping up a few salted beef strips and boiling them until they were tender again, taking all the leftover vegetables from the day before and layering them one after the other, and finally, topping the whole thing with two potatoes, which she had smashed and creamed to the best of her ability. Piping hot and seasoned with garlic and a few herbs she had dried the month before, she was ready for her fourth meeting with the captain.

"Come in, Andrew," Doran sang. Of course, he knew the only person it could be was his sailor, coming to bring his dinner. Anne didn't understand just how much the captain enjoyed the company; although she never ate with him, she figured it was nice to have someone to talk to just the same.

Anne was dreading this dinner most of all, and as she entered the captain's cabin, she was sure once Doran tasted her latest dish, he would take her off the project. And though she hadn't wanted to create a meal in the first place, she was still terrified of failure. "Captain, I am sorry to report I have completely run out of vegetables. Therefore, I am afraid this meal will be less than great."

Doran merely nodded and prepared himself to be served. She never suspected he already knew "Andrew" was going to prepare some of the best foods for the Harvest. With what meager ingredients she had aboard the ship, she had concocted some of the most interesting and rather tasty dishes. So, he was quite pleased with the way things had turned out.

Anne tried not to look at the captain as she prepared his plate and then moved around the table to place the napkin on his lap before bringing the food before him. Next, she went to the captain's desk to retrieve his cup, which she sat to his right, filled with water. Nothing ever changed in this routine; each night was the same as the last. Doran would then ask her to explain what he was about to eat, and she would describe what she had done. He would begin the feast, and she would stand off to the side, answering whatever questions he posed.

However, this night proved different. As she turned to retrieve the captain's cup, she tripped over the leg of his chair, bumped into his shoulder, and landed in his lap. Immediately, a wave of heat welled up inside her. Never before had she sat on a man's lap—well, except perhaps her father's when she was very young. She thought the sheer embarrassment would kill her. Quickly, she leaped from his lap, smoothed her sweaty hands down her overcoat, and made the apologies. "Captain, I am so sorry. I should have been paying attention. I swear, it will not happen again."

Doran laughed—a roaring, thunderous laughter, which shook the cabin. "Andrew, you're one of those men who becomes so rigid when things don't go exactly as expected!" Anne saw that he thought the entire thing was hilarious. What she didn't know was that Doran had been waiting for something like this to happen all week. People often enjoyed when someone who seemed so perfect makes a mistake. "Andrew, I'm fine. Calm yourself, lad. You are far too old for your age." Doran brought his laughter down to a chuckle. "Now, come, tell me about this meal."

Still slightly shaken, Anne quickly placed the cup of water to the captain's right, made her way to her nightly position, and explained the meal. "As I said earlier, sir, I'm afraid this meal is not my best. Since we are out of or never had many of the traditional Grand Harvest ingredients, I was forced to use what we generally keep on board." Then she told him what he was eating and how she was forced to prepare it.

Doran ate as he usually did, with a few bites intermittent with a bit of conversation. They usually talked about the ship, the crew, Andrew's love life—or lack of one. However, again, this night was different. The captain told Anne to sit while he ate. Then, when he spoke, Anne felt rather uncomfortable.

"So, Andrew, after our last run to Île-de-L'est, we will be docking at Berton's Wharf. Have you a place to stay while we are there for the holidays?"

Anne had, of course, thought of options, but nothing had been made solid yet. She had written to a few of the more reputable saloons with apartments but wasn't expecting a response until they arrived in Hampton. She hoped she could afford one or another. And Anne had heard *Survivor* was one of the first ships to leave port after the frost, so the length of stay would hopefully be affordable. "I have written to a few places and await their replies."

"I see," the captain stated nonchalantly as he continued to eat. "So you have no family in Ryland?"

"None I would feel comfortable imposing upon."

"Well, perhaps I can suggest a few places. You see, many of the men onboard are in the same boat, pardon the pun, and most of them lodge together in a friendly little inn called the Sleepy Bear. Those, however, who choose not to stick with the group either travel or reside in the Happy Horse or the Three Stars."

Anne felt this was good information to have but not for the reasons Doran would have believed. It was nice to know where everyone stayed, so she could *avoid* those areas. She wanted some time alone, to be *herself*, even if it was behind closed doors. "Thank you for the suggestions, Captain. I'm sure they will come in handy."

Chapter Seventeen

Schemes d'Orianna

Orianna had always known how to get under her brother's skin, just as any younger sister did. The trick, however, was to pull off her farce without being discovered. Invitations would need to go out early enough for the desired number of people to arrive, but not so soon that Nolan would catch the faintest hint or slightest wind. Preparations would have to be done in the greatest amount of secrecy—not even her parents could be allowed to know until two days before. The only good thing about the timing of the event was that it would be the same as the Royal Christmas Party. Therefore, her parents would anticipate the servants magically transforming the Amber Hall, their most elegant ballroom, from its usual finery into the glittering magnificence meant to warm the heart and bedazzle the eyes. So, from that preparatory standpoint, the king and queen would not be suspicious. The only true tip-offs would be the number of tables, the amount of food, and the extra decorations she'd ordered. Although, she hoped, if they even bothered to notice such things, she could convince them she felt Nolan should have an extra special holiday to welcome him home.

The princess smiled devilishly to herself as she thought of Nolan's face when he entered the ballroom. Would he pale? No, that seemed rather unlikely. Perhaps he would run and hide. Amusing though that would be, Orianna knew better. No, Nolan, poor boy, would suffer through it, much to her delight. He would rather endure all sorts of horrors than insult their guests, and this was where she hoped to gain all her pleasure. Knowing deep down he would wish to do nothing more than avoid so many people, and it was she who would trick him into the very situation he often evaded, bringing tears of merriment to Orianna's large eyes. Oh, she may have had to work overtime to see to his duties as well as her own, but during the Christmas party, she would make Nolan work harder than she ever had to keep up with his duties.

Smiling to herself again, Orianna got back to the fabrics from which she would choose the perfect curtains to witness the perfect revenge. Then she would return to the mundane preparations for the Grand Harvest dinner, a less exciting affair.

Although this was her first holiday with the de Rangers, Laveda could not get into the spirit of the season. Over and over, she replayed her parents' story in her mind. Three years she and her sister had suffered, and for what? The pride of someone she didn't know, nor would she ever wish to know?

Sitting outside to do her homework, as she usually did since the summer heat had made way for the cool autumn breezes, Laveda glanced up at her favorite tree, which was now beautifully dotted with gold, rouge, and copper. She wondered what would have happened if she had never met Andrew? Would her mother's friend eventually find her? Would she have ever learned the truth behind her parents' disappearance?

A soft breeze wafted ever so gently across her face and soothed away her burning questions. She closed her eyes and leaned heavily against the trunk of her study buddy. Life, she decided, was not about the *what-ifs* but about what was and what would be. She had been given the chance to have a better life and was determined to do everything in her power to achieve the happiness she now knew was denied to her parents.

Having forcefully made up her mind, Laveda reopened her eyes and returned to her studies. Sometimes great achievements had to begin with the simple unbearables, like homework. In her new frame of mind, not even mathematics could bring her down.

Henry watched Laveda from where he was crouched in the garden and couldn't stop the wave of sadness that overcame him. He felt as though the autumn change had not only transformed the world into the magnificent shades of golden glory but had also placed Laveda at a height no mere gardener could ever hope to surmount. There were few secrets in a manor of this size, and if all rumors were true, Laveda and Sophie were related to the royal family. Not to mention that the all-too-horrid Oren de Vinay had been struck by her beauty.

"Hhhh," he sighed to himself as he continued to pick vegetables for the Harvest dinner. There was no use in wishing for something or someone so completely unattainable. He knew there was something special about her the moment they'd met, so it was only a matter of time before the rest of the world noticed too.

Chapter Eighteen

Dreadful Fruitcake

"Ahoy there!" the captain shouted as he bounded down the ship's plank to greet Master Wemilo. The two men embraced and clapped one another on the back before turning to Kenward who also wanted to greet his father.

On the dock as well, among the crowd of working sailors and passersby, was Kismet. The eldest of the Wemilo daughters was looking rather fetching in her long, straight striped skirt and long-sleeved cream ruffled blouse. Anne knew the entire outfit had been put together with the utmost care and consideration. Every thought given to detail, from the simple shoes to the necklace of natural stones had come together in an ensemble made to please *her* eye. Anne could only sigh to herself as she thought of the work the young girl had put into such a lovely set and how it was all done in vain.

Walking down the plank—slowly as not to rush into uncomfortable matters—Anne suddenly felt Devin's arm come around her shoulders. Never before had she wanted him to be so close as he was now, and she wished she could curl up in his embrace and forget Kismet was waiting. And the feeling surprised her. *If only the world followed our hopes and dreams to the letter.*

"For all the attitude and strength you possess, I know you're not looking forward to our stay in Hampton." Anne didn't know Devin had spoken to Dyson about the *Survivor's* last trip to the island and could better understand why Anne preferred Île-de-L'est. Anne figured he had seen the look on her face when she noticed the pretty, young lady awaiting their arrival. Only Devin would understand why she was so uncomfortable with being so adored. She was sure she had made the same face in light of the adoration he'd bestowed upon her while in school.

After all the hellos, accepting her mail from a carrier, and a particularly indifferent chat with Kismet, Anne was off to the Wemilo homestead while the others bothered with unloading the cargo. It was two days until the Harvest, and she had much to prepare. She needed to discover what ingredients were at her disposal as well as what she could purchase or catch on her own.

Madame Wemilo was awaiting Anne on the doorstep with outstretched arms, and Anne could do nothing but smile as she stepped into the older woman's embrace. It was nice to be around ladies who were not attracted to her, and she felt as though she drew strength from the presence of women.

Much to Anne's surprise, Madame Wemilo had traded, bought, or harvested many of the items Anne needed to prepare her meal. The only items she would have to get herself were a few ducks, candied fruits, and apples. However, the lady of the house quickly informed her the duck she wanted to use was not native the island. *Surely, one of the native birds will suffice.* With all that being said and done, Anne got to work.

The first thing she had to do was find a few willing Ryland helpers, people who would understand what she was trying to accomplish and would possess a desire to help. The first to join up was, of course, Devin . . . followed by Bêrk, Neville, and much to her surprise, Dyson. Not having much of a desire to kill anything, Anne sent Devin and Dyson in search of at least six plump birds. Neville was asked to go through the potatoes and find the best ones for mashing, while she and Bêrk took up the task of finding candied fruit and apples. The day was melting away, so, Lord willing, if she got all of her items together, she would have tonight and the following morning and afternoon to do nothing but cook.

To Anne's delight, by late afternoon, all was in order, and she had more help than she could have hoped for. Devin and Dyson, making a sport of duck searching were able to interest several other crew members in the hunt and came back with ten fat but rather odd-looking fowl. Neville had gone through a barrel of potatoes with nothing bad to report, and she and Bêrk had found the fruit, although quite expensive, for which they had been searching.

With the shopping and hunting over, Anne and her chosen helpers, along with five newcomers, including Jerah, began the prep work. She, Bêrk, and Neville cut up beef and lamb, cut corn from their cobs, peeled and cut the potatoes, and broke enough beans for the eight shepherd's pies to be made. The other seven who stayed behind unfeathered and salted the birds.

Once the birds were done, they were then wrapped twice in a type of burlap cloth and taken to the cool cave Madame Wemilo suggested they use for storage. Then the seven hunters became two as all save Dyson and Jerah headed back to the ship. The two remaining men cooked the beef and lamb combination and split the meat into eight portions and placed them in their respective pans before returning to the ship themselves. Neville layered on the corn, followed by Bêrk with the snapped beans, and finally Anne, with the potatoes she had mashed to top off the little lovelies. The pies were then covered and also placed in the cave.

With the main part of the meal prepped for the following day, Neville and Bêrk headed out to the ship. Anne was the only one remaining and didn't happen to think much of it until Kismet arrived.

"Hello, Andrew." The younger girl smiled up at her. "Is there anything else you need help with?"

Anne felt the weight of her gaze and was nearly smothered; however, there was nothing she could do. Had she been a man, she may have welcomed Kismet's attention, or if she could tell the girl the truth, then the girl would stop wasting such loving glances upon her fellow maid. Anne let out a small sigh; she could neither be mean to the child nor dismissive. It was her own fault that she was in this situation, and she would merely have to put up with it.

"Well, all I have left to do before tomorrow is bake two fruitcakes for the head table, then I'll see if your mother needs anything. But I suppose if you help me with the cake, we could help your mother sooner rather than later."

When Kismet's face lit up, Anne knew she had probably made a mistake, but there was no turning back.

Over the next two hours, Kismet and Anne made the two fruitcakes and assisted Madame Wemilo with her final prep and the cleaning of the kitchens. The entire time, Anne did her best to avoid Kismet's roaming hands and keep her comments as benign as possible. She didn't want Kismet to misread any of her words or intentions; it was the most exhausting part of her prep.

There is no rest for the weary cook when there was a party requiring mountains of food. Anne had only slept four and a half hours before rising and heading back to the Wemilo homestead. The night before, she had helped the madame and her crew shell more beans than she had ever seen, bake five dozen pumpkin fritters and seven loaves of sweet bread, and then watched as the men buried three fat hogs with herbs and hot coals. Now, with a bag of nice clothes for later, it was back to the house to finish her meal and help the madame.

Since the family had but two small coal stoves (not nearly enough to help feed the army of people who'd be arriving), Luam, Kenward's younger brother, helped Anne dig a coal pit for the shepherd's pie. Then she was off peeling potatoes from sunrise until nine, when Neville and Bêrk arrived. Neville took to finishing the potatoes, while Anne and Bêrk worked on the honeyed carrots. Around eleven, Bêrk and Neville traded places because Neville could no longer stand the sight of potatoes. So, in large pots over controlled wooden fires, Neville cooked the carrots, and Bêrk mashed the potatoes, while Anne began her family's traditional dish of apple yam casserole.

Anne wasn't sure just how far back the tradition went, but she knew her great-grandmother felt it wasn't a true harvest without the spiced, sweet dish. And the recipe was so sacred, not even Verna was privy to the casserole's secrets. Every year, her mother rose early in the morning to bake the dish before the manor cook was awake, to safeguard the riddle to which only she, and eventually Anne, knew the answer. Because of this, Anne had to find a secret place to make the two casseroles. When everyone seemed preoccupied, she stole away, only to reemerge with two medium-sized pans of the glorious hodge-podge of deliciousness.

Now, only needing to cool the fowl, she acquired the assistance of Kenward and Luam to grab and string the birds over the prepared fire pit. Still wrapped in burlap and cool to the touch, Anne was reassured they would be just fine for the feast, so they each grabbed several birds, Kenward having one more than the other two, and went to her spit. There they secured the unlucky fowls to a long stick which, afterward, was placed over the growing flame Luam had started. Having thanked the men for their help, Kenward and Luam took their leave and let Anne get back to administering to the birds.

By five o'clock, all the food was nearly done. Madame Wemilo had a battalion of helpers and expressed there was no need for the young *man*, Anne, to waste anymore of his shore time worrying over the meal. Anne, though feigning injury, was delighted to have some time to relax and get ready for the feast. From her previous visit to the island, she remembered a secluded spring that always promised a warm bathe.

Before leaving for her private puddle, Anne checked on her food once more. The finished creamy potatoes and sweet carrots were being kept warm in shallow holes filled with cooling coals and wood. Dyson, who had taken over for Bêrk, was tending to the birds, keeping them warm without cooking them further, and basting them with a sweet and spicy sauce Anne had made, combining honey, wine, and peppers. The pies and casseroles, finally done, were cozy in their make-shift oven, and the fruitcake was secure in Madame Wemilo's pantry. All said and done, Anne thanked Dyson for his help and went to bathe.

So far from the homestead and with no one around to spot her, Anne stripped down to her luxurious self and basked in the moment's freedom of her true iden-tity. She gently, slowly, caressed her breasts and lovingly smoothed her hands over her entire body. She loved having her hair free from its braided constraints and reveled in the fifteen minutes she had before redonning her masculine costume. With a small sigh of regret, she had to admit: she missed feeling like a lady.

At six o'clock, the frenzy began, but Anne was not fazed in the least. There were three long tables set up for the food, huge blankets spread over the sand for all the guests to sit, and a long white cloth set up as the head table. Quickly, people ran back and forth, covering the unclothed tables with curried squash soup, seafood stew, salted fish with rice, beans and rice, sweet bread, glazed mixed vegetables, spicy eggplant, Anne's fowl, mashed potatoes, shepherd's pie, and honeyed carrots. The fruitcakes and apple yam casseroles graced the head table along with the shrimp casserole and coconut custard furnished by Madame Wemilo. Each blanket also had its own supply of ginger beer and pumpkin juice.

Anne was amazed by the sheer amount of food on display, and her delight grew when the guests arrived. There were so many people, young and old, sailors and farmers. Almost overcome with excitement, Anne nearly forgot she needed to find a place to sit. However, before she could get too far from the head table, the captain grabbed her by the arm.

"Ah-ah. I can't have my chef sitting with the crowd. You, Bêrk, Devin, and Dyson shall join me at the head table."

Anne was shocked. It was such an honor to sit at a head table, or in this case, the head blanket, but she didn't understand why she was asked. Now, if they knew who she truly was, then she would expect to be asked; however, as they knew her, she was no more than a servant. Surely, the captain would rather have the senior members of the crew sit alongside him.

"Captain, Devin, Bêrk, and I are fairly new to the ship's complement. Wouldn't some of the more senior members be better suited for such an honor?"

Doran, having released Andrew as he spoke, crossed his arms before making his reply. "No. I believe the seats of honor should go to those who labored with such care and consideration to bless us with reminders of our home. Besides, I've already made up my mind, and your place has been set."

Astounded, Anne walked back to the head and made a closer inspection of the blanket. Before each plate and wooden cup, there were small clay name plates, which could be seen by the crowd. Master Wemilo was at the center, and to his right, Madame Wemilo and their children: Kenward, Luam, Kismet, Alcina, and Callidora, in descending birth order. Then to the host's left, Anne could see the captain, Jerah, Dyson, Bêrk, Andrew, and Devin's names written on the same sort of clay plates in order of seniority. She couldn't believe she had missed seeing them before now, but then again, she had been a bit amazed by the sheer size of the event. At any rate, staring at them now and allowing what the captain said to sink in, Anne suddenly realized someone was missing.

"Captain, I hate to bring up an oversight, but if you wish to honor everyone who worked hard on the feast, shouldn't Neville be included?"

The captain laughed, clapped her on the back, and then pointed out a specific blanket. When Anne followed his finger to its point, she spotted Neville, sitting with several members of the crew, grinning from ear to ear behind a clay plate bearing his name.

"If you haven't noticed, he hates attention," the captain said while still chuckling. "So when he saw his name at the head of the feast, he quickly snatched it up and scurried off before anyone could stop him."

Anne had to smile at the image of the slender man of nearly twenty-five summers grinning proudly, happy with the knowledge he could be at the head with all the others if he chose.

"My dear family and friends," Master Wemilo began the feast once everyone was seated and the runners had filled all the plates and cups of the head. "It is a great blessing that we have come together for this glorious feast. Now, as it is our custom to allow the honored guest to say a few words before the meal, I ask Captain Doran of the merchant ship *Survivor* to lead us into our feasting."

The captain stood and hugged Master Wemilo, who then regained his seat on the blanket. "My friends, I would like to begin by recognizing the chefs and helpers who put this feast together for our enjoyment with a round of applause."

The entire area before the Wemilo farm broke out in a thunderous ebb and flow of clapping and cheering, with a few people standing to show the sound of hands coming together in joy was simply not enough. It took some doing to get the crowd back to their previous mumble, but with Master Wemilo's help the crowd was returned to their low hum of excitement.

"Thank you," Doran chucked. "Now if you would join me in a short prayer—we'll say our thanks before stuffing ourselves silly."

Again, the crowd responded, this time with laughter. However, when the captain bowed his head, the throng silently obeyed the unspoken command.

"Dear Lord," his voice carried across the field hungry mutes, "we thank you for bringing us together this holiday season and for all the food you have blessed us with this evening. We pray you will bestow such graces upon us the following year, just as you have done in this one, and we praise you now and forevermore for the kindness you have shown us in the past, continue to do in the present, and with the hope you will find us worthy in the future. Our love to you, dear

Lord, on this marvelous Grand Harvest day, amen." And with that, the frenzied feeding began.

The feast was a true success. The party enjoyed three heaping courses because of the abundance of food provided, and then everyone, having had their fill, were lying about, lazily savoring their desserts. Everything had been delicious, and Madame Wemilo, as well as Anne, had never been so pleased.

Of course, Anne's pleasure had little to do with the crowd's enjoyment but was wholly centered on that of the captain. Captain Doran had praised her time and again for the meal she had prepared and completely forgot his tongue when he tried to describe the amazing tastes that had come together in the apple yam casserole. Therefore, it was safe to say Anne had blushed more than a few times that evening, and though her behavior went unnoticed by the happy throng, and even to Anne herself, every shy gesture, every subtle warming of her face, and every loving glance was picked up by Devin.

Devastated and heartbroken, Devin realized, whether Anne knew it or not, she was in love with their captain. She noticed every little thing he did, heard every word he said, and hung on every one of his praises. Had Annie ever given him half the attention she now bestowed to Captain Doran, he would have been the happiest man alive, and he would carry that happiness through his life to have died a contented man. Instead, she chose to give her heart to the captain of a merchant ship. Was he a gentleman? Was he well educated? What will he do when he learns Andrew's true identity? It was anyone's guess.

"Ah, the heart is ever blind," the poet muttered under his breath.

"Hmm? Devin, did you say something?" Anne questioned as she took a bite of fruitcake.

"I was just musing over your obvious love and adoration for Captain Doran."

Then is when it happened: the unimaginable. Anne had taken a larger bite than she had thought and mixed with the shock of Devin's proclamation, it had become lodged in her throat. She couldn't breathe. Shock, fear, and panic mingled in a cloud of blurring emotion. She tore at Devin's clothes but couldn't tell if she held him or not. Confused. She was so confused.

Then, she felt something hit her and suddenly her lungs were on glorious fire; the rum laden chunk of fruitcake shot from her mouth, and she was lying in Devin's arms, gasping for air. Her eyes cleared as tears rolled down her cheeks, and her breath slowly became regular again. Closing her eyes, then opening them again, she realized Devin was sitting before her, holding a cup of water. Therefore, she immediately realized, it could not be his arms around her. Confusion yet again made a complete muddle of her mind, and she slowly looked up to find Doran's concerned expression looking down on her.

Chapter Nineteen

Revenge and Love?

Anne sat in the galley trying to read over the letters she had received from potential lodgers, but to her great frustration, her mind would wander back to the words that continued to echo in her ears. ". . . you are in love with Captain Doran." Devin's voice went round and round in her mind. She had tried to ignore it; she had tried to wish those words were never spoken; she had even tried to pray them away, yet nothing worked. No matter how ridiculous she felt the statement was, it lingered in her heart and festered in her mind.

"Stop it, Anne," she spoke aloud to herself before trying yet again to focus on the task at hand.

There were five inns that had answered the inquiries she had set forth before their ship had left Île-de-L'est; however, three of them were the ones the captain (she sighed) had suggested a few weeks ago. And the other two, though very nice, were a bit out of her price range. She could stay at the Whispering Willows, but all her money would be spent on lodging alone. They served a sizable breakfast every morning, however, so if she was desperate, she could possibly get by.

The true question was whether it was more important to have privacy or money, for if it were money, she could suck it up and stay at one of the inns Doran (another sigh) had suggested. *Doran . . . hmm.* She wondered if he would be staying in an inn for the holidays. She smiled as a light dream of her dancing with him on Christmas day filled her mind and blinded her eyes—so much so, she hadn't heard or seen Bêrk enter the room.

When Bêrk pulled up a chair, the spell was broken, and her mind was made up. Whether it was through fear or a true desire to be herself for a while, Anne would never know, but she decided privacy was what she needed and desired most.

"Wow, Andrew, where were you?" Bêrk spoke as he sat down. "Don't think I've ever seen you smile like that before.

Anne cleared her throat before lying. "I was just thinking about Christmas and how much I was looking forward to carolers and a nice Christmas ham."

"Ah, that *would* bring a smile to your face. Heavens, it brings one to mine!" The other man chuckled. "Well, until then, it's back to salt beef and crackers. Let's start on chow."

Relieved that Bêrk had believed her fib, Anne quickly gathered her letters and started to work.

Orianna had finally done it. She had just approved the perfect invitations to the upcoming Christmas celebration. The tea-length ecru, beautifully woven heavyweight linen paper was embossed on the bottom with a lightly colored pearlized sprig of holly. Not to mention, the calligrapher would be using gold ink to convey Orianna's message.

Family, Friends, and Subjects,
Her Royal Highness, Princess Orianna-Loni
Cordially invite you and your families
to a

Royal Christmas Ball
At Caardea Palace
On the 24th of December
In this, the Fourth Year of Peace

Guests will please arrive promptly
At 7:30 that evening
And dressed in their best apparel

All Ladies are Welcome
With or Without an Escort

This celebration is a Surprise
For His Royal Highness Prince Nolan

Therefore, Her Highness Expects
Everyone to Keep the Secret

(Should the surprise be spoiled,
Her Royal Highness
shall take it upon herself
to cancel the event.)

Once the invitations were completed, the calligrapher and his staff would then place tissue atop each invite before stuffing them into their addressed envelopes.

Orianna was expecting the invitations to go out within the week, allotting everyone invited two weeks of preparation. It was enough time for the ladies to come up with their best evening gowns, but not so much time as to enable them to send word to extended family and have them join the festivities. Timing was everything.

The menu consisted of deer, boar, and fish and would be accompanied by such holiday favorites as roast duck, sweet ham, spiced yams, buttery baked young potatoes, minced pies, pumpkin pies, pecan pies, fruitcakes, and so much more. There was enough food to feed three armies and each member of the Royal Navy. Orianna had also given the palace chef plenty of room for experimentation—so long as the traditional foods were also present. Oh, how her mouth watered as she thought about all the delicious delights that would be prepared for the evening.

Red drapes with a golden swirl pattern and pulled back with golden cords would be hung in the ball room, and the floor was to be covered in pounds and pounds of tiny white pieces of paper to give the impression of snow. There would be six trees about the room, each covered in sparkling silver, gold, and transparent ornaments. Mistletoe would be hung at every entrance and exit. The tablecloths were silver swirls atop gold, and the placemats were a metallic green. So the only question left to answer was that of the silverware. Should she use silver to play up the swirls in the cloth or gold to match the cloth's background? She and her events coordinator would be going over this last detail that afternoon before she supervised the cleaning of the chandeliers.

As for now, however, it was time to see her seamstress about her party gown and then her brother's tailor about the suit he was to wear. As for Nolan's attire, she wasn't quite sure yet, but hers she had envisioned since the previous Christmas dinner. It was to be made with white satin, layered with a sheer, shimmery fabric covered in tiny crystals to reflect the candlelight and give the effect she was sparkling. She wanted to be the mirror image of how she imagined a snow princess to look, and in doing so, be the most beautiful woman at the ball.

Orianna was just imagining flocks of pretty little men falling all over themselves to get to her when there was a knock on her door. Annoyed back to reality, she screeched a horrid, "Come in!"

"Sorry to disturb you, Your Highness, but 'tis the very minute you asked me to be here," the lady who had knocked spoke curtly.

The princess dully eyed the older woman at her door. Maya, her seamstress, was nearly twice her age, and in being so, had always spoken her mind in the most respectful manner she could muster. However, Orianna knew Maya liked working for her mother far more than she enjoyed working for her—partially because she hated being told what to do by someone younger and partially because she felt Orianna was a disrespectful spoiled little brat. The funny thing was, the curter Maya was to the princess, the more rotten the princess became.

"Ah, so it is, Maya. Oh, and I see you have brought Isaura with you. Need a young set of eyes to help you go over my designs?"

"My eyes are as sharp as they have ever been, Your Highness, but I thank you for your concern." Maya did not seem thankful in the least. "No, I have brought Isaura with me to show her how a ball gown is made from start to finish, then perhaps one day, she will take my place."

Orianna smiled as she pulled out her drawings. "Oh, Maya, if you were only so lucky."

Ever since the Sunday she had met Oren de Vinay, the letters had come, sometimes once a week but usually twice. Laveda wasn't sure how she felt about the young man's *supposed* feelings toward her, but somehow, she believed they were all wrong. Some days, she couldn't believe he was writing to her because she was so far beneath him; then other days, she wondered if he was only writing to her because of her apparent lineage to the throne of Île-de-L'est. Either way, she wasn't comfortable with their correspondence and had even told him so in one of her replies. Yet the letters still came, much to her chagrin and to that of the de Rangers.

Another curiosity was why the de Rangers carried an underlying distaste for not only Oren but his entire family. At first, she thought she was just imagining things, but it became quite clear as the letters streamed in. They were concerned about something. Usually, when the family would not talk about an issue, one could ask the servants, but even they had lost their tongues.

Laveda sighed as she looked into her vanity mirror. Tuesdays were always slow for her. Sophie was into her studies; the de Rangers had hired a tutor for her. And Laveda usually finished her homework the day she received it. Therefore, there was nothing for her to do until the next morning. Bored and tired of her own thoughts, she decided to see if George and Henry needed any help with the yard work. A bit of fresh air might do her some good.

Laveda found Henry and his father in the back of the manor raking leaves and cutting back some of the shrubs. George, seeing her approach and knowing her all too well, immediately disappeared into the shed and produced a rake.

"Was wonderin' how long it would take you to join us," he laughed.

Laveda smiled at the older man. To think he had once been appalled by her desire to help with the manor chores. It had taken her months to convince him to allow her to assist, and he then heard how she often helped in the kitchen too. Once he had accepted her as one of their own, she was no longer just a guest of the manor; she was like family.

"Well, I am very sorry I have kept you waiting." She gladly took hold of the offered gardening tool.

George chuckled. "Ah, you're forgiven. Now, if you truly want to work, you'd better get to helpin' Henry. If not, try to look as though you're doin' somethin' useful, and try not to distract the boy too much!" He gave her a little wink before turning back to the shrub work.

Laveda loved getting out of the manor whenever an opportunity presented itself, but it was even better when she had something to do and people to do it with. However, if she truly admitted it to herself, she actually liked spending time with Henry more than anyone else within or without the manor house. He was always kind to her and spoke to her as if she were his equal. Of course, the de Rangers were always very kind, but they (and Andrew . . . if she were to admit the entire truth) seemed as though they were above her—not so much as to speak to her like she was a servant but as if they were parents speaking to their children. There was none of that tone with Henry.

"Ah, so the loveliest lady of the manor has decided to get her hands dirty." Henry smiled as he tossed her a look over his shoulder.

Though Laveda smiled back, her words feigned dissatisfaction, "Oh, pooh! I'm sure I work as hard as you, and since when did I become a lady?"

Henry stopped raking to turn and look at the girl who was now but a few feet away. "You've always been a lady in my eyes, but with all of your schooling and new clothes, I'm sure the rest of Ryland, if not the world, has realized it too."

The intensity in Henry's eyes took Laveda's breath away, and she could feel the heat rising to her cheeks. She neither knew what to say nor what to do, so she looked away. Then, slowly, she took her free hand and touched her cheek.

Meanwhile, Henry was silently berating himself for being so forward with a lady who was surely meant for someone else. Instead of waiting for Laveda to say something, he moved away to rake a different section of the yard.

The two of them raked the leaves in silence until Verna came to tell Laveda she should ready herself for dinner. Nodding, she placed her rake against a tree before walking up to Henry to tell him where she had left it. When she touched his shoulder to get his attention, she was shocked by her desire to hug him. Shaking it off, she dropped her hand, told him about the rake, and swiftly made her way to the comfort she knew she would find within the manor.

Henry turned in time to see her disappear into the manor house, and his heart sank. Their friendship would never be the same now—all because he couldn't keep his mouth shut.

Chapter Twenty

Home for the Holidays

our days, Anne, four days. Surely she could keep her wits about her for four days. Then she would be safe in the secluded inn, able to relax and be herself without fear of discovery, and perhaps shake whatever love nonsense Devin had placed in her head.

For an entire week, Anne had experienced trouble with concentration during the day and had endured many restless nights. Her mind kept filling with images of her—her true self—laughing, dancing with, and sometimes even kissing Doran. And much to her dismay, the crew was noticing her lack of attention. Marid was even treating her differently.

But Anne had other things to worry about, and with Christmas only a week and six days away, she had to prepare herself for the loneliest holiday, at least *her* loneliest holiday, ever.

Devin had asked her to come home with him; he even promised to help her keep up her façade before his parents. But then she couldn't be herself, and she was so looking forward to basking in her feminine nature. She had even set a few dollars aside to purchase some nice soap with which she could bathe. Her plan was to rise early in the morning, bathe in the boarding bath, then fly back to her room to enjoy herself. Ahh . . . four days. She could wait four days.

Well, it was amazing how quickly time could fly. Four days went by a lot faster than Anne had envisioned, and they were presently docking in Ryland. Oh, it felt so good to be home. She smiled to herself.

Not having enough money for holiday gifts, Anne had bought a few nice cards to send and a birthday gift for her father. She gently placed the items into her burlap bag atop her clothes and blankets and made her way back up top. Once above deck, she noticed much of the crew was already making their way off the ship. Devin, however, was talking to Doran as he waited to escort her to her lodgings. Seeing them together tied Anne's stomach in knots.

"So, Andrew," the captain began as she approached, "Devin tells me that you have decided to take up lodgings in town. Did any of my suggestions meet your approval?"

Anne had no desire to chat with the captain, especially about where she was staying, but she couldn't think of a polite way to get out of answering his question. "Yes, they were all very nice and inexpensive, but I decided I would like to spend some time away from the crew." There, she effectively told him that she had not chosen one of the inns he had suggested without giving away where she would be staying.

"Really?" He raised his brow. "So where *are* you staying?"

Dang it, man, why must you know everything, she thought. Instead, she smiled and answered, "The Whispering Willow."

"The Whispering Willow," he exclaimed. "Surely, I don't pay you enough to stay there!"

"Just barely. So where are you staying?" Anne asked flippantly, noticing it made Doran a bit uncomfortable.

"I'm staying with my family," he replied rather gruffly.

Family? Surely, he wasn't married—or was he? Suddenly wanting to know more, Anne went fishing. "Oh, that's nice. But you don't seem happy about it."

"Let's just say," he was smiling now, "that I may be staying in the closest place to the underworld during such a religious time." He clapped both *men* on the back. "Well, I wish you both a very merry Christmas, and I'll see you next year."

"Until next year then." Devin extended his hand to the captain. Doran gave it a firm shake before doing the same with Anne. Anne tried to keep her wits about her during this goodbye, and outwardly, she believed she had succeeded. Although, inside, she felt a great sadness about this parting. She knew the feeling was completely ridiculous, but no one can tell the heart how to feel, not even its owner.

Devin and Anne descended from the ship as quickly as they could, though beset with what felt like a thousand goodbyes, followed by hundreds of hand-shakes and claps on the back, and at least three dozen "Merry Christmases." Anne was so overwhelmed by the time they hit the dock that she feared a nap was in order.

The air in Ryland was crisp. The wind whipped off the water and across Anne's face, so much so that she had to squelch the desire to unbraid her hair and use it as a shield against the elements. As she and Devin neared a slightly more respect-able area of town, Anne had ultimately decided the air rumored the upcoming weather. "So, do you think it will snow tonight, Devin?"

"I haven't the slightest—though, I hope not. The Good Lord knows I hate traveling in the snow, and since you refuse to stay with my family during the hol-iday, I will be forced to endure the weather to visit you."

Anne gave her companion a sideways eye roll before responding. "Oh, such a hardship should never be borne by so good a man." Her voice dripped with sarcasm. "Do allow me to relieve your burden by saying that such a journey is wholly unnecessary."

"What? And force you to spend the entire holiday season alone? No, Annie, I cannot allow it." His voice held no humor and was very matter-of-fact in its making.

Anne stopped to have a serious moment with her friend. "Listen, Devin, I am terribly sorry things cannot be the way you wish them to be between us—really I am. I swear you are the most wonderful man I have ever met, and the past few months aboard *Survivor* have been near perfection since your arrival. I just—"

Devin cut her off, "I know, Annie. I'm finished with trying to convince you I am the most amazingly sexy, incredibly intelligent, and incurably humorous man you will ever meet in your life. I mean, if you cannot handle what I have to offer, why should I force you into overwhelming greatness? Besides, Captain Doran is an *okay* fellow, but I must offer a bit of advice about your relationship."

Anne shook her head, and when Devin did not continue on with his advice, she raised a questioning brow. Devin went on, "Marry him before your parents find out you have fallen for a merchant. Sooner or later, you will have to reconcile with them, and I would hate to find you have run away, yet again, because they did not approve of your par amour."

Anne made a face at him that she hoped conveyed, *What, are you insane?*

"Hey, don't look at me like that. I have a life, you know. I can't waste it away island-hopping after you. I need to find a lady who can handle all of this." He waved his hands over himself.

Anne laughed. "Devin, I swear, if we were alone, I would give you the greatest hug there ever was or ever will be in existence." Then, tearing up a little, she said, "Thank you for being such a wonderful friend."

Consumed by the emotions of the moment, neither Anne nor Devin realized they were being examined by a scrawny blond man who merely watched yet said nothing.

It took a few moments for Anne to notice Lindsey's presence; she wasn't sure if it was the stillness of the air around them or the weight of the young man's gaze that brought her out of her feelings, but she suddenly looked up, and there he was. She smiled and waved him over.

"Devin, I would like you to meet a fairly new friend of mine, Lindsey. Lindsey, this is my dear friend Devin." Then, with a knowing tilt of her head followed by a wink, she added, "He knows what you know."

Devin shook Lindsey's hand before whispering a question to Anne, "You told him you're a maid?"

She shrugged. "I didn't have to. He just knew, which I have to admit made me very nervous at first. However, when you joined *Survivor* and didn't notice, I figured if I could fool you, I could fool most anyone."

Lindsey beamed at his companions before handing a note to Anne. She took the note and read it to herself.

My Lady:

I know you will not be spending this holy season at the home of your family, but it is unwise for you to spend it completely alone. Therefore, allow me to be at your disposal at this time. I will do whatever it is you ask, and I am fully prepared to pay for your residence as well as stay outside your door for protection. Just name the place, and I will follow.

Yours,

~ Lindsey

Anne shook her head and smiled. "Lindsey, this is not necessary. I swear I'll be fine. I'm quite looking forward to being alone. I haven't been myself for some time now, you know. Besides, where did you get money? Oh, never mind it doesn't matter." She shrugged it off, smiling.

Devin gently took the note from Anne and read it. Lindsey began writing feverishly, and while he was preoccupied, Devin gave him an odd glance before turning to Anne. He whispered, "Do you trust this fellow, Annie?"

"Yes, of course. Well, I have only met him once before, but if he truly wished to ruin me, you would think he would have done so by now," she whispered back.

"Well, perhaps you should take him up on his offer. I am a bit worried about you staying on your own, and he already knows who you really are. He seems harmless, and you say you trust him."

Anne rolled her eyes. "Devin, this is not an issue of trust. I simply wish to be left alone."

"Well, I, for one, would be more comfortable with your staying with this Lindsey chap. I know you don't want me to check up on you every day we are in town, but I will if you don't do something to protect yourself." Devin crossed his arms before his chest. "Think of it this way: If I visit every day, people will get suspicious of my rather strange behavior, and it will soon come to light with whom I am visiting."

Anne was thinking about the picture Devin had painted before her when Lindsey handed her a new note.

My Lady, you must listen to me; a woman alone is most vulnerable. I cannot, in all good conscience, allow you to simply cast off my offer. And if you refuse to change your mind, I will simply follow you around town and find a way to sleep at your door. Please, I beg you to come to reason.

Anne read the note, and Devin did so as well, just over her shoulder. "He makes a good argument, Annie."

"Of course you would think so, but what of him? Surely, he has someone else with whom he should be spending the holiday?"

Lindsey shook his head vigorously.

"Well, it would appear he does not." Devin smiled devilishly.

Looking from one to the other, Anne realized she was involved in a losing battle. It was apparent Lindsey would not back down and Devin would agree with her muted friend until she gave in. So there was only one thing to do.

"Fine. Fine. I will accept your offer but with a few minor changes." Lindsey nodded enthusiastically. "First of all, we shall share a room." When Lindsey shook his head violently, Anne told him it was her way or not at all. Then she went on with her contingencies. "We will share a room as well as the price of the room. I will not have you spending the full amount, then sleeping on the floor outside my door. It isn't right. Second, you will have to allow me some privacy from time to time. I have spent far too many months surrounded by others and look forward to some quiet time. And third, you must refrain from treating me like a lady when we are out in public."

Lindsey did not seem to care for the rules she had set forth, but when Devin told him he would get no better offer, he reconsidered.

"Smart man. I know stalking her seems the better way to go, especially if you are intent on having your way. But she truly is hard-hearted and would most likely have you arrested for harassment."

Anne scoffed, "I wouldn't dare!"

"Of course you would," Devin smiled, "Like you said, it's your way or not at all." Devin then grabbed her bag and continued his way up to the street.

Orianna was working diligently on her letters to their subjects. Although she often complained about the task, she actually liked doing it. She loved it when people genuinely wanted to know her opinion, and then there were always the return letters from children (which were far too few) that made her smile.

She once received a letter from a little darling by the name of Tamah. The sweet girl was so sad to find that Orianna's brother was a prince because she just knew a princess must marry a prince. She had written to say she could not imagine the despair Orianna must be feeling at the prospect of having to marry her brother, especially since she had three brothers and wasn't particularly fond of any of them. Orianna had laughed so hard that she could not finish her letters that day. Instead, she called for her carriage and went out to set the saddened six-year-old straight.

Ah, she supposed it wasn't the task she minded; it was the sheer multitude. She used to do her letters for an hour or two each day; however, these days, she could only manage to get to them every other day. The rest of her time she spent seeing to Nolan's duties: overseeing tournaments, going over their soldiers' evaluations with her father, etc. Then there were the usual boring teas, long talks with advisors, and making a royal appearance wherever her parents chose not to appear.

"There," she said as she signed and sealed the final letter. "Well, it only took me a little over four hours. I suppose it could have been worse."

"And yet it still can be."

Orianna jumped at the sound of the male voice coming from behind her. Angered that she had nearly fallen out of her chair, she turned to scowl at the intruder.

"Ehh, sis! You know, if you're not careful, you may get stuck with that horrible look on your face." Nolan strolled lazily over to her before producing a letter from his inner coat pocket.

"You're certainly home early." She snatched the letter from his hand. "Homesick?"

Nolan lazily tossed himself on a nearby chaise and placed an arm over his weary eyes before mumbling, "Don't be ridiculous."

Orianna gave Nolan a reproachful glance before opening her final letter. She couldn't believe he was already home. But though she was annoyed, she was also grateful to have the holiday preparations completed. If he showed little interest, which was likely, he would not notice the magnitude of the event until the guests arrived. By then, it would be too late for him to pull out of the festivities without disgracing the crown. She smiled as she began to read her letter, and before she knew what was happening, her grin widened.

It appeared the men she sent in search of Mademoiselle Solène of Île-de-L'est's friend, Samara, had found her. She was still on the island of Île-de-L'est but no longer working for the royal family of D'Ecart. She was now working as a nanny for an influential family. Not wanting to peak Nolan's curiosity, Orianna gave a little sigh and lazily wrote a response to the naval officer who had sent her the letter. She was quite sure the de Rangers would make an appearance at the Christmas Eve festivities, so now she merely needed Samara to join them. Therefore, she asked the officer to extend the invitation to the nanny—and to ensure she did not refuse.

"Finally, the last one," Orianna commented, more for Nolan's benefit than her own. "Well, there is always more to be done, so if you would excuse me . . ." She made her way out of the room, correspondence in hand.

Nolan looked up for a moment, rolled his eyes, and returned to his previous position.

The Whispering Willow was a rather nice building and not at all like the other lodges in the area. It boasted a wraparound porch and a large entryway with a chandelier and elegant molding. The rooms were also larger than most, or so Anne had heard from the other guests. The dining area looked nothing like a bar; although it had a small one at the furthest end, by the back door. The entire inn was decorated with the holiday in mind, so it was warm, cozy, and smelled delightfully like cinnamon and cloves.

Anne and Lindsey had been lucky enough to obtain a room with two beds and its own bath. It was quite a bit more than Anne could have paid by herself, but with Lindsey covering half the price, she could cover meals and have a little extra money left over—just enough, she presumed, to make herself presentable for Sunday morning service at St. Ursula's. Well, not enough to be allowed to sit, but she could stand with the commoners in the back. Although she was not usually fond of attending service at the very opulent cathedral, she had to admit they had the most wonderful choir during the holidays. And it just wasn't Christmas without a trip to St. Ursula's.

Anne closed her financial book and went out to find a dress for the event. Lindsey told her he would be out for the rest of the afternoon because he had been delivering holiday packages for money, and as Christmas neared, he would spend more and more time away, which was perfectly fine with Anne. It allowed her time to finish her Christmas cards, wrap her father's birthday gift, and mend some of her clothes—and all the while, her hair would be down and her breasts unbounded. She sighed to herself as she thought how wonderful it would be to feel like a lady again. Ahhh . . . but until then, it was back to her masculine wears.

Anne rose from the tiny desk near the window and braided her hair. Slightly saddened by the act, she wondered how much longer she intended to live her life this way. Although she knew her parents would accept her back, she could not return to them now. She had tasted freedom. And to return to the old life was simply out of the question. Then she thought of Doran. If he knew who she really was, what would he do? She wasn't foolish enough to think he would marry her on the spot, but if he did, then what of her? She would not sit at some home for months on end, waiting for him to return.

But working on a merchant ship was getting to her. She cared even less for the profession of a merchant's wife. She feared she would always be lonely and would always wonder how he was fairing.

No, she thought, *not at all the life for me.* She would just have to go on as she had and wait for something—anything—to happen.

Once her hair lay like a thick rope on her back, she rebound her breasts and left for the marketplace. Perhaps a little fresh air would do her some good.

Laveda couldn't believe she would be attending a ball at the palace! How marvelous! To think, last Christmas she and Sophie had shared a hard loaf of bread and a cookie, and this year, they would share a feast meant for royalty. She could barely believe this was real!

Reyna was taking them—Ethana, Sophie, and herself—to the marketplace for dresses. She said there simply wasn't time to have Cipriana design and make four dresses for such a grand event.

The excitement radiating from every inch of Laveda was electric and lent to the excitement the rest of them felt inside the carriage. Never before had she been so happy to attend anything. She wondered if Ethana still got giddy over the prospect, but then, remembering how Ethana said Anne had begun to dread them as her eighteenth summer drew near, Laveda wondered if it caused the younger de Ranger girl's excitement to dwindle. Laveda could very well understand Anne's despair, suddenly being forced to be more proper, to be quiet, to keep her views to herself, and to dance with every eligible boy there. From what Laveda had heard of Lady de Ranger, she could imagine how suffocated she must have felt.

"Well, here we are," Reyna said, as their carriage slowed to a halt.

They had arrived before the most popular boutique in the marketplace. Laveda was both ecstatic and nervous about this shopping trip, and her exuberance brought a smile to Henry's lips as he opened the carriage doors, allowing the ladies to exit. Reyna and Ethana slid out with ease; then Henry's father, George, with Laveda's assistance, lifted Sophie and carried her inside. Laveda noticed the sweet smile covering Henry's face and made an inquiry.

"Find something humorous?"

It was the first time she had spoken to him since the afternoon she had helped rake leaves in the garden. She didn't know that he had made sure their paths had not crossed.

"No, not at all." He smiled at her with his whole heart.

Beneath his smile, Laveda felt warm, despite the blistering wind that wound around them. The mere tenderness of his gaze added a lovely shade of coral to her cheeks, and her heart beat ferociously.

"Laveda, my dear, please hurry," Reyna's voice knocked her back into the present.

"Yes, of course," Laveda called back. "Excuse me." She nodded to Henry before taking her leave.

George watched the young girl disappear into the warmth of the boutique as he held open the door for her. He also noticed his son did the same but with a noticeable twinkle in his eyes. "Watch yourself, my boy," George warned his son as he joined him by the carriage.

"What do you mean?"

"You know precisely what I'm talking about. Henry, she is a nice girl, but she is also not meant for you. So don't go about mucking things up, you hear?"

Henry kicked the ground as though it had uttered the words he had not wanted to hear, then he answered his father: "Of course not."

Anne missed shopping with her mother and sister. Even though she wasn't fond of the *idea* of shopping, it had been nice to go out, just the three of them, and spend time together. It really had been the only form of female bonding they practiced because, most of the time, Anne had been more interested in her father's affairs.

Mmm, funny how things in our lives develop. Anne never believed the day would come when she would long for the company of her mother and sister over that of her father. In fact, she missed Ethana so much at that very moment; she thought she could hear her voice in her head.

Wait!

Anne slowly turned toward the familiar ring, and to her surprise, Ethana stood a mere five paces from her. Startled, Anne quickly stashed herself behind a tower of hat boxes.

"Mother, look here. Would this not be a wonderful color on Sophie?" Ethana asked as she lifted the edge of a beautiful marigold-colored fabric. "Oh, it would be lovely with gold threading and that crystal pin we saw as we walked in."

"I think you're right, Ethana. It would look lovely with Sophie's complexion. . . . What do you think, dear Sophie?"

Anne looked on curiously as a young girl sitting rather awkwardly in a nearby chair nodded in agreement.

"Yes, it's beautiful, but do you think I would be allowed to wear such a prominent color?"

"Prominent? Yellow? Oh, Sophie, no."

Laveda agreed with her little sister. "But Baroness, surely it is almost gold." Anne knew Laveda had come to live with her family after the incident at Swinfen's, but it was still shocking to see Laveda not only with her family but also looking very much like a proper lady.

"And so what if it is?" Anne's mother rebuked. "It's not as though you're peasants—you're actually related to the royal family!"

That last comment caused Anne to nearly topple over. Surely, Laveda had not fed her family a fistful of lies! She leaned forward to better hear them all.

"That is not yet confirmed." Laveda seemed to be choosing her words carefully. "Sophie and I have no proof of our parentage, so why should the royal family believe us? No. I would much rather have Sophie in a less prominent color. Please excuse me, but I cannot have us walking around as though we are demanding our *supposed* birthright be recognized."

Anne watched her sister's response. Ethana frowned, and Anne knew that look. She thought Laveda was clearly upset, and as their mother was about to press the issue further, Ethana placed a hand on Mother's shoulder, as if to say, *Mother, please let it be.* Then Ethana moved toward Laveda and hugged her. "It's okay. There are plenty of lovely dresses here. I am sure we can find something to everyone's liking."

Laveda, a little teary-eyed, hugged Ethana in return. Anne's heart ached with a bit of envy.

Then Laveda turned to Mother and, in a hushed voice so low Anne had to strain to hear her, said, "I'm sorry, Reyna. Please understand it was only a few months ago that Sophie and I were living off of crumbs and wearing rags. Now, you're all telling us we are related to the royal family and that our parents were a part of some tragic love story. It's still difficult to believe after so many years of suffering."

To that, Anne's mom smiled and nodded her understanding before holding up a lovely green frock. "I'm sure Sophie will look just as lovely in this . . . if not more so."

Anne sat breathless as she watched the ladies resume their shopping. She wondered who Laveda's parents were and why the four of them were in such a tizzy over finding the perfect dresses.

Her answer came when a young girl approached Anne, exclaiming how she couldn't believe the royal family had invited nearly everyone in town for a holiday ball. "How wonderful it will be." With a wink, the girl added, "I hope to dance with the prince!"

Anne smiled and got back to her perusal of the older, lower-end dresses, now making sure she avoided the de Ranger party to the best of her ability while in the tiny shop.

A few minutes later, Anne watched Ethana held up a beautiful silver gown that sparkled brilliantly as she stood looking in a mirror, her mother's face appearing just above her right shoulder. "It's beautiful, my dear."

"Yes," Ethana said as she placed the dress back on the rack from where she had found it. "However, I'm afraid it was made for the one who is no longer with us."

Anne thought her sister's voice seemed a bit sad.

"Yes, it would have accented Anne's eyes beautifully." Her mother warmly stroked her hair. "Come now. We must find you something."

Anne waited for them to move to another section of the boutique before turning to look at the dress. It was exquisite. Ethana always had such wonderful taste. The gown was classic in its make: floor length, with cap sleeves, and a heart-shaped bodice. However, it also had a hint of sassiness—a "come hither" look—in a sort of naughty way that screamed her name. However, what did not scream *Anne* was the price tag. The dress was more than three times the amount she had to spend. She sighed and decided on a much simpler dress, one more in line with her purse. Besides, there was no need for such a dress if she intended to avoid attention. She smiled to herself. Even if she hadn't left home, she wouldn't wear such a dress to church, lest she was prepared to confess *something*.

Chapter Twenty-One

Snowflakes on Noses and Warm Winter Wassail

*A*s Christmas day drew closer, Anne had to admit she was feeling a little lonely. Everyone in the market was either shopping for gifts or buying ingredients for a special holiday feast. There were carolers gracing the entryways of stores and homes, hoping to not only entertain but to sing their way into a warm cup of tea, cocoa, or the highest prize of all: wassail. Each day she ventured outdoors, she was enveloped in the warmth of holiday cheer, only to return to her quarters at the end of the day, which were devoid of any such merriment. So today, she decided to sit on the porch until the cold threatened to freeze her bottom to her chair.

Now and then, the lady of the inn would bring her a complimentary cup of tea and warn her she was going to catch her death. Anne tried to pay her the first time she brought the tea, but when she went for her purse, the lady simply shooed her, saying she'd rather have the rent, and if *he* died, she would have to scale back Christmas dinner. Anne had laughed, but she knew, despite her words, the older woman was actually bringing her tea simply to be nice.

Anne wasn't sure how long she had been outside when Devin arrived, but it had to have been at least two hours since the sun was beginning to touch the neighboring rooftops.

"Ahh, someone tell you I was on my way?" Devin dismounted and one of the stable boys came to care for his horse.

"No. I've just been getting a breath of fresh air."

Devin looked at her skeptically. "Fresh air? You must be having a laugh. It's so cold out here, your lungs are more than likely cursing you for introducing icicles to your insides."

Anne laughed. Then, noticing Devin was quite cold himself, she grabbed her teacup and saucer and made her way inside.

Even though it was nearly time for supper, there were few people in the den area since everyone was out on the town doing whatever they needed to do to prepare themselves for Christmas day; therefore, it was not difficult to find a place to sit.

"So, how have you been, my friend?"

Devin hung his coat before coming to sit next to Anne. "Busy. I'm sorry I haven't made it here sooner, but I had no idea I would be preparing to attend a royal ball."

"Mmm, yes, I've heard the royal family has invited nearly everyone in town, as well as almost every influential family just outside the city," Anne said.

"Yes, well, it's quite annoying if you ask me."

Devin never did like balls. He hated dancing and small talk even though, if Anne's memory served her correctly, he was quite good at both. "Why is it so annoying? You will be enjoying some of the best food ever created, be introduced to all sorts of interesting people, and have the opportunity to dance with no less than a dozen swooning ladies."

"Okay, I'll give you the food, but the talking to arrogantly pretentious people and dancing with silly, empty-minded girls is not my idea of a good time."

Just then, a serving girl joined them. Devin ordered a whiskey for himself and a hot apple cider for Anne. A little annoyed that he hadn't asked if she would have liked a whiskey as well, Anne gave him a rather hard look.

The glare, though quick and short, did not miss Devin's notice. "Don't look at me like that," he whispered. "Just because others don't know what you are does not mean I am going to treat you as though you are what you would have them believe."

Anne rolled her eyes. "Devin, why have you come if you were going to be in such a retched mood?"

To that, the young man sighed—a full-body, spirit-cleansing sigh. "I'm sorry, it's just nothing has gone the way I had hoped since being home. I have not worked on my travel guide for Hampton, nor have I had a chance to visit you, and I feel all I have been doing is wasting my time on completely meaningless frivolity!"

"You know, Devin, a ball isn't completely worthless. You can make some helpful connections—perhaps find a publisher for your book?"

Devin wasn't convinced. "Well, if you think it's so great, why not take my place?"

"Ha! Now you're having a laugh. You know I can't show my face around a place like that."

Just then, the serving girl arrived with their drinks. Anne and Devin enjoyed their libations in virtual silence, Anne somewhat reflective and Devin somewhat sulky. Although Devin was not in the best mood, Anne was glad to have him around. It was nice speaking to someone who truly knew her.

Taking another sip of cider, Anne glanced up to peer out the window, and much to her surprise and sheer delight, she noticed it was snowing. She loved the snow.

"Oh, Devin, look!"

Her companion looked out the window and scowled. "Great. Can this holiday season get any worse?" He then raised his glass to his lips to take another sip of whiskey.

Anne smiled. She had never seen this side of Devin before and liked it. She had often wondered how he could always be so steady, so mild and even-keeled. But now, here he was: irritable, grouchy, and marvelously ghastly.

"What are you smiling at?"

Anne leaned toward her friend. "I could just kiss you, you know?" Then she stood up and strolled over to the window to get a better look at the frozen confetti fluttering down from the heavens.

Devin sat dumbfounded for several heartbeats before joining her by the looking glass. "What did you mean by that?"

"Mmm?" Anne turned toward him and upon seeing the shock sitting squarely on his face, she knew immediately what he was asking. "Oh, the kiss thing. I merely meant that I like seeing you so horribly unsettled. You have to be the most composed person I have ever met, and to be honest, I was beginning to wonder if you could even get riled up at all."

"Hmm." His eyes were trained on her while hers were on the snow. "You don't consider our disagreements aboard *Survivor* to count?"

Anne smiled. "Ah, you're right. I had not considered our time on *Survivor.* Perhaps I simply do not care to be the object of your displeasure." Then, bringing her brows together, she said, "Devin, is it just me, or is the snow coming down rather quickly?"

Devin turned his attention to the window to find, to his greater displeasure, the snow rocketing down in a fury. Soon, the roads would be much too treacherous for travel. "Devils! I should retire."

Devin walked across the room to place his glass upon a side table before reaching for his coat. Anne turned her back on her rapidly forming wintery landscape to stand near her friend. She was sorry to see him go so soon, but knew, for him, it was now or never.

As Anne and Devin walked out of the den, he handed her enough money to pay for their drinks before they made their way to the front door. However, before they could open it, Lindsey was blown inside by a gust of unforgiving wind. The poor soul looked frozen, both inside and out, and his usually cheery face was drawn, chapped, and extremely red. It took some time for him to notice that Anne and Devin were watching him thaw, but when he did, he seemed fairly ecstatic.

Devin patted Lindsey on the back as he pulled away from his embrace, but in freeing himself, he made Anne his next victim.

Anne smiled, "Okay, Lindsey, that's quite enough." She, too, pulled away.

"Well," Devin began, "it was good to see you both, but I really should be on my way."

To that Lindsey disagreed. He quickly threw himself before the door and wildly rummaged through his clothes for his notepad.

"Lindsey, I really haven't the time for this." Devin tried to move his wiry companion.

Lindsey, however, did not budge. Instead, he wrote feverishly with blue fingers. Anne wondered how he could write at all since it looked as though each digit might snap off like bony, ice-finger twigs on a frozen tree.

He passed the note to Devin.

Exasperated and more than slightly annoyed, Devin read the note aloud. "Mustn't go. Roads too bad. Visibility non-existent." Devin smiled as he folded the note and gave Lindsey a firm pat on the back. "Thank you for the warning, my friend, but I really must be on my way."

"I'm not so sure about that, Devin. Please take a look." Anne had gone to the window as Devin read Lindsey's note, and it did seem quite dreadful out. The snow was coming in angry swirls and though it was now dark, the lampposts were not lit.

Devin joined Anne by the window and sighed, "You have got to be kidding me."

"Afraid not, young man," the lady of the inn had joined them. "My husband has just come in and says we may be in for a rather rough night. He believes everyone will be staying where they are until morning."

Anne turned toward the woman. She knew this was sure to hurt her business since they counted on everyone lodging there to be eating there as well.

"Unfortunately," the lady continued, "I haven't a room to offer to ya." She was speaking directly to Devin.

"If you don't mind, my lady, Mr. Levenax can lodge with us for the night, and I shall compensate you whatever you deem worthy of his stay." Anne felt the woman would not mind the extra person in her room, but just in case she did, the money would help to soften her displeasure.

"Such a sweet boy you are, but that won't be necessary. What sort of person would I be if I made you pay for your discomfort?" Then, running her hands down her apron, she continued, "Supper will be ready soon. We are having a hearty venison stew, country loaf, and a warm minced pie."

Since Devin was too shocked to speak, and Lindsey never spoke, Anne muttered a simple, "That sounds delightful," before returning to the den. Lindsey and Devin followed her.

Once inside, she wandered to the window as if in a daze. It was as though something was calling to her, something from deep within, and something she could not ignore. So there she stood without a word, watching the whirling snow in deep thoughtless contemplation until she was called away to supper.

Nolan loved the snow. The peace it brought him was unimaginable. He sat by the grand window of the library, his book dejected on a nearby table next to a wassail-less goblet, and he watched in enlightened quiet. He wasn't thinking of anything at all, but for some reason he was happy. So happy that the feeling welled up within him and expressed itself across his handsome face. What drew him to the window was more than the dancing snow; it was like a pull from within, drawing him closer. He knew not exactly what it was, nor did he care. He just knew he didn't want to leave until the snow had stopped. However, that was not to be.

"What happy thought has caressed your sweet face, my son?"

Reluctantly, Nolan turned to meet his mother's gaze.

"I've not seen you thus since you were a boy. Surely, a simple sprinkling from Heaven hasn't made you smile so."

Nolan had no desire to speak with his mother, but it was not possible to *shoo away* the queen. It wasn't that he did not love her; he just felt this moment was sacred, somehow, and he didn't want anyone to ruin it. "The first snow is always special, Mother."

The queen sat across from her son and glanced out the window. The raging swirls had calmed, and the wind was making the glittering flakes dance to and fro. The view was spectacular and looked soft and hazy, like a dream.

She glanced at Nolan and smiled. "You could be a great king one day. I just wish you could see it. But there is something missing, my son. Something akin to courage. . . . No, that's not it."

There goes my peace. But Nolan knew what his mother meant. He even knew what it was. He lacked faith in himself. In the past, he had taken command of the troops, but the thought of running an entire country frightened him. Why? He hadn't any idea, but Nolan knew his mother hoped he would find what he needed before it was too late.

He felt his mother's eyes upon him, and they burned like flames to ice. He dared not meet her gaze because he didn't want to get into a row. He always knew what his parents thought: *Why won't he be the prince we know he could be?*

What they didn't know, and could not seem to understand, was he did not have it in him. He couldn't run a country; there were just too many aspects, too many things to consider. Orianna was better with details—her memory nearly flawless—and she, despite her grumbling, wanted it. Oh, how he wished she would marry so he could be free to abdicate with little to no fuss. *Ha. No fuss!* Who was he kidding? His parents would have a royal fit, but what could they do?

"My dear," his mother began, "I know what you're thinking, and it will not work. Orianna is wonderful, but she would rule through her feelings. And can you imagine how much the people would suffer if the stitching in her ball gown wasn't quite right?"

To that Nolan could do nothing less than throw his head back and roar with laughter. His mother, on the other hand, brought a delicate finger to her lips and released a royally modest giggle.

Chapter Twenty-Two

The Invitation

Though they had stayed up late dancing, singing, and carrying on, Anne and her friends were up before daybreak. Devin wanted to make sure he would arrive home in time for breakfast, and Lindsey had to revive his role as Santa to ensure last minute Christmas deliveries found their way into designated naughty-free hands. Unfortunately for Anne, their departures left her alone—again.

Not knowing what to do, she assisted the lady of the inn with her chores, cleaned her quarters, and devised a plan to go to church the next morning, as well as planned a brief visit to Indira. Before returning to Ryland, she had decided to stay away, but being back now, and with Christmas around the corner, she was feeling a little nostalgic. So, after deciding to go home while the family was at the church, she'd completed her tasks for the day. With nothing left to do, she paced around and fretted. If she were to spend the holiday with her family, it would mean the end of something greater. She couldn't imagine leaving the ship.

The ship, she sighed. Whenever she thought of the *Survivor,* an image of her captain haunted Anne's mind, making a muddle of her brain. She spent many nights awake, wondering what he was doing and who he was with. No one seemed to know where he was staying or anything about his family and not knowing was driving her insane. She had to do something. She had to get out.

Grabbing her jacket and the scarf left behind by Devin, Anne barred herself against the bitter cold and made her way to the market.

Nolan had stayed up late, speaking with his mother. He had always known his parents wanted him to rule, but he didn't know they knew he was scared. The thought of making decisions for so many people and having to contemplate the future of the entire country truly frightened him. His mother told him he was not the only one to have those feelings, and it was those worries that would make him great. She said worrying in the manner he was would ensure he reviewed all options before deciding anything. Nolan had not thought of this argument before, and it had kept him up for most of the night. Even when his body finally collapsed with exhaustion, his mind continued working. Therefore, when he rose with the sun, he felt as though he had never slept.

Despite his lack of energy, Nolan rolled out of bed and began his day. His valet had already drawn his bath before leaving to make ready his clothes. Nolan was always amazed by Gilmore. He possessed a great intuition concerning what Nolan needed. For instance, the prince never took his bath in the morning because bathing helped to soothe and relax. Nolan felt the morning should start with something invigorating, like a brisk walk about the grounds. Today, however, this bath was welcomed and surprisingly enough, desired.

Nolan lowered himself into the copper, claw-footed tub and marveled at how wonderful the water's warmth did just as he thought it would: relax him. He closed his eyes, and for a moment, he thought he would sleep, really sleep, but there was something he was forgetting. Something was nagging him in the back of his mind. *What is it?* Then it hit him, "Gilmore!"

Nolan shot out of the tub, and his valet was there in an instant with a towel. "No. Don't worry about me, please. Gilmore, I need a carriage right away."

"Your Highness, the carriage is already waiting for you," the older gentleman replied as he strolled over to retrieve the prince's robe.

Nolan was dumbfounded. Gilmore was always one step ahead; it was as if he were a seer of some sort. "Gilmore," Nolan began as he shrugged into his robe, "what does my father pay you?"

"His Majesty the King is very generous, Your Highness."

Nolan smiled as the gentleman left the bathing room to sharpen a blade for his shave. Nolan sat before the mirror in his apartment and waited for Gilmore to begin. "Well, my friend, whatever your wage, I am going to make sure my father doubles it."

It was freezing out, but Anne dared not return to the inn. She could not tolerate being by herself right now and wondered why she had opted to stay in an inn so far removed from her shipmates. Surely, they were having a bit of fun. But then she thought of all the time she had spent over the last week with her hair down and her breasts free from restraint, how often she awakened without fear of being discovered. It truly was the best gift she could have given herself.

She really did miss being a maid. She missed the pampering, the clothes, the flirting. She smiled to herself as she wondered if Doran would respond to her subtle glances and innuendos, or perhaps her teasing smiles, were she to show up in front of him as herself.

His lips . . . oh, he had beautiful lips. She wondered how they would feel upon hers, and suddenly, she was no longer cold. Her lips tingled, her heart raced, and her hands, though chapped by the bitter cold, began to sweat.

"Sir," a man said, frightening her back to the present.

Anne nearly lost her tongue when she realized she had just been approached by a royal footman—regal and dressed in the traditional royal blue breeches and coat. "Yes. May I help you?"

The man bowed his head and lifted an envelope in a gesture suggesting she should receive it. Glancing left and right, not knowing quite what to do, Anne finally obtained the letter from his hand. However, she did not open it.

"It would please the crown," the boy began again, "if you would attend the upcoming ball."

"Ball? No. I mean, are you sure you have the right person?"

"You are Andrew Pallas, are you not?"

Well, Anne could not deny that this man had found the correct person, but Andrew was not acquainted with anyone at the palace, not even the lowliest of servants. "Yes. I am Andrew Pallas. Though, may I ask to whom I owe this invitation?"

"Ask all you might, but I am not at liberty to say. I was merely told to give you the invite and to inform you to dress your best." He clicked his heels together.

Dress her best! *Dearest Lord, help me.* She had not thought of this situation, but before she could decline the invitation based on her current financial reality, the footman had read her mind and begun to speak. "The envelope should contain sufficient funds for you to attain the proper attire." Again, he clicked his heels.

"Well, I suppose I can find no reason to stay away. Please inform your mistress or master I accept the invitation and look forward to our meeting."

They both bowed before the younger man took his leave.

Nolan watched from his carriage as his footman addressed Andrew. He had been looking for a gift for Orianna when his carriage passed the boy near the bakery. Since Andrew seemed so out of sorts at the time, Nolan just had to invite him to the Christmas ball, did he not? Oh, who was he kidding? He would have invited him, anyway. He had already thought about sending an invitation to the Whispering Willows Inn but had decided against it. He supposed it was improper for him to invite Andrew and not the rest of the crew, but then again, it wasn't as ship's captain that he was inviting the young man. But as a friend. At any rate, it was lucky for him that Orianna had left extra invitations with his driver.

"He has accepted the invitation, Your Highness," the footman said when he returned.

"Wonderful. Did you tell him in what manner to dress?"

Without eye contact, the footman said he had told Andrew all the prince had wished him to know.

"Excellent. Well, then, I suppose we are off to the jeweler. Mustn't forget a gift for the princess."

Anne watched as the royal footman returned to the royal carriage, briefly spoke with the royal inside before going on his royal way. She wasn't quite sure whose carriage it was, exactly. Of course, the royal family had many, but everyone had their favorites. For example, the princess was always seen in a luxurious carriage drawn by four white horses. This carriage, on the other hand, was not so grand. It was still magnificent, and surely designed for the royal family, but it lacked the ostentatious detail of the princess's. It was a black Clarence-style carriage with the royal emblem on the side and gold toppers at the four corners of the roof. She'd barely caught a glimpse of the inside, which had silver and royal blue curtains with silver and gold tassels. It was beautiful.

Errr! What was she going to do? She turned the invitation over in her hand. She could not decline, but she equally could not go. What if her family recognized her? No, worse . . . what if they revealed her before Doran? He said he was a friend of the royal family, so surely he would be in attendance. Oh, what was she to do?

Just then, Lindsey exited the bakery with a small brown bag. He smiled when he saw her, and she was just as happy to see him. Perhaps he could help her work out this awful dilemma.

"How was your shopping venture, Your Highness?" Gilmore asked upon Nolan's return.

"Excellent, Gilmore, just excellent. The packages shall be coming up soon, and I would appreciate your making sure they are properly dressed for the holiday."

Hanging Nolan's coat as he spoke, Gilmore assured the prince he would see it done and notified him his family awaited his presence in the library for tea. Not wishing to make them wait any longer, Nolan made his way to the library at once.

"Good afternoon, family!" Nolan gave everyone in the room one of his winning smiles.

"Wonderful! The court jester has arrived. Have fun avoiding your duties today, brother?"

The king and queen rolled their eyes. He figured with their reaction that Orianna had become a huge nuisance. She likely had little nice to say about Nolan, whether he was around or not, and she was probably bemoaning the harsh role the Fates had dealt her.

"Actually, dear sister, I was seeing to some of my holiday duties, and . . . unless you're nice, you'll never know what it is I have done." He strolled over to his mother to kiss her upon the cheek, sent his father a nod, then turned back to Orianna. "Oh, yes, before I forget, I invited a friend to the ball. Do you think it will be any trouble to add an extra place at the table?"

"Add an extra place?" Orianna feigned real annoyance.

Nolan sat in the open armchair next to his sister and across from his mother before responding. "Oh, come on, sis, don't make me beg. I know the ball is tomorrow, but surely something can be done. Besides, it is Christmas—have a heart."

It was Orianna's turn to roll her eyes. "Fine. Since it's Christmas. So what's her name?" Orianna had pen and notebook ready.

"*His* name is Andrew Pallas." Nolan accepted a teacup from the serving girl.

"Ah, of the Southerings? They are a good family, indeed. How did you come upon them without invitation?"

Nolan took a lazy sip of his tea before answering. "To be honest, I'm not sure from where his family stems. I merely know he is a delightful gentleman whom I would like you to meet." Another sip of tea.

To this comment, the king smiled at the queen, and Orianna blanched.

"You've invited someone for me?" She couldn't believe he had done this to her. She should deny the gentleman entrance based on this fact alone.

"No, Orianna, I didn't ask him to come over and marry my too serious, overbearing, vindictive younger sister. I do like the man, and even if I didn't, it's Christmas; a lump of coal would have sufficed."

Orianna's face was red with anger, and she wasn't breathing. "You think that's funny? Do you honestly believe I will make an acceptation for your friend now, brother?"

Trying not to laugh, Nolan apologized. "I'm sorry, Orianna. I simply wanted to have a friend over for the holidays. And to be honest, I know you will like him."

"Oh, really?"

"Yes. He is a decent gentleman with an outstanding moral fiber—"

"Oh," Orianna was standing, "and *you* would know all about outstanding moral fiber!"

Unperturbed by Orianna's apparent anger, Nolan continued to sip his tea. "I must say, I have learned a thing or two over the past several months. Some, of which, have proven you right on several counts. You see, Andrew shares your views on many issues and has shamed me more than once without intending to do so." He then leaned forward to grab a tea biscuit from the table. "This alone should be enough to recommend him to you."

Orianna didn't know what to say, so she looked to her parents for some advice. However, neither had anything to convey; her mother shrugged her shoulders, and her father was smiling at his son. She simply couldn't win when her opponent was as near perfection as Nolan.

"So you really believe I should go?" Anne was completely taken off-guard by Lindsey's advice; she had been sure he would say the opposite. But there they sat, in front of the bakery, eating sweet rolls, and trying to decide what she would do tomorrow.

"But what of my family? What if they notice me? What if . . ." she trailed off because Lindsey had handed her another note.

You MUST attend this ball, and you must go as your true self. It is time you were seen. You need to be seen.

"What do you mean, *I need to be seen*? And have you lost your mind? I cannot go as myself."

This is your destiny. You must see it through to the end, and if you're always hiding in the inn, nothing will happen for you.

"My destiny? Huh, you're having a laugh, right? I mean, you truly find this funny?"

When Lindsey shook his head emphatically and then looked at her with earnest, she acquiesced. "Okay, let's say I decide to go. Where will I get ready? How will I get there?" He handed her another note.

Hand me the money; tell me what you need and allow me to take care of the rest. Please trust me on this. You must go to the ball even if for a moment.

Anne thought about what Lindsey was suggesting and had to admit she did wish to go. It would be nice to be half of herself again, even if it were for a few moments—to laugh, to dance, to eat pheasant. This had been a very lonely holiday so far and perhaps being invited was a Christmas gift for her straight from Heaven . . . without Santa as the middleman. And if she were found out, perhaps she could just disappear again. She would merely need to make sure Doran did not discover her true identity.

"Okay. I'll go."

Chapter Twenty-Three

Indira

Anne rose with a smile just as the sun peeked over the horizon. It was Christmas Eve and time to get ready for church, so she rolled out of bed and strolled over to the clothing hutch in the room. Her smile widened as she gazed upon her silver dress, the one Ethana had chosen for her the other day at the boutique. She had given Lindsey all the money she had received and asked him to buy her the dress, a large snowflake comb made of silver and crystals, and a small bottle of gardenia- and honey-scented lotion. The rest she told him he could use for whatever he needed to do to help her. Oh, she couldn't wait to wear it, but for now, the modest olive dress she had purchased several days before would do.

Since Anne had taken her time to bathe and wash her hair the night before, she only had to get dressed and be on her way. Now, if only it were that easy. Tapping her index finger upon her lower lip as she thought, she decided the best way to get ready would be to wear her masculine clothes downstairs, dress in the stables, and then head to church. That way, no one would see a lady leaving her room, and it wasn't likely that anyone would be in the stables at this hour since most people would have left by now to claim a decent seat. So, not wanting to miss the choir, she quickly dressed, gently folded the olive frock and wrapped it in her coat, then finally made her way to the stables.

Just as she had thought, there was no one there. Anne picked a horseless stall and with the speed of lightning, removed her top and bindings and replaced them with her dress. She then unleashed her hair and tossed it about to give it some body. And finally, she packed her things into her bag next to her father's birthday gift. Since the church was nearly a mile off, she would have to hurry to be sure she got inside the church.

Although Anne was quite late when she arrived, she squeezed into the very back of the cathedral. The choir was already singing "Gloria in Excelsis Deo," and the sound was marvelous. St. Ursula's choir was recognized everywhere, and at Christmastime, people came from all over to hear them. Looking around, Anne noticed this year the crowd was rather lean compared to years past. *Hmm, must be the snow.* After that thought, she let go of all other thoughts and surrendered to the melodic tranquility that enveloped her.

"Gloria" gave way to "Ave Maria," then more from Father Gillies, and finally the Hallelujah Chorus: Anne's favorite. Chills ran through her and tears welled in her eyes, but there was something else.

She felt as though she were being watched, as if someone had recognized her. Panic and fear replaced her serenity, and she discreetly allowed her eyes to rove over the parishioners, trying to find the one who had broken her concentration. It didn't take long to find him. For within seconds, Anne's eyes locked with those of her father.

She could tell he wanted to get up and approach her, but he was too far in the middle to accomplish the task without gaining the interest of the worshippers. Seeing his agitation, Anne smiled at him, raised her right index finger to her lips, and then motioned for him to pay attention to the choir. At first, she wasn't sure that he'd turn back to the front, but the moment he did, she slipped back out the way she had come.

Back in the wintery chill, she made her way home to Indira. Since it was Christmas Eve, service would not end for another two hours, at least. It was just enough time to get there, drop off her father's gift, and head back to the inn without anyone being the wiser.

Thaniel knew he should not have taken his eyes off of Anne, but what was he to do? He couldn't stare at her for the next two hours. Thaniel bowed his head in grief; he dared not turn back around because he knew she was gone.

"Thaniel, dear, are you okay?"

Hearing Reyna's voice made Thaniel realize he needed to regain his composure and get through the service. Nothing would be gained by telling his wife he had just seen their runaway child, so he simply lifted her hand to his lips, kissed her fingers, and returned his attention to the choir.

Anne trudged through the snow for what seemed to be forever. She had never before realized their manor was such a great distance from the market, but the biting winter wind made her rethink her position. "Oh, come on, Anne, it just over the next hill," she spoke her encouragement aloud. "Just a few more minutes."

Anne never gave up and never took a break; she simply wanted to get there, so when she did finally arrive, she nearly cried. Deciding to go through the back door, which led to the kitchen because it was always the warmest room in the manor, she slipped inside and gladly greeted the warmth. As she suspected, the fire was going, and Verna had a pot on. *Soup!* she thought as she removed her shoes and laid them near the fire.

She knew she shouldn't stay long, but she needed to warm up, to rest—just for a little while. Anne stiffly moved toward a low wooden stool next to the butcher-block table. It was where Verna usually snapped beans and peeled potatoes and was the closest to the fire. Shrugging the chill off, Anne relaxed perhaps a bit too much, and upon her crossed arms she laid her head on the table. So relaxed was she that she didn't realize she was near sleep when someone's arm was swung around her throat.

"Who are you, and what are you doing here?"

The mind can be a little off sometimes. For the first thing Anne thought was, *Wow, Henry is much stronger than I ever would have imagined.*

"I asked you a question!" Henry's arm tightened.

Coughing now, Anne realized she should speak up else her parents find her dead upon their return. Therefore, in a strained voice, she tried her best to call off her assailant, "Henry," coughing and sputtering, "for Heaven's sake, let go."

Henry couldn't make out the entire sentence, but his name was rather unmistakable. He let go.

Anne grabbed her throat and turned around to see Henry close by and Verna behind him with a rolling pin just in front of her chest.

"Lady Philana!" the older lady screamed as she dropped her culinary weapon of choice and ran to give her a hug.

"Well, hello to you too." Anne embraced the lady with a smile and gave a wink to Henry.

"My Lady de Ranger," Henry bowed, "I . . . I'm sorry—I had no idea. If I had known I would—"

Anne cut him off by simply raising her hand. Then she also hugged him. "It's okay, Henry. I can imagine the start I must have given you both."

Having looked Anne up and down, Verna could not hide her shock over the girl's appearance. "Me, dare, gerl, what are ye wearin'? Shurely, ye've not com to bad ends?"

Anne laughed. "No, dear Verna, I am quite well. Granted, I've not much in the way of gold, but I've plenty enough to live in a happy manner."

"Happy? Are you happy, milady?"

Henry was always so formal, and his manner toward her reminded Anne, sadly, of the life she had left behind. Her new life, void of the all the propriety of the old, had made her more appreciative of the little things. She liked being treated like a lady and missed being recognized for who and what she was. Also, she felt familiarity was what she needed right now. Perhaps it was the holiday or having been away from home for so long, but she needed to be near people who knew her.

"Please, Henry, for today, call me Anne. And yes, I am happy." She smiled. "Of course, I do miss all of you, but otherwise I am well."

The rest of the time Anne was home, she had a meal, laughed with the staff, and learned more about Laveda and Sophie. She found it funny how she should know less of someone she had met first. The entire prospect of Laveda being the daughter of Llewellyn and Solène was amazing. Her life would then turn out to be one from which legends were made: ill-fated lovers, abandoned children, poverty, prostitution, salvation, and a triumphant ending. It was marvelous. Although, there was one area of concern: Oren.

Anne didn't like the fact that Oren was writing to Laveda regularly and had a feeling there was some sort of ulterior motive involved. His family seemed to be the worst sort of haughty royals; they looked down on anyone they deemed beneath them. Therefore, it was clear to Anne that the only reason for Oren's interest in Laveda was her connection to the House of D'Ecart, the Île-de-L'est royals. She also worried about what he would say or do when he found out where Laveda had lived and what she had been doing for the past three years. Whatever he did, she was sure it would not be good.

After a little more than a half-hour, Anne decided it was time to go. Her shoes were not completely dry, but they were warm, so she did not mind slipping them on. Verna had tried to talk her into staying, but Anne's persistence ultimately silenced her on the subject; although, as a consolation prize, she was permitted to *force* a basket of food upon her. Finally, after leaving her father's gift and offering more than a dozen hugs, she bundled for the cold with basket in hand. Anne was ready to go.

"Well, I suppose I should be on my way."

"How far ye goin'?"

"I shall be fine, Verna. I am only headed to the marketplace."

To that, Verna grabbed a jacket from a hook nearby and threw it at Henry. "Take her tu da market, boy."

"No," Anne quickly rebuked the idea, "that won't be necessary."

Henry knew why she wished to go alone, but he was not about to allow her to walk all the way back to the market in this weather. So, ignoring her, he placed on his coat, and retrieved his hat and gloves from the small mudroom just off the kitchen. Once he was ready to go, he returned to fetch Anne.

Duke Saben had a clear view of everyone who had attended church that day, and an especially good view of the young lady in which his son was interested.

She was quite pleasing to look at, but he did not care for the fact that she was on intimate terms with the de Rangers; he was sure that family would ruin her. He didn't believe they would speak ill of his family, but he was positive they would pass their abnormal ideas onto the poor girl. Something would need to be done to curb that from happening.

When the service ended, Saben stood with his family and began to make his way out of the cathedral when the perfect idea came to him. He would speak to the king. Telling his wife he would meet her at their carriage, he then headed for the front of the church as fast as he could; however, by the time he arrived, they were gone. Disappointed, Saben moved to rejoin his family but noticed the princess's carriage from the corner of his eye. Surely, he could convince her to have the girl removed from her current residence.

"Your Highness," Saben bowed just outside the princess's maroon and gold carriage, even as he thought about his niece's impressive style. Her carriage was a beautiful shade of the deepest red. There were images of Artemis in the woods on the doors and plenty of ornate detail in the finest gold along the top, upon the wheels, and on the dash.

"Duke Saben," Orianna greeted her guest in a petulant manner. It was bad enough she had to share her carriage with her brother, but to suffer another speech from Saben about his *captured* lands was more than she could bear. "Dear friend, I have told my father of your concerns; however, as the land you are now missing once belonged to Sagedor, he says he simply cannot find reason to renegotiate the treaty."

Maddened by this information but not wanting to show his anger to his niece, Saben brushed the topic aside and got on with his new order of business. "I am sure his Majesty, the King, did all that was in his power without causing undo harm to the fragile truce we share with our northern brethren. However, this is not the reason for which I have come."

Curious but wary, Orianna gave her father's half-brother her full attention. Prince Nolan, whom the Duke had not noticed sitting across from the princess, did the same, with the greatest amount of interest.

Seeing he now had Orianna's full attention, Saben continued. "I am sure you have heard that the children of Princess Solène and Sir Llewellyn are residing with the de Ranger family." When the princess nodded her awareness, he went on. "Well, the de Rangers are a respectable family, to be sure, but as the girls are of upper royalty, perhaps it would be best if they were hosted by . . . how shall I say . . . a more noble line?"

Nolan watched Orianna as she seemed to contemplate this rather absurd suggestion. Duke Saben, in Nolan's opinion, was the worst kind of elitist, and it appeared he felt the de Rangers, though noble, were not members of their exclusive group of peacocks. He could not tolerate such snobbery. "And how, do you propose, we should remove them from the de Ranger's hospitality without seeming . . . discourteous?"

Saben jumped at the sound of Nolan's voice; until then, he had not noticed the prince's presence. "Your Highness! I am sorry; I did not see you sitting back in the shadows."

Nolan, on the other hand, was quite pleased he had caught Saben off-guard. "Yes, well, I am sure it is easy to miss that which you are not seeking. So, now that we are all aware of who is present, perhaps we can get on with your request. As you have said, the de Rangers are a well-respected family—kind and honorable— and most people are quite fond of them. This being said, why should we rob their guests of such fine hospitality and the de Rangers of their treasured companions?"

Though Orianna had never approved of Nolan's evident favor for the de Rangers, she had to admit that he had a point. She could not see any way to take the girls from their home without seeming uncouth; there was simply no reason for it. In fact, the de Rangers, from what she had heard, should be commended for taking the girls in and caring for them as if they were their own children. Besides, she was still not completely convinced they were the lost heirs to the Île-de-L'estan throne.

"My dear friend," Orianna spoke up before Saben had the chance to give Nolan a reply. "I am afraid my brother is correct; there is little cause to have these ladies removed. Furthermore, their identities have not been wholly substantiated in my mind, and until we know with absolute certainty they are who they claim to be, I shall treat them with the same amount of courtesy I permit all others."

That was it. Saben had lost. "Yes, Your Highness. It was, after all, merely a suggestion." Saben nodded his defeat toward the prince and watched silently as the royal carriage pulled away from the cathedral. Seething inside, he knew he had to step up his plans, and from this point forward, he would further include the prince in his schemes.

Thanks to Henry, Anne had arrived back at the inn before church had even let out. Not wanting him to see where she was staying, she had him drop her off in the marketplace and then made her way down an ally too narrow for a carriage to follow. Although, if she really thought about it, she didn't think Henry would follow; he was always true to his word.

Before rushing into the inn, she made sure to change clothes in the stables. Then, running up the stairs, she decided she would pack her things to ready herself for the ball. Running through the mental list she had devised to keep herself organized, Anne knew exactly what she needed to do once she had closed her door behind her.

First on her list was her attire, so she grabbed the lovely silver dress, then the boots Lindsey had brought for her, placing them in the bottom of the dress bag. Although the boots were a bit worn, Anne was lucky Lindsey had come across them as another young lady tossed them into the street. Dress boots were expensive, and she would have had to go without. The next thing she packed were her adornments: the comb for her hair and her beautiful amethyst, crystal, and pearl set, which she had Verna fetch for her while she was home.

Ah Verna, Anne thought as she placed the earrings, necklace, and bracelet in the matching purse that came with the dress. The poor dear believed Anne was going to sell the set for money; she could see the sadness written all over the woman's face. Anne smiled. She hadn't bothered to correct the older lady because to do so, she would've had to concede she would be attending the ball. And that simply would not do.

Anne packed her rouge, hairbrush, and other miscellaneous items until everything sat ready by the door. Then she waited. Lindsey said he would come and take her some place where she could get ready. She wasn't sure where she would be going, but she was quite eager to get there.

Chapter Twenty-Four

Unfit Outfit

"You can't be serious!" Nolan stormed out of his chamber with Gilmore trailing after.

"Your Highness, this is the latest trend in men's clothing. Your sister wanted you to have nothing less than the very best."

"My sister wants nothing less than to humiliate me!" Nolan had never been so filled with rage. He was wearing stockings, and his breeches were far too short and tight. And the color! Nolan was so angry; he didn't bother knocking on his sister's chamber door.

Orianna was in the midst of her usual before-ball pampering routine. There were five ladies waiting on her—one on each arm, rubbing them with lotions; one applying a clay mask to her face; and one holding a large bowl beneath her hair as the last poured fresh water over it.

"Glenda, who has entered?" Orianna questioned lazily.

Before Glenda could give a suitable response, Nolan was yelling for everyone to get out. Frightened, all the young ladies abruptly ended their tasks and shuffled out of the room. Abhorred, Orianna sat up and glared at her brother.

"What the—"

"My sentiments, exactly! What the—" Nolan cursed and motioned to his attire.

Orianna smiled at him, turned back in her chair, leaned her head back, and closed her eyes before responding. "Ah, Nolan. What you are wearing is the latest trend in fashion. Every man at court wears something quite similar to that. Of course, I made it a little more suitable for your rank and status by choosing the gold color and adding a bit of satin and lace."

"Orianna, what man in his right mind would be caught wearing this much satin and lace!?"

To answer this, Orianna faced him. "Listen, if you do not like it, you can go naked for all I care. Perhaps next time, you will be sure to make yourself available for consult." Then she turned back around. "And now, Nolan, if you would, please do send my ladies back in when you leave."

That was it. He had been dismissed. Nolan wasn't aware when he had lost the upper hand in the argument—or in the relationship—but he was sure there was nothing left to be gained. He returned to his chamber.

Anger and confusion led Nolan to pace up and down the rooms of his apartments. He only had a few hours before guests would arrive, yet he had nothing to wear. He supposed he could wear his trouser suit from the previous year, but he was sure his mother would object, as would Orianna. It was too late to make a purchase, and he had sent his usual tailor home early.

Suddenly, Nolan was awakened from his clothing despondency by Gilmore's soft rapping.

"Come in!" he bellowed.

"Your Highness, I know there isn't much time before this evening's event, but perhaps there is something else we can do." Gilmore moved to the side to allow an older lady to enter the room. "Your Highness, this is Maya. She is the palace's head seamstress."

Nolan eyed the older woman carefully. "Do you actually believe there is time to construct another costume?"

"Your Highness, I believe we can come up with something slightly more to your liking and still keep with the latest fashion. However, if we are going to do this, we must act quickly."

Feeling this was his best alternative, Nolan agreed.

Upon the family's return home from church, the head cook gave the baron his birthday gift and told him it was from his daughter.

In response, Reyna said she could not believe Anne had been home while they were at church, and she was angry with Verna for not having tied the girl down to a nearby chaise.

"Thaniel, we must put forth a search team. She must still be in Ryland!"

Thaniel hugged his wife and told her no. He knew Anne would not be found, and he was realizing she would return only when she was ready. Although she looked worn when he'd spotted her in the church, she also looked happy and at peace.

"What do you mean no?" Reyna pushed away from Thaniel and looked him in the eyes.

"Reyna, I didn't want to say anything, but I saw Anne at church this morning." Reyna's eyes doubled in size, but Thaniel continued on before she had time to interrupt. "Darling, she looked well, happy. She's not ready to come home, and I think we should allow her all the time she needs. We betrayed her trust last summer, and it is going to take time for her to forgive us."

"So what then? We just wait? Thaniel, it's dangerous out there for a girl with no connections, no money. How is she living? What is she doing to sustain herself?"

Thaniel did not wish to think of the numerous improprieties Anne could be involved in. All he cared about was that she was alive and seemed healthy. "I don't know how she is caring for herself. However, I know Anne is strong and resourceful, and as she seemed well. We must conclude she is fine." He hugged Reyna again. "Knowing she is well enough to provide gifts is good enough for me. Now, let us keep this to ourselves and get ready for the ball. There is no need to weigh down Ethana's merriment by bringing up something she cannot change."

Verna, who had been present for the entire interchange, nodded her agreement and left for the kitchen. Reyna and Thaniel walked slowly up the winding staircase to their bedroom, hand in hand.

Ethana, Laveda, and Sophie were so excited to be back from church, they were out of the carriage as soon as it pulled up to the front of the manor. Each of them was so exuberant, nothing could stand in their way or stop them from getting ready, so they blew past Verna in the doorway, expressing their inability to eat along the way. Then they flew up the stairs, Ethana first, followed by Laveda, with Sophie on her back.

Ethana looked over her vibrant marine-colored gown, with its sweetheart neckline and swirls of black detailing. She felt it was the most beautiful dress she had ever owned because it was not only beautiful but also expressed an elegant maturity she felt had begun welling up within her. Several months ago, she would have thought this ball was the greatest event of her life, and she would've been dreaming of dancing with the prince alone in the gardens. Now, she was excited but more because it was Laveda's and Sophie's first ball, and she wanted them to have the grandest time.

Ethana moved to her vanity, where she chose a beautiful onyx pendant and teardrop earring set to go with her dress. Then she lifted a small velvet box containing her favorite pearl set, which she intended to loan to Laveda. Sophie, on the other hand, was to wear her mother's dainty emerald set she had received as a girl. Smiling as she thought how beautiful they would all be, Ethana decided she would help the two younger girls get ready before she readied herself.

Chapter Twenty-Five

Orianna's Revenge

It was eight o'clock and nearly time for the royal family to make their grand entrance; however, much to Orianna's dismay and expectations, Nolan was late. She looked out over the crowd of people from behind the mass of curtains veiling her and her parents. Everything had turned out just the way she had planned it, and she couldn't wait to see the look on Nolan's face.

There were masses of eligible ladies twittering all about, and the electricity they were exuding could be felt by all. Orianna smiled as she envisioned her brother running from bands of frantically adoring female subjects. She could barely contain the giggles dying to be released when, suddenly, her mother spoke.

"Oh, sweetheart, you look fabulous!"

Orianna smirked as she turned to glance at the golden monstrosity she had made for her brother to wear, only to find he was not wearing it. Instead, Nolan was sporting a lovely deep green suit. She looked him up and down and couldn't believe he had found enough time to find more suitable attire—and such fashionable attire at that.

"So," Nolan gave a little turn, "does the princess approve?"

As he entered the curtained area, Nolan knew Orianna must be fuming inside, and seeing the shocked look on her face made everything he'd gone through worth it. After speaking with Maya, and realizing the older trends *were* coming back in fashion, he acquiesced to the breeches—over pants—idea. Then there was the color to contend with. Maya had all the royal colors: gold, silver, royal blue, and various shades of purple readily available, but Nolan wanted something that screamed Merry Christmas! Gilmore, whom Nolan now considered a magician, found a seamstress not too far from the palace and bought two types of fabric, a green velvet and a cranberry satin, while Maya and her daughter got busy taking Nolan's measurements. Upon his return, Nolan could not decide which he liked better, so Maya had suggested they use the deep green velvet for the breeches and coat and the red satin for the waistcoat. Then, to tie the ensemble together, Nolan would wear a shirt and pair of stockings in winter white, both of which he already owned.

"Where did you get that suit?" Orianna could only breathe her question.

"You never told me Maya was such a talent, and her team of seamstresses . . . amazing!" Then he offered Orianna his arm. "Shall we? After all, we are a bit behind schedule."

Orianna gave Nolan a glare but took his arm just the same. They got into position, with the king and queen in the front, prince and princess behind, and the announcement was made.

"I now present to you His Royal Majesty King Bohdan, Her Majesty Queen Zorina, and their children, their Royal Highnesses Prince Nolan and Princess Orianna-Loni."

Two by two they slowly descended the great staircase leading into the ballroom, and much to Orianna's pleasure, Nolan faltered upon seeing the crowd.

"How many people did you invite, dear sister?" Nolan asked with a side whisper between nods and smiles.

"Oh, just everyone of importance throughout Ryland and a few notables from Île-de-L'est, not to mention I made room for your Mr. Pallas and Kenward."

"Ha! Made room for? As if you would notice two extra people in this throng!"

"Tsk, tsk, brother. Make sure to smile; you don't want to seem upset." Orianna grinned from ear to ear.

It was a few minutes after eight when Anne and Lindsey arrived at an old abandoned church located within the royal grounds. Anne had never seen it before and wondered how Lindsey had come to know about it but didn't ask. She merely dismounted her horse, compliments of Lindsey, and went inside. Lindsey also dismounted, then grabbed her bag and quickly ushered Anne away from the front entrance. Anne had learned not to ask too many questions of her companion because it took too much work to discover the answer. Therefore, she simply followed.

Lindsey led Anne to a back door, which opened to reveal a long, narrow staircase and just inside, on the wall, a torch, which Lindsey lit. Once the door was shut behind them, Anne followed her friend down the stairs to a small cellar and storeroom. It was so cold, Anne couldn't help but shiver, but it was also private, so no one would be drawn here to investigate.

Lindsey placed Anne's bags in the storeroom and drew a curtain to separate it from the cellar. Then he lit two candles, gave them to her, and motioned for her to enter the storeroom.

There was a small table there. It was old and showing signs of rot but still good enough for what she needed to do. Anne placed the two candle holders upon the table and began her task.

With the swiftness of a hare who had heard tales of the tortoise, Anne shed her masculine self and rejoined her natural being by working her way into her feminine undergarments. Since her dress had layers upon layers of full petticoats, she would not be able to do much once she put it on, so despite the bitter cold, she would have to do her hair and makeup without the warmth that came from being fully dressed. Beginning her next task, Anne pulled out a piece of broken mirror she had found several months ago while in Sagedor, and watched her reflection as she swept up her hair and secured the snowflake comb around it—and again to add a blush of color to her lips and cheeks. Then she massaged the honey gardenia lotion over her arms and legs, slid her feet into her stockings and boots, and put on her jewelry. Then and only then was she ready for her dress, which she managed to get on after a bit of difficulty. However, she still needed help. Since the back of the dress laced up, she needed someone to pull the laces tight and tie them up in a pretty bow. She had tried to do it herself but couldn't get the laces tight enough. Finally, she asked Lindsey to assist her.

Less than an hour later, Anne was ready to go. Lindsey had done an excellent job helping her with the dress and then had gone up to retrieve the horses. Anne cleaned up the mess she had created, packed Andrew, her lotion, and the rouge in a sac, blew out one of the candles, and grabbed the other before heading up herself. When she got to the head of the staircase, she noticed Lindsey had placed the torch back on the wall, so she blew it out, along with her candle, and stepped out into the winter chill.

Much to her amazement, Lindsey stood before the door and next to a carriage! It was a rather old and very simple carriage, but it would be quite superior to riding in on horseback. Anne couldn't believe how wonderfully everything was coming together. It was as if this was simply meant to be. She closed the door behind her and hugged Lindsey before sliding into her chariot.

Devin looked around the room in utter astonishment and shook his head. It appeared every single lady in attendance had gone completely mad as they followed the prince from one end of the room to the next, doing everything within their power to get him to ask them to dance. It was pathetic.

His parents had given him a lecture on how he wasn't getting any younger, and it was time to think about settling on a career and starting a family. "The Levenax family is quite the minority in these parts, my boy. It is up to us to set this right," his father had said. As for his mother, she was beside herself with joy when she realized Philana-Narie was no longer an option—due, of course, to Anne's recent unapproved holiday. Therefore, on the way to this event, Devin had promised his parents he would try to find a *suitable* young lady. Looking around now, he was wondering just how he could stay true to that promise.

Ah, well, he thought, *At least the food is top-notch.* Deciding to refill his plate with a variety of tasty vittles, Devin sauntered over to the buffet. However, once there, he glimpsed a rather striking young lady wearing a deep blue gown. Her beautiful blonde hair was pinned up with tiny black beads, exposing a graceful neck with creamy pale skin. Devin was drawn to her but noticed she was interested in someone else—another young couple off in the distance.

"She is lovely."

Ethana turned to see who had interrupted her thoughts. The gentleman behind her was gathering fruit and cheese from the buffet. He looked familiar, but she couldn't quite place him. "I'm sorry?"

"The girl you see with Lord de Vinay. She's lovely. However, he'd be a fool to choose her over you." Daring to look up from the buffet, Devin glanced at the beauty before him and introduced himself. "Please, pardon my directness. I am Devin Levenax."

Ethana smiled and blushed a little. "A name I know as well as my own, Mr. Levenax. Although, I must profess I am not at all surprised by your candor; however, the target is of some uncertainty."

Devin gave the girl a little smile. "I don't think I understand your meaning. Please, enlighten me."

"Of course, sir. Hmm, was it not a year ago that you were singing the praises of my beloved sister? Whom you ever so affectionately called 'Annie'?" Ethana suppressed her laughter as she watched, almost instantaneously, the recognition wash over Devin's face.

"Dear Heavens! Ethana?" When the lady nodded, Devin began his apologies. "I am so sorry. I had no idea. I mean, dear . . . how you've grown!"

Ethana had to laugh, a small polite laugh. "It is very good to see you too, Devin."

"Ethana, if there is anything I can do to make amends, please say it. It will be done."

Ethana thought a moment while she glanced over her sister's former suitor. He was actually quite handsome, and if she remembered correctly, Anne had been quite fond of him—in a friendly sort of way. Then, looking back toward Laveda and Oren, she noticed to her dismay they were now dancing. She sighed. "Well, Mr. Levenax, how is your waltz?"

The look Ethana had given the two lovers on the floor did not evade Devin's notice, and somehow, it hurt. "I am a bit rusty, but if you don't mind a stumble or two, I am all yours."

Ethana smiled at the arm bestowed as he placed his plate next to the strawberries on the table. She then wrapped her arm around his, and they were off.

Nolan was in Hell! He had never danced so much in his entire life and yet the army of ladies ready to drag him across the floor continued to grow. Orianna would pay. She knew he detested large events because of situations like this. Everyone knew the dream of every maid (fair or not) was to marry a prince. Therefore, being thrown into this gauntlet of adoration was sheer torture!

"Perhaps you should hide awhile. Give your feet time to rest."

Nolan swung around to meet the little voice that had just acknowledged his pain. A young girl no more than nine or ten was sitting on a chaise just to his left. She was a pretty little thing, dressed in a lovely clover-colored frock and smiling up at him sympathetically. He kneeled to greet her. "What is your name, sweet angel of mercy?"

"Sophie Reis, your Highness."

"Reis, is it?" Nolan raised his brow as he remembered the conversation between his uncle and sister outside the church. Though he was young when Sir Llewellyn disappeared, he could still pick out similar traits in the child's face. "Well, Miss Sophie, why are you not dancing with the little people?"

"I cannot, My Lord. I am a cripple, you see. Therefore, dancing is quite out of my area of expertise. Although, I must say, even without this preferred form of soiree recreation, I am having a splendid time. Never before have I seen so many lovely ladies and handsome men in one room."

Nolan laughed. "Ah, Sophie, your viewpoint is rather refreshing, to say the least. I don't—"

"Your Highness?" Nolan was interrupted by yet another group of voracious ladies. "We were wondering if Your Grace would like another turn about the floor. It is said they are to begin a branle in a few moments."

Nolan rolled his eyes at Sophie, then whispered, "Haven't I danced enough for one evening?" then stood to answer the throng's fearless leader. "I am afraid, Miss . . ."

"Penaworth," the girl beamed.

"Ah, Miss Penaworth, I'm afraid I am saving myself for Miss Sophie here. You see, I shall not dance with anyone else until I can devise a way to dance with my dear friend."

Miss Penaworth glared at Sophie, and Sophie blushed and looked away. The group of ladies loosely reigned in their disappointment as they curtsied and went their separate ways. Nolan stayed rooted next to Sophie.

"So you are not to dance for the rest of the evening, then?"

"Perhaps. Then again, perhaps not. It really depends on you."

Sophie looked quite perplexed. He figured her thoughts centered on the fact she had just informed him she was unable to walk, let alone glide gracefully across a dance floor.

Nolan gave her a warm, caring smile as he knelt beside her. "My dear, merciful Sophie, if I devise a way for you to dance tonight, will you do me the honor of accepting me?" Having lost her tongue, Sophie could do no more than nod her head. Nolan's smile broadened, and he lightly kissed her upon the cheek.

Devin stood on the balcony and breathed in the frigid air, but he didn't feel a thing. All he could think about was Ethana. The entire time they had danced felt like a dream. She laughed at his jokes, teased him, and apparently forgot all about Oren. She was amazing, smart, funny, and beautiful. He just couldn't believe he had never noticed her before. Then again, with Anne around, who would notice Ethana? Anne was incredible. When she entered a room, everyone noticed, and with Ethana standing in her shadow, she was likely overlooked.

"But Anne's not here now, is she?" he muttered to himself.

No. She wasn't . . . and because she wasn't, he was given the chance to dance with the most beautiful girl at the ball, and if all went as he had hoped, perhaps his parents would have a word with the de Rangers about their younger daughter.

Devin was smiling to himself when someone bumped into him. He turned to see what was happening and realized the prince appeared to be on the run. Trying not to laugh, Devin decided to help the poor man out.

228

"If you are looking for a place to conceal yourself, you may want to try hiding behind that group of topiaries at the other end of the balcony. It's rather lucky that you chose to wear such excellent camouflage, Your Highness."

Taking Devin's advice, the prince hid behind the topiaries, and Devin turned his back on the balcony door. When five anxious ladies burst through the doors, he turned back around lazily to greet them. "Well, hello, ladies."

The leader of the pack ignored Devin's playful attempt at seduction. "Have you seen the prince, Mr . . ."

"Levenax, Lord . . . Devin Levenax. No, I have not seen Mr. Ballroom, but since you're all here, why not forget him, join me, and let the fun begin?"

Each lady made her own little sound of disgust and returned inside.

Devin smiled. "All clear, Your Highness."

Nolan emerged from his hiding place and joined Devin, overlooking the view of the garden. "Phew. Thanks, Devin. I don't know how much more I can take."

Now just recognizing the voice and the facial features speaking to him, Devin glanced over at his companion, and much to his shock and amazement, realized to whom he was really speaking. "You're welcome . . . Captain?!"

Nolan closed his eyes and sighed. He had forgotten Devin was one of his crew members. He had hoped to keep his identity a secret for another year before giving up the ship to become more involved with national matters, but what now? Devin was a good man; perhaps he could trust him. "Ah, I've been caught."

Devin couldn't believe his ears. He thought the prince might deny his claim and pretend he had never been on a merchant ship. He certainly wasn't expecting . . . well, this.

"Your Highness, might I ask why you work aboard a merchant ship?"

"Well, my friend, I will tell you so long as you keep my secret." When Devin agreed, Nolan continued. "All right then, if truth be told, it's boring here, and I wanted to get out, do a bit of traveling, and perhaps have an adventure or two."

Devin couldn't believe he was having this conversation. Boring or not, wasn't it the prince's duty to stay at the palace and oversee, well, whatever it was a prince oversaw? Didn't he have important decisions to make? Wasn't there some sort of king-in-training course he needed to take? Confused, Devin had so many questions.

"How long have you been captain of the *Survivor*, and how much longer do you intend to keep this up?"

Nolan shrugged. "I've been captain for a year and a half now, and I had hoped to make it permanent. However, due to recent events, this year may be my last run, so I intend to turn the ship over to someone else when I leave. Hmm, perhaps Dyson . . . or maybe Andrew if he can prove himself a leader."

Devin chuckled. *If the prince only knew.* Funny how he seemed to know everyone's little secrets. Then something dawned on him. "Your Highness, what about Kenward?"

"Ahh, Kenward. Well, you see, Kenward lives here. He is somewhat of a temporary member of Ryland's Royal Army and my personal bodyguard. Therefore, leaving him the ship would not be feasible."

Ah, another secret! Devin wasn't sure he could take any more. First Anne, then the prince, and now Kenward? "Okay," he sighed, "now that I seem to know all the secrets swirling around this year, what now? I mean, will you still allow me to serve aboard your ship?"

"If you'd like, but allow me to be clear on one point. I will not be blackmailed. If you expose me, I will simply pack up, come home, and have you arrested for treason. Therefore, there is nothing to be gained."

Although the prince said this with a smile, Devin knew better than to consider it a mere joke and gave it the same weight as all things of great importance. "Yes, sir. I mean yes, Your Highness."

"Good man. Well, now that you know everything there is to know, I suppose I should welcome you into my inner circle." Nolan extended his hand and Devin took it for a firm handshake.

Although Devin and Nolan believed they were having a private conversation, there was one other who was privy to the secret information they shared. Walking out onto the balcony through the jarred door in his search for Laveda, Oren had heard everything, and it was the break for which he and his father had been waiting. With this information, he was sure his father could hatch a superior plan to regain their captured land from the north. Overjoyed by his discovery, Oren's search for Laveda ended, and he went in search of his father.

Chapter Twenty-Six

Before Midnight

A nne stood nervously outside the ballroom doors. Since she was nearly three hours late, there would be no one to announce her on this lower level, and for that, she was grateful. But she wasn't sure if she should even be there, and if she left, what if the person who had sent her the invitation came up to her later and asked Andrew how he had enjoyed himself? She wouldn't be able to give any sort of straightforward answer, other than she did not attend when she had promised she would.

"All right, Anne, it's now or never. You can do this; I know you can," she spoke to herself. She entered the ballroom with as much confidence as she could muster, and once inside, she was glad she had come.

Dressed in silver, gold, reds, and natural greens, the ballroom was quite the tribute to the holiday. There was mistletoe in every archway, and so much snow-like paper, the room felt more like a wintery fairyland than a royal ballroom. The front of the room was for the royal family as the king and queen could be found sitting at the long table, enjoying various holiday treats and conversing with other upper royals. The center of the room was covered with merry dancers, and around them were beautifully decorated tables—some empty and others occupied with whispering lovers. This was her element. Anne had always loved social gatherings, and after having been alone for so long, she was ready.

Just as Anne decided she would love to dance, she spotted Devin. Oh, she couldn't wait to see the look on his face. Attempting not to make eye contact with anyone, lest they immediately recognize her, she made her way across the room to Devin.

"May I have this dance, sir?" Anne lowered herself into her grandest curtsey.

Devin turned around only to see the top of the head of the girl asking. At first, he was going to decline, but when the girl rose, he nearly spat his drink all over her. He grabbed Anne by the arm and dragged her to the balcony.

"What in the glorious heavens are you doing here?"

"Taking part in the holiday festivities."

Devin rolled his eyes. "Annie, you shouldn't be here. You'll be seen!"

Anne turned to look back into the ballroom. As far as she could tell, no one was looking their way. "Devin, there isn't anyone with the slightest interest in us. Every lady is swarming Prince Nolan, and every gentleman is entranced by Princess Orianna-Loni."

Devin followed her gaze and realized she was correct. The prince had found himself yet again trapped by a large mob of salivating young ladies, and the princess had her fair share of hopeful suitors. She was a complete vision in white and silver, she looked like an alluring ice princess, desirable yet unattainable.

"She is quite beautiful is she not?" Anne asked as she marveled at the princess.

"Yes, she is lovely. But . . . she isn't *the most* beautiful lady in the room."

Anne, thinking Devin was speaking of her, blushed ever so lightly; however, she said nothing. "So, how about that dance?"

"I don't know, Anne."

Just then, the prince took to the floor. He was holding a child—*was that Sophie?*—in his arms and twirling her around the dance floor. The girl looked so happy that the disappointed looks on the faces of the other young ladies in the room became humorous.

"Oh, come on. No one will notice us with the prince dancing nearby."

With a sigh, Devin finally acquiesced, and they, too, took to the floor.

It was just as Anne suspected; everyone's eyes were on the prince and his partner, Sophie Reis. Verna and Henry had told Anne that Sophie was a cripple and so felt sympathy for the girl, but she was also proud of the prince, who bothered to show her any form of attention. It really was kind of him.

As for her own dance, Anne could tell Devin simply could not relax. The entire time, he was rigid and purposely avoided half of the dance floor. In the beginning, she believed he was just trying to keep her from the people most likely to recognize her, but the way he kept his eye on Ethana made her question her first assessment.

"Devin, is there something you should tell me?"

"Hmm?"

"You've a very watchful eye when it comes to my sister. Tell me, is she *the most beautiful lady in the room?*"

Devin's eyes darted to Anne's, and his face became a shocking shade of red.

Anne giggled softly. "Ah, my poor friend, captured once again by a de Ranger lady."

"You are not angry, then?"

"Angry? Of course not. Ethana would be perfect for you; she's clever, sweet, pretty, and deep down, I believe she is more adventuresome than she appears. Although, lucky for you, she has a steadier nature than I, to be sure."

Devin breathed a sigh of relief. "I am going to ask my parents to speak to your parents later tonight. Do you think she would be interested? After all, I wasn't very successful with you."

Anne rolled her eyes. "Ethana has good taste. Believe me; she would certainly swoon for you long before she would swoon for the captain of a cargo ship."

Devin gave her a little twirl then pulled her back into his embrace. "Anne, Captain Doran is a fine gentleman, and since we have been home, I have gained more respect for him and his *position*. Therefore, if you can win him, I am sure you will be the happiest woman in all of Ryland."

"High praise, indeed, Mr. Levenax! Now, why have you had such a complete change in opinion?" Then, thinking more intently about what he had said, something dawned on her. "I'm sorry, did you say you have seen him since our return?"

Devin sighed and tried to dodge her question. "Well, not exactly."

"Devin, you have either seen him or you have not." When her friend refused to look at her, she came to the only conclusion she could. "You have seen him!"

"Annie—"

"Mercy . . . is he here?" Anne's eyes darted around the room.

The music stopped and Devin ushered his former beloved across the floor to the banquet tables, where he handed her a plate. "Here, eat something."

Anne placed the plate back on the table. "I'm not hungry. Please, Devin, is he here?"

"Yes, but what does it matter? Are you going to just waltz up to him and say, "Hello, Captain, it's me, Andrew . . . well, no, because I am actually the *missing de Ranger girl!*"

"Of course not. I just—I don't know . . . I just want to see him."

As Anne and Devin argued back and forth about the whereabouts of Captain Doran, Laveda noticed their heated interlude from across the room. It was obvious Devin was quite familiar with the lady with whom he spoke, but she did not understand why he should show Ethana so much favor when there was such a lady readily on his arm. Wondering who she was and wanting Ethana to know what was happening, Laveda found her friend and brought her attention to the couple at the banquet.

"Pardon me," she interrupted the group in which her friend was speaking. "Ethana, might I have a word?"

Ethana humbly excused herself from the group and moved off with Laveda. "Is there something wrong?"

"To be honest, I am not quite sure." She looked Ethana in the face. "Do you happen to know the lady speaking with Mr. Levenax?"

Ethana looked in the direction in which Laveda had nodded. At first, the lady's back was to her, but moments later, she caught a glimpse of her face, and her heart seized. "Dear heavens, it cannot be!"

"Who is it?"

"Laveda, please keep this to yourself. Do not bring her to anyone else's attention. We do not want to scare her off."

Seeing the seriousness engraved on Ethana's face, Laveda nodded. "But who is she?"

"My sister," Ethana breathed as she moved toward the table.

Anne and Devin were so preoccupied, neither of them saw Ethana walking toward them.

"It's good to see you, Anne," Ethana's voice cracked in a way that let Anne know she was trying not to cry.

Anne froze and closed her eyes. Devin was right; she should not have come. She reopened her eyes and looked at her friend. He was as white as a sheet, and he wasn't looking at her but around her; she supposed he was looking at Ethana. Finally, taking a deep breath, Anne turned around.

Upon seeing Anne's face, Ethana burst into tears and threw her arms around her sister. Anne, frightened someone would see this display, asked Devin to help her move Ethana to the balcony. Releasing herself from Ethana's embrace, Anne took her by one arm as Devin took her by the other, and they moved to the outside.

On the balcony was a loving couple hidden off to one corner. Not wanting to disturb them and not wishing to be disturbed, they moved to the other side of the floating garden.

"Ethana, please breathe." Anne cupped the younger girl's face in her hands and smiled at her.

"Oh, Anne!" Ethana hugged her again. Anne looked over Ethana's shoulder toward Devin and asked him to bring them a few drinks. Then, once again, she pulled herself away from her sister's embrace.

"Ethana, it's okay. Really, I am fine."

Swallowing hard, Ethana looked her sister up and down and smiled when she recognized the dress Anne was wearing. "I knew you would look beautiful in that gown."

Anne smiled. "Well, you always had impeccable taste."

Then, more seriously, Ethana asked all the questions Anne assumed she'd been wondering over the past six months; like where was she staying; how was she supporting herself, and when was she returning home?

Anne tried her best to comfort Ethana's fears, but she would not answer her questions directly. However, the more Anne dodged her, the angrier Ethana became. "Anne, why will you not come home?"

"I can't. Ethana, there is just something I must do."

"Or someone she would like to catch." Devin had returned and passed Ethana a champagne flute and then one to Anne.

"What do you mean? Anne, what is he saying?"

Anne rolled her eyes and swatted at Devin. "Don't listen to him; he hasn't the slightest idea of my intentions."

"Ha, don't I? Ethana, I may not know exactly what Anne is planning, but I do know succeed or fail, all will be said and done by this time next year."

"Devin, what are you talking about? I will continue on my path for as long as it takes!"

Devin hugged her, "Annie, there are some circumstances simply beyond your control."

Ethana watched the interlude between her sister and the man she had been focusing on all night, and her heart sank. *Who would remember Ethana with Anne around?* she mused to herself.

Anne noticed Ethana no longer looking at them and suddenly realized what her sister must be thinking. She quickly but gently pushed Devin away and asked him to allow her some time with her sister. Devin reluctantly left the two ladies alone but mentioned he could be found gathering food at the buffet.

Anne then took Ethana's hand as she divulged her secret. "My dear silly girl, Devin is yours."

"I don't know what you mean," Ethana denied her feelings.

Anne smiled. "Ethana, I am in love with someone else. And, though this brought Devin some pain at first, he has since felt nothing but kinship toward me. Truly, we have been like a band of brothers ever since he found out. In fact, when I arrived here tonight, he told me you were the most beautiful lady in the room."

Ethana looked up at her sister, her eyes shining with new hope.

"And Ethana, you have my blessing. Devin is a *good* man, and when he gives of his heart, he does so completely."

"Are you sure there is nothing between you?"

"I swear it upon the life of the one I love," she said, then giggled.

Ethana hugged her sister so tightly that Anne believed she might never take a breath again; however, as soon as that thought skirted across her mind, her sister released her. And they were chatting quite happily, as only sisters could do.

Devin had left the balcony doors slightly ajar so he could keep an eye on the de Ranger girls from the banquet table. For he was intensely curious about what Anne would say to Ethana. He silently prayed Anne would not ruin him in Ethana's eyes; although he could not think of anything she could say to turn the young lady against him. Lowering his eyes as he took another sip of his champagne, he had not noticed the prince, who had joined him, until he looked up and found his view obscured by a dashing figure in evergreen and cranberry.

"Your Highness," Devin bowed halfheartedly.

"Devin." Nolan smirked rather humorously. "You've been watching those ladies for quite some time now. So, which is to your liking?"

Devin looked up at the young monarch and confirmed that he was, indeed, smirking. Rolling his eyes, Devin eventually gave a response, "I was once quite enamored with the darker of the two, but it is the fairer who has given me reason to speak to my family."

"Ahhh, she is rather pretty." Then, looking more closely, he said, "Ethana de Ranger, is it?"

Shocked, Devin shot the prince a questioning glance.

"I am a friend of her father's." He chuckled. "Ah, but who is the lady conversing with Miss de Ranger? Now, she is stunning." He rubbed his chin. "I am amazed she hasn't been on the floor all night."

Not thinking, Devin slipped. "The *real* Miss de Ranger, Philana-Narie, she is."

Nolan's face went blank, and it was then Devin realized what he had done. "Your Highness, dear Lord, oh please, do not tell anyone. Annie simply wishes to speak with her sister."

Nolan couldn't believe what he was hearing. Was Devin truly asking him to look the other way and pretend he had not seen her? "Have you gone mad? Her parents have been beside themselves with grief for many months. What better a Christmas gift could they receive besides the return of their daughter?"

"Sire, please, you don't understand."

Nolan wasn't listening; instead, he was surveying the crowd in search of Thaniel de Ranger. "Stay here, my friend, and keep an eye on the girls."

The moment the prince left his side, Devin sprinted toward the balcony, arriving in mere seconds. Anne and Ethana ended their conversation and gave him odd glances.

Speaking as quickly as he could between pants, Devin told Anne she should retire. "The prince . . . the . . . he knows you're here. He's gone . . . to inform . . . your father."

"What!? How?" Anne knew the question was of little importance, but it slipped out just the same.

"Anne, go. I'll make your excuses to Mother and Father."

"Good idea." Devin seemed to have regained his breath. "But you should go now, before it's too late. Ethana, I need to get back to the banquet before the prince finds out I have left my post." He then hugged Anne goodbye and lightly kissed Ethana upon the cheek before taking his leave.

"What does he mean by his post?"

"I have no idea, and apparently, I haven't the time to find out!" Anne laughed. "It was so good to see you, dear sister, but I suppose I need to be going."

"You will take care and continue to write?"

"Of course, I will." She hugged Ethana. "Please give my love to everyone and tell them I shall be home soon." With that being said, Anne ran back through the ballroom, out the doors, and back down to where Lindsey waited with the carriage. Her only regrets were she hadn't the chance to dance with the prince nor spy Captain Doran, and unlike Cinderella, she was not able to stay 'til midnight. Nonetheless, she felt happy.

All the commotion in the ballroom to find Anne brought a smile to Thaniel's lips. He lazily took a sip of his wine before placing an arm around his wife's shoulders. Then, he placed his glass upon a table and led Reyna to the dance floor.

"Thaniel, what on earth?" Reyna said when ushered forward.

Thaniel chuckled. "You do know they will not catch her?"

Reyna smiled. "It is just like Anne to cause a scene."

Reyna laughed as Thaniel led her into a music-less waltz. Party guests looked on as the parents of the missing girl appeared unconcerned about the sighting of their daughter. The baron and baroness, and even the second daughter, were all smiles.

"I miss her, Reyna, but this . . ." He laughed. "This is the girl we raised. As I said before, she'll come home when she's ready."

Reyna nodded. "She hasn't missed a ball yet. Perhaps we can plan for her to come to the next?"

Thaniel hugged his wife. "And stay until the end."

Acknowledgments

I don't care what anyone says . . . there are so many people involved in making dreams come true. People who inspire, people who uplift, people to drink with, and people who lend you strength, knowledge, reason, or a laugh when needed . . . oh . . . and cash. ☺. The people below were not only instrumental in this book becoming a reality, but in my personal growth and development. I love you all dearly. This is for you . . . for us.

My amazing daughters, Brontë and Hywel. My best friends, Alfreda, H, KT, Stephanie, Ramona, Matt & Laura, Brit, Marifer, and Carolina. My sister, Abena, and my *brother*, Daniel . . . I couldn't have done this without you guys. My dear friend, Ubah for inspiring this tale and her sister Hina for telling me it was worth the paper it was written on. My cousin-in-law, Amanda. Posthumously, my best friend Reggie B. Miller and Dr. Joseph Garrison. Mary Baldwin College's English, Art, and History departments. Dr. Martha Walker previously of MBC and currently of Notre Dame of Maryland. And finally, my work family at Landmark Builders; with a special shout out to Rebecca, Melanie, Sally, Sean, Aden, Montgomery, John Kinlaw, Lane, and Tito.

To the Morgan James Publishing team, thank you for believing in this story.

One more loving shout out to Reggie. He believed in me when I didn't believe in myself and begged me to show the world the person I truly am without fear, without reservation, and with pride. It took me more than twenty years to get it, and I am immeasurably sorry he wasn't here to witness my awakening. I miss you Reg—but don't miss watching *Knight Rider*.

About the Author

N krumah Mensah comes from a long line of oral storytellers. Wanting to keep her stories going outside of the family, to share with others, Nkrumah began writing them down. Later, after a long and winding road, she chose a degree in English from Mary Baldwin College, where she had several poems published in the school literary magazine. Years later, after two children and a move to Greensboro, North Carolina, she published another poem in *We Are Greensboro* magazine. *Anne of Survivor* is her first foray into novel writing.

A free ebook edition is available with the purchase of this book.

To claim your free ebook edition:

1. Visit MorganJamesBOGO.com
2. Sign your name CLEARLY in the space
3. Complete the form and submit a photo of the entire copyright page
4. You or your friend can download the ebook to your preferred device

Print & Digital Together Forever.

Snap a photo   Free ebook   Read anywhere

Printed in the USA
CPSIA information can be obtained
at www.ICGtesting.com
JSHW080036221124
E13829100002B/4

9 781636 984520